The Evening Star

Book Two of the Star Saga

S.E Dymek

ISBN: 979-8-9906015-1-2

Printed in the United States

First edition Oct 2023

Second edition 2025

This book is a work of fiction

Dedication

To Aaralyn, Ivy, and Caiden. My biggest inspirations for everything I do. To my husband, Aaron, who is my biggest support.

Acknowledgements

I'd like to thank my parents, close family, and all my inner, dearest friends who listened to me babble about ideas and were willing to read them. I love you all. Thank you to all my readers!

About the Author

S.E Dymek is an upcoming author who has published **The Alpha's War Series:** Including Between the Alpha's War, Breaking the Alpha Council, and The Beta's Betrayal **The Star Saga:** Including The Morning Star, The Evening Star, and The North Star available with Barnes and Nobles, Amazon, Kindle, and other book selling sites. She is also published on several ebook platforms. She has a passion for writing romance novels including paranormal romance novels and fantasy. All of her works include twists and turns, keeping her readers on their toes. She is a mother of three and loving wife. When she is not writing; she is working as a veterinary technician. Born and raised in Rhode Island, she has found her second home in Texas.

Follow her on social media:
Facebook: S.E Dymek
Instagram: sedymek
Tik Tok: @sedymek

Website: www.Sedymek.com

Chapter One

Voyage

*C*laire stood tall, with her shoulders back as she stared into the mirror. Her reflection looked back at her and showed a strong and capable person. She studied her face, her big sky blue eyes filled with seriousness, her golden blond hair pulled back in a tight ponytail. She pressed her lips together as she had been up for hours. She repeated everything she needed to do in her mind. What route she was going to take, how long it should take her and how to hold herself in the company of the crew. She did not realize how long she was up until the golden rays of the sun peeked through her window. She had paused for a second just to watch the sunrise out of her window. The gold light danced across the tops of waves, it always captivated her. She glanced back to the mirror and stared hard at it. As if the Claire in the mirror had answers for her or would tell her she got this.

"Claire bear, how long are you going to keep staring yourself down?" Morgan's voice filled her room.

"I-I just. I don't know." Claire whispered and tore her eyes away from the mirror.

"Well I do. You got this. You know you do, stop second guessing yourself." Morgan said firmly to her.

Claire let out a small breath and turned to Morgan. Morgan already had her arms open for her. Claire stepped in and wrapped her arms around her. Morgan squeezed her back in a tight hug.

"I am so proud of you." Morgan whispered to the top of her head.

        The words tugged at Claire's heart, that was all she wanted. She wanted to make them proud, uphold their family name. She pulled back and nodded to Morgan as she took a deep breath. She reminded herself that she had gone on several trips since childhood with Gavin and Morgan. She had seen and done so many things. Their ship had touched almost every ocean so far. She glanced about her room and things she collected from each trip stood out to her. She knew how to sail and had seen Gavin and Morgan negotiate with people a million times. Morgan was truly a great negotiator while she hit people hard and fast with knowledge and facts. Gavin could sell ice to an eskimo with his charm.

        "I know. I just don't want to let you and Gavin down." Claire whispered her fear, her voice shook a little as it came out.

        "Claire, you are not capable of doing that." Morgan said as she kissed the top of her head.

        "We wouldn't let you go if we didn't believe in you. Now do you have your papers?" Morgan asked as she took a step towards the door

        "Aye." Claire said as she took them out of her back pocket and waved them at her.

        Morgan reached for them and began to look them over. Making sure everything was in order. She double checked the content of the letter and ensured the seal was on there. Morgan nodded and handed them back to her. Something slammed into Morgan's leg.

        "Ariadne." Morgan muttered as the curly red headed little girl giggled and held on to her mother's leg.

        "Auntie going?' Ariadne asked Claire her bright eyes looked up at Claire.

"Aye but I'll be back soon enough to torture you some more." Claire said to her as she knelt down and snatched her up.

The little girl screamed as Claire began to tickle her. The sounds of her laughter echoed through their home. Ariadne kicked and flapped her arms around like a wild seagull as Claire attacked her. Morgan smiled as she watched the two. Claire scooped her up into her arms and began to carry her out of her room. The little girl laughed as Claire tossed her over her shoulder and carried her down the stairs.

"You two need to quit making so much noise or you'll wake your brother." Morgan scolded them.

Claire and Ariadne giggled quietly as Claire set her down on the kitchen floor. Gavin stood by the kitchen window with a small smile on his face as he overhead the scene.

"You ready?" Gavin asked Claire.

"Aye. I won't let you down." She said with a nod.

"I know you won't. You are more than ready." Gavin said with a nod to her.

Claire's eyes got teary. The faith that Gavin and Morgan had in her meant the world to her. They did everything for her growing up and now she wanted to thank them

"So about ships. The angry seagull is a fine ship." Gavin began, a wicked smile on his lip.

"That's not the name of my ship." Claire said through gritted teeth.

"Aye but it is lass. You named it yourself. You told me when you were finally able to go off on your own. Your ship would be named the angry seagull." Gavin said, as he tried to keep the laughter hidden in his voice

Claire sighed and rolled her eyes. She had said that but she was ten at the time and loved seagulls. Her ship was not called that at all. She loved her ship. Gavin had got it for her when she was sixteen. It was the first ship she had taken out into the water. She had called it Twilight to follow suit with The Morning Star. It was definitely a smaller vessel but she knew it like the back of her hand.

"Anyways, Morgan and I were talking. Your ship is a great ship and all but you should take The Crown." Gavin said, as he glanced over to her and waited for her reaction.

" Really are you sure? You don't need her?" Claire said as her face lit up.

"No and I would feel better if you took her." Gavin said as he shifted from looking out the window to look at Claire. A smile on his lips.

Claire rushed over to him and wrapped her arms around him. Gavin laughed and squeezed her back. The Crown was Gavin's second pride and joy. If she sailed that into dock at the trade post no one would ever question her.

"Now when you get to your destination; don't you dare let anyone or any man try to over talk you. Or talk to anyone else. You are the captain of the ship. You are in charge. You make the trade deal and if you don't think it's good enough, don't take it. If they are rude or disrespectful to you, It won't hurt my feelings if you set them straight and if they don't want to trade because of that. Well then the Queen will deal with them." He said as he placed his hands on her shoulder.

Claire nodded to him as she listened to his words. A smile on her face as she did. Gavin was a man meant for a different time. He never once let the fact that Morgan or herself be treated less than equal. He would kill a man if they ever disrespected either of them.

"And if the crew don't listen….throw someone overboard. That always works." He smirked and winked at her.

"Gavin." Morgan's voice came from behind them as she shook her head.

"Love." He smiled wickedly at her before he turned back to Claire.

"Now the crews have already switched ships and your supplies are over there. They are just waiting on their captain." He said as he squeezed Claire's shoulders again.

Claire wrapped her arms around him and hugged him fiercely. Gavin had become the father she never had. He believed in her and taught her everything she needed to know. He squeezed her back. After a few seconds she let go and stepped back. He turned her towards the door and nodded for her to go. On her way to the door Ariadne grabbed her leg and Morgan stole another hug.

Morgan let go of Claire and stepped back. She gave her a nod to let her know once more she got this before she handed her the bag for her trip. Claire looked down at Ariadne. She reached down and ran her hand over the top of her head.

"Look after your little brother and listen to your mother." Claire told Ariadne who nodded fiercely

Morgan leaned down and unwrapped Ariadne from Claire's leg. Morgan's stomach knotted as she watched Claire head out the door. This was by far one of the hardest things Morgan had to do. Gavin noticed Morgan's mood shift and he walked over to her and embraced her.

"Love, she will be fine. She is smart, brave and tougher than the both of us." He said. As he pulled her in for a hug. Morgan inhaled and nodded knowing he was right.

"Come Ariadne let go light the candle." Morgan said, as she scooped her daughter up.

$Claire$ made her way down the path toward Adriane's Crown. The ship was a beautiful cherry-colored wood and just like The Morning Star, it had etches of gold detail throughout it. Gavin took pride in the small detail of his ships. The sails were enormous and brilliantly white. The top mass held the flag, a simple crown surrounded by stars. The Queen's flag flew in the back corner of the ship letting others know that the ship was protected by the Queen. Gavin and Morgan had done well for themself and for the past few years had a contract with the Queen being her official trades associate.

Claire walked up the walkway to the ship. The men on board all came to attention the minute her feet hit the deck.

"Captain on board." The call was shouted out across the ship.

Pride surged through Claire as entered the ship. She kept it to herself and walked on to the ship. She nodded to them as she walked past them as she made her way to the helm. Jacob waited for her there as he gave out orders.

"Captain." He smiled seeing her.

"Jacob." She nodded.

She took her spot next to him as she overlooked the crew. Most of the men had been sailing with her for a few years now. They respected her and saw her as an equal. She worked hard for that. She never backed down from any task. Always proved she could do more or do something better than any of them. She would never ask them to do something she wouldn't do herself.

"Jacob set our course. We set sail immediately." She said loud enough for the crew to hear her.

The men waited for Jacob to shout the official route and they quickly got to their stations. Sails were dropped and anchors began to rail in.

"You've got this Captain." Jacob whispered to her. He knew how important this journey was to her, She smiled at him.

"Jacob takes us to sea." She smiled as she gave him an order.

"Aye, Aye Captain." He grinned back.

Claire's stomach flipped with excitement as Jacob pulled The Crown out into the water. The dock disappeared and Jacob pointed the ship toward the open ocean. He began steering to the open ocean. Claire tried her best to contain all the emotions that washed through her. She glanced back at her home nestled in the cliffside. I can do this, I will make them proud, she reminded herself. The glow from the candle lit in the window made her smile. She would be back soon and return with everything they needed. She

said a silent goodbye to her family and turned her attention to the horizon.

He stood at the helm of his ship and looked out over his crew. His fingers drummed on the railing. He sighed loudly, his first mate glanced at him, his eyebrow raised up as if asked what was wrong. He became aggravated. The crew was impatient. They needed something. He didn't have much time either. The Pirate King would want his quarterly payment soon and he was already behind. If you owed him things never ended well. He clenched his jaw frustrated. How did it come to this? He thought. He was doing so well for himself and then this scum came about with an army of pirates and demanded that he was to be paid for the use of the sea. He blew him off at first but he quickly obtained the man power and named himself king.

"Fuck." He whispered under his breath.

They hadn't seen another ship in some time. He was already wanted in several areas close by, He could not dock the ship and go on land to get his money. They needed a score and a good one. His men grew tired of being poor and bored.

"Captain?" Jonah asked him softly, as he sensed his frustration.

"What?" He grumbled.

"What's the plan?" Jonah said in a low voice. He did not want to anger the captain.

He growled loudly and slammed his fist down on the rail. The crew below jumped at the sound of their captain's anger.

"The plan...The plan… The fucking plan is we find a ship and we loot, rob and steal from them." He yelled as he stormed off.

He reached the cabin door and nearly missed the handle to open it. He almost just barreled through it. He slammed the door behind him as he tried to slow his breathing. He needed a way out. He couldn't keep living to sever some fake king. He loved the sea for the freedom of it, now some nutcase thinks he owns it. He needed to find a way to free himself and the sea. First he needed to settle some of his debt to him before he ended up dead.

His eyes fell on the desk in the center of the room. An old map rested on it. He walked over to it. He smiled faintly as he looked down at the map. They never did go after the treasure. If he knew the way he could settle everything.

"Jason, you would know what to do if you were here." He whispered to the empty room.

He sunk into the chair at the desk and studied the map. He remembered Siren's Gulley all too well but the route and map, and how to get there was a blur. He put his face in his hand. He had two days before he needed to meet the king. He needed some type of payment.

A soft knock at his door made him look at it. The sound echoed in his cabin. He grumbled softly as he debated whether to acknowledge the knock or not. He waited a few seconds.

"Aye?" He said, his voice annoyed as he spoke.

Jonah walked in with a small smile on his lips as he approached him. He looked at Jonah confused, why the heck is he smiling? He waited for Jonah to say something.

"Captain, there's a ship coming our way." Jonah smirked.

Thank God! He thought as he stood up and looked at Jonah to make sure he heard him right. Jonah nodded again.

"Get the boys ready," He smiled brightly.

He had positioned his ship near some cliffs. It was hidden that way if ships passed, he could ambush them before they had a chance to respond. Jonah nodded quickly and walked out to the upper deck to give out the captain's orders. This will at least keep the Pirate King at bay for a little bit. Maybe give him enough time for him to come up with a plan.

He walked out onto the upper deck to see what type of ship. His eyes narrowed and he frowned as he saw the Queen's colors posted on the back of the ship. This ship was protected by the Queen. He groaned. Normally; he liked to keep a low profile and not draw anymore attention to himself; like attacking ships associated with the royal navy but it was too late. He glanced at Jonah who also spotted the Queen's colors. Jonah's face also flashed a glimpse of worry. He shook at Jonah with a small smile, they couldn't let this one go. It meant their survival.

"We have to." He muttered to Jonah, his tone let Jonah know that it was not up for debate.

Jonah dropped the topic immediately and turned his eyes to the incoming ship. He glanced at the captain. A devilish grin appeared on his. Jonah said a small prayer to himself as he hoped everything went well. Now they wait.

Chapter Two

Attack:

Jonah watched the captain as his stomach dropped. His eyes focused on the flag that held the Queen's colors. The ship they were about to attack was under the Queen's protection. It made his stomach twist and he felt nauseous. There was no going back from this. If they attacked the ship, it would make them enemies to the crown. His eyes searched for his captain. He understood why the captain was doing it, if they did not acquire treasure anytime soon to give to the Pirate King they would all be dead. But now, they were between a rock and a hard place. Jonah;s eyes searched the ship for the captain one last time. He wanted to make sure he did not miss an opportunity to resend orders. He spotted him, his knuckles white as he stood at the helm and squeezed the wheel. His eyes locked with Jonah and he saw concern. He watched the captain's lip go thin and he shook his head. There was no other choice; they had run out of options.

The unsuspecting ship slowly made its way towards them. Jonah glanced at the crew below. They were ready, they looked almost hungry like they've been bored for too long.

"Get ready boys!" The captain yelled to the lower deck.

The men grumbled excitedly. Cannons were out and grappling hooks waited for the signal. The men twitched as their eyes fixated on the ship. Just a few more minutes and they would unleash hell.

The sun that reflected brightly off the ocean blinded Claire as she steered the ship. Her eyes squinted at the horizon, it made her face hurt. The sun was hot and she needed something. Jacob came by and plopped a hat on top of her head. She grinned at him as she used one hand to tuck her hair up under it.

"Thank you." She smiled at him.

He nodded to her. Claire looked out at the deep blue sky. She had decided to take one of the short cuts Morgan had discovered. It was one of the reasons their trade business did so well. The route would save them half the time. Most didn't take this way due to the cliff sides. It was hard to judge the shallow areas, no one wanted to risk wrecking. Gavin had taught her how to watch the waves swirl and pull to tell where the edge was. The crew was relaxed as they made their way. They trusted her. She felt pride in that.

"Captain!' A shout rang out from the crow's nest.

Jacob glanced forward and Claire's eyes narrowed over the helm to the open ocean as she tried to see what Adam saw. She was confused as there was nothing there. What was wrong, She glanced back at Adam about to call out to him.

Then it all happened so quickly. Another ship pulled up beside them. She was shocked. The ship came out of nowhere. She glanced at Jacob. As Grappling hooks started to fly from the other ship. The hooks pulled and locked the ships together. The metal of the hooks hit and wrapped around the railing. The cling noise chimed through the ship and sent fear through Claire.

"Cut the Ropes!" Claire yelled as she pulled the wheel hard in the opposite direction of the enemy's ship.

The ship creaked as it tried to follow orders but there were too many ropes that held it to the other ship. Claire narrowed her eyes at the ship. It had jet black sails with a crescent moon on them. At the end of the crescent moon a star dangled off of it. Claire felt a strange feeling of deja vu. Did she know this ghostly ship? She looked down at the lower deck and the men who frantically tried to free the ship. Each time a rope was cut another rope magically appeared. They clearly had done this before.

"This can't be freaking happening." Claire mumbled to herself.

Claire studied the ghost ship, her eyes set on the man at the helm. She locked eyes with this man. He had a grin on his face. He was proud of the scene that unfolded in front of him and he enjoyed it.

"Enough of this." She muttered to herself

"Hold tight, back away from the rail!" She ordered the men

Claire pulled the ship hard away from the ghost ship and then in one hard swift movement she slammed the ship back into the ghost ship. Aloud crash noise echoed out. The wood of the ship creaked and cracked as they smashed into each other. The sound of it sent a chill through the air and the world went silent. No one would risk injuring their own ship, if the ship broke they all went down. The man held on their breaths caught in their chest but trusted their captain.

She pulled back again and then slammed the ship back into it. The ropes held the ships together began to break loose. She smiled as she watched her plan slowly work. Her men were scattered on the floor of the lower deck as they tried to help free The Crown from the ghost ship. Her eyes locked eyes with the man again. His grin faded and he looked a bit taken back. The blows to the ship she had delivered sent his men to the ground, they were dazed and confused. For a minute no one was able to keep on their task. Claire's crew used this opportunity to get their feet and cut ropes.

"The ropes get up and get the ropes off." She yelled down to the men who looked lost.

The men scrambled to their feet as they began cutting the ropes that were left.

"Board the ship! Now!" She heard a deep chilling voice yell across the ghost ship.

They were going to board them. Chills were sent down her spine as she tried to think of what to do. She needed her ship free and away from his. His men began to swing their way over, using ropes. Ladders were being placed across the two ships and men began to climb them. She was not prepared for war. Sailing, trading,and negotiating; yes but pirates. She felt the acid burn her throat. She needed to do something. She watches Jacob as he locked swords with a man who made it onto the ship.

"Cannons!" She yelled down to the men.

A noise like thunder began to rumble below the deck as the men rolled the cannons into place. Claire watched the captain's eyes narrow as he tried to figure out the sound. Then as it dawned on him, the Captain's eye shot to his crew, like he didn't accept Claire to order cannons.

"Get on that ship now! Shut it down!" His voice echoed off the cliff sides.

Claire gritted her teeth. She knew the cannons were not prepared so they had to be set up and double checked. She could feel sweat as it beaded across her forehead.

"Get those ladders off the ship." She yelled but the crew was too busy as they tried to defend themselves, no one was free.

She had to do it herself. She left the helm, it wasn't like she could steer anywhere right now anyways. She raced down the stairs. The sound of swords clinking together filled the air. Claire ducked around an active battle between one of her men and one of his. She could feel his eyes as they followed her. She ignored the anxiety he gave her as he watched her every move. She threw her shoulder into a man who had one of her crew members pinned. The man stumbled back off balanced, the crew member took the opportunity Claire gave him and regained his stance. She reached the ladders as men started to climb across them. She gritted her teeth and gripped the ladder with both hands. She used all her strength and began to push the ladder away from her ship. The men began to yell as it rocked them back and forth. One man tumbled into the ocean while the other began to back track. As the weight became less and less Claire gave one fierce push and the ladder tumbled into the ocean.

"Stop him!" The Captain yelled.

The men aboard the crown heard their captain's orders and eyes turned to her. The ones that could step away from their fight did. One down, three to go. She thought as she raced over to the second ladder. She tried her best to ignore the men coming at her. She trusted her crew and knew they would do their best to intervene if they could. She needed to stop the flow of incoming men. She grabbed a hold of the rungs of the ladder and began to shake them. She knew that she did not have the strength to push the ladder off the ship. There was too much weight on it. She gritted her teeth and then shook the ladder with all her might and one man tumbled into the ocean. The other man began to climb quicker towards her. She bit her lip and tried harder to shake the ladder again. She felt someone behind her and turned ready to fight. She balled her hand into a fist and swung around. Her fist was caught by Adam, he had a big grin on his face as he looked at her.

"Captain it's me, Let me help." He said as he let go of her hand grabbed the side of the ladder.

They both began to rock the ladder, the men that climbed across it, held on for dear life. Their grasp waved and with one big shake, the man finally went into the ocean. Claire and Adam pulled the ladder towards them and then dropped it into the ocean. As it splashed loudly into the sea, Claire turned and smiled big. Her plan had worked.

"Two to go." She announced to Adam and then took off running ahead of him to the third ladder.

Adam followed after her as Claire as she began to work on the third ladder. Adam's stomach twisted as he watched a man slowly approach Claire from behind. She wasn't paying attention as she worked her hardest on the ladder. The man's sword was drawn as he got closure. He raised it above his head. Adam's body panicked as he rushed across the deck after Claire. The man brought his sword down as he went to strike Claire. A fast cold breeze of air brushed across Claire's back and the sound of metal as it clashed together rang in her ears. Claire turned slightly, not sure what she was about to see. Adam had locked swords with the man. The man looked at Adam with disbelief. Adam and the man's sword were locked together as they struggled to get loose from each other. Claire was becoming frustrated; she clenched her jaw before she brought her fist back and then forward. Her arm brushed against the entwined swords, the metal scraped against her skin as she drove her fist into the man's face. She drove her fist into the man's face. A loud pop was heard as Claire's fist connected with his nose.

He let out a cry as his hands went to cover his nose and the sword crashed to the floor. Blood flooded his hands as he cupped his nose. Claire ignored him and went back to working on getting the ladder loose. Adam chuckled before he took the hilt of his sword and smashed the man in the back of the head. The man didn't even wince, he fell forward and hit the ground with a thud.

He squeezed his fist so tight his knuckles went white. He clenched his jaw as he watched the ladder splash into the sea. Anger boiled in the pit of his stomach. Who was that man? How dare he run everything. He was so small in stature and the crew seemed to protect him. He was someone important to them but yet his own shadow was bigger than the small man. He walked through the battle on the deck like it wasn't even happening. His only goal being to ruin the advancement of incoming men. He watched the third ladder go plunking into the ocean. He growled, that's it. He thought as he began to move away from the helm. He could not wait any longer. Any minute those cannons would be ready and his attempt in paying off his debit will be gone. He marched his way across the lower deck, his eyes locked on this small statue of a man. His hand wrapped around a rope. The men on his ship were loyal. If he could get this tiny man captain, he was sure he could end all the fighting and he could have what was his, with less mess. He gripped the rope, he ran back a few paces and then ran forward throwing himself overboard. He swung across the distance between the two ships and landed neatly on his feet.

As soon as his feet hit the deck and he was upright a man ran at him. He didn't even flinch but he simply moved out the way. The man couldn't stop himself and ran right past him. As he rushed by he smirked and raised his sword handle, he hit him hard in the back of the head. The man stumbled forward and collapsed. The man looked down at him and grumbled. He was already robbing the Queen's ship; he did not need to add murder to the list of charges he was making. His eyes searched the deck for the small man. He had lost track of him for a mere second. He spotted him working on the last ladder. A man stood protectively

In front of him, locked in battle with one of his crew members. He walked across the deck like he was full proof. Nothing phasing him. He stepped around or through men fighting. He drew his blade as he came closer to the man bouncing the ladder. The man protecting him began to panic as he could not get free from the battle he was in soon enough. He grinned widely as he approached the man. He placed his sword on the side of the man's neck and gently pressed the cold steel to his neck.

"Checkmate." He smirked as he saw the tiny man stiffen.

A hush fell over the deck. As if something magical happened everything stopped instantly. Both crews stopped. His own crew was confused but this man who he now held captive, his crew was worried. He felt a rush of triumph flooded him as he realized he had won, so simply.

"Alright gents! Drop your swords! And your Captain lives!" He said his smirk turned into a grin.

The sounds of swords hitting the deck was music to his ears. He watched the man in front of him shift, and he pressed the sword harder into his neck. He knew he was looking for a way out and he had to make him realize there was no escape.

"Now I wouldn't do anything stupid." He snickered as he waited for the man to realize that this was it, everything was over.

"I will be taking all your jewels, coins, and anything of value as soon as possible. The quicker you're done emptying your valuables the quicker we will be on our way and no one will be hurt." He said, as he shifted his sword slightly.

The metal pressed into Claire's neck and she cringed. There was no way this was happening. The words You've gotta be kidding me screamed in her head. She played out everything that she could possibly do, every action she could take. Something had to be there, anything to get away from this man. She was so angry. This was her first solo trip, this ship was her responsibility, this cargo was her to deliver. He wasn't getting anything. Her body shook but not from being afraid but from the rage that coursed through it. She turned slightly to face the man who held the sword to her throat. The blade stung as it left a small cut against her skin as she moved.

The man was taken back as a small cut formed in the man's neck as he turned around to look at him. As he did a wind blew and the hat the tiny man wore. A flash of blond hair whipped out in the wind. Her bright blue eyes stared him down full of rage and they burned into him. He was a she. That's why the crew was protecting him so fiercely….he was a she! He tilted his head. Why did this woman look so familiar? Before he could continue to think her finger pressed into his, the center of his chest. He looked down at her finger and then to her, confused.

"What exactly do you think you're doing!?" Claire yelled as pushed on his chest.

"This ship is protected by the Queen herself? Do you have a death wish pirate?" She continued to scream in his face.

Claire stared at him baffled, her chest raised and fell quickly as she tried to control herself from shaking. The anger and rage that rushed through her made her body vibrate. He did not answer her, just stared at her. That only fueled her anger. He probably never had a woman yell before. She dug her finger into his chest hard as she went to talk again. He winced at that last poke she gave him. He shook his head annoyed and then swatted her hand away. He watched her face turn red from the action but he still studied her. He knew her. Who was she? He didn't remember any blondes. He never really fooled around with blondes or at least not recently. He grumbled softly. His hand was going to capture hers and the weapon she was turning it into. He caught her by the wrist and basically growled at her to make her stop.

"I would suggest you stop doing that" He growled back at her.

Her sky blue eyes snapped up to his. He was almost taken back as he got lost in them. He blinked a few times. He was at a standstill with this woman. He wasn't sure what to do. His eyes traced and studied her face.

" I strongly suggest you go about your business and get off my ship." She growled back at him.

Who did this woman think she was? Her strong will reminded him of someone from long ago. Fiery red hair flashed into his mind. She had her attitude. He smiled softly thinking of Morgan...Morgan. He glanced back at this girl's face and his eyes widened.

"Claire?" He whispered barely loud enough for her to hear him.

Chapter Three

Encounter

Claire froze, her eyebrows frowned at the sound of her names. Her eyes narrowed as she locked eyes with him. His cocky grin turned into a warm smile as he dropped his sword away from her neck. She stepped towards him, closing the space between them as she studied his face. Her eyes looked over every inch of his face. His hazel eyes were called to her. Each freckle of gold in them sparkled pulled at her heart and his tousled bronze hair reminded her of a young boy she used to know.

"Claire." He repeated her name as if he needed to confirm that she was who she was.

"Jackie?" She whispered, unsure of the words that floated effortlessly out of her mouth

"Aye it's me!" He said excitement bursted out of him as he grabbed a hold of her and wrapped his arms around her.

She hit his chest and the instant feeling of home wrapped around her. Jack had been a safe place for her when she was young. He had helped, cared and distracted her when they were on The Morning Star. If it wasn't for him, she would have lost herself when things got dark. He was her best friend then, even after they left the ocean. He had always been there for her and then they grew up and he was just gone. He had said he would be back. He never did. She had waited for him. Every third weekend of the month, when he would normally return. She had waited for years, he had left one time and then stopped coming. Sadness replaced

the excitement. She pulled back from his chest and looked at him. She was still processing everything. This was her Jackie? She had thought the worst. He chose not to come back to her.

"What the heck are you doing out here? Whose ship is this?" He said as she pulled back; the need to hug her again and not let go overwhelmed him. He had thought about her every day for so long.

"What the heck am I doing? What the hell are you doing?" She said as anger came rushing back, she waved her hands violently around at the other pirates as she spoke.

"I'm a pirate….doing pirate things." He said and he sounded like a boy that was confused.

There was silence behind them as the men from both crews watched the strange encounter take place. Jack's crew was confused as they watched their ill-tempered captain put his sword away. There was excitement and happiness in him that they had never seen before. Claire's crew was still on edge and watched her every move as they waited for a command.

"Pirate! Pirate things! Really Jack! Did you not see the Queen's colors! Did you not think?" She said as she jabbed him in the chest with each sentence.

Jack took a step back completely confused and not sure how to respond as this small woman stabbed him with her finger. A shock noise went through Jack's crew. No one touched the captain like that. The noise snapped Jack out of being stunned. He remembered he was a pirate, a captain, and his whole crew was watching. He became slightly angry. He had a ruthless image to uphold. He snatched Claire by the wrist. She looked a bit surprised at first but quickly recovered. She pulled her hand back but Jack wasn't letting go.

"If you're Captain then let us go!" She growled.

"Well first I need to speak to your Captain and I will be taking some of the ship's valuables." He grinned.

"What are your terms?" Claire asked, as she straightened herself up.

"Terms? Gorgeous, I need to talk to your Captain for that. Now which one of you lads back there is captain?" Jack asked as he turned around and stared at Claire's crew.

"Ah Jacob!" He smiled seeing Jacob.

Jacob nodded as he came forward. Claire smirked and folded her arms across her chest and just waited.

"Aye Jack. It's good to see you, unfortunate circumstances though." Jacob said, as he reached Jack.

"Unfortunately indeed. Now I know you must be captain. I will be generous and not take everything you got but I need a good amount of gold or coins or something I could trade for that. What do you have?" Jack said as he put his hand on Jacob's shoulder.

"We don't have much. Some coins and some spices. We are on our way to trade and develop a trade deal." Jacob said, shrugged.

"Shit." Jack grumbled.

"Well I'm sorry but I got to take your coin. I'll take your coin and your crew can go free deal, tradesman?" Jack smiled.

"I'm sorry Jack but I can't make any deals. I'm first mate not captain." Jacob said a small smile on his face as he glanced back at Claire.

"Then bring the man to me. I'm growing annoyed and when I get annoyed people die." Jack said, his voice deadly.

"You've already spoken to her; Jack." Jacob said not being able to control the smirk on his face.

"Her! Bloody hell." He groaned as he turned around to see Claire with a grin plastered on her face.

"Your captain!" He grumbled.

"Aye Love, I am." She said as she mimicked his previous tone.

He exhaled and pinched the top of his nose in frustration. He was growing tired of everything.

"Your coins love, get them to me and your crew can go." He growled, as he dropped his hand back down.

She went back and forth on it. They didn't need coins to get to the trading post but they would need someone to resupply for the journey back.

"Half of the coins." She said as she narrowed her eyes at him.

"This isn't a negotiation, Claire Bear. I'm taking your coins and graciously letting your crew go." He said as he stepped in her his anger began to boil.

"If you take all of our coins we won't have any supplies for the way home." She said as she met him half way in his stance.

"Half your coins and you stay." He smirked.

"Me stay? Are you crazy?' Claire said her eyes widened slightly.

"Crazy, Aye most likely. Jacob will go make your trade deal. We will meet back here and I'll take the other half that I should take now. You're going to make a deal so I know you will be getting coins from that. So on your way back we can trade more coins for you to come back to them." Jack smiled wickedly.

"You know you're not just stealing from the Queen right now. You're taking from Morgan and Gavin. This is their company and their livelihood." Claire said her voice full of disappointment.

"Well this is my livelihood." He said through gritted teeth, the words she had spoken stun but he pushed the feeling down.

"I can't believe this is how you turned out. Fine deal." She snapped as she held her hand out, her eyes judged every inch of him as if she was repulsed by him.

"Excellent. It's a deal." He smiled brightly, as he took her hand and shook it.

As they shook hands Claire squeezed so hand, as if she could break his hand in hers. Jack didn't act like he felt anything at all.

"Claire you can't do this." Jacob said as he stepped to her.

Jack clicked his teeth and stepped in front of Jacob, his hand wrapped around his sword threateningly.

"Jacob, go retrieve my belongings and half of the coins from our ship. I am making you a temporary captain in my place. When you return I will resume my role as captain until then you are in charge." Claire said, as she spoke around Jack.

Jacob shook his head and went to protest the order that Claire gave. She narrowed her eyes at him and ordered him again silently. Jacob let out a sigh of frustration and gave in. He turned sharply and made his way to the captain's quarters, his footsteps echoed throughout the silent ship. Claire rubbed her brow annoyed as she turned herself from Jack. She ignored him completely. She had decided at that moment she would give him the cold shoulder until her imprisonment was over.

She clenched her hands into fist at her side as she thought about her being stuck on his ship. How she would miss her voyage. Rage surged through her. She dug her fingers into the palm of hand. It made her blood

boil. She had to remain calm, she was captain. She closed her eyes and took a deep breath in. She held it until her lungs burned. Even still all she could think about was how easily it would be to toss him overboard. She could feel a vein in her neck throb as her heart pounded in her chest.. She could murder him right now.

A soft touch on her shoulder stirred her. She jumped slightly but regained herself. Jacob stood in front of her with a weak smile on his face. He hated this too. She could see thoughts of how he could get her out of this swirl around his head. Claire shook her head no and reached out and took the bags he held.

One of the bags let out a jingle, her stomach twisted as she knew it was the bag of coins. She slung the bag that held her clothing over her shoulder. She gripped the bag of coins tightly in her hand and looked at them. Her eyes full of hate looked at Jack. She shook her head and chucked the bag of coins at him. It hit him hard on the chest and he caught them as they bounced off of him. He clenched his jaw as he was about to say something. Claire ignored his look and turned to Jacob. She was going to make sure he knew he was not worth her time.

"The plans for the trade negotiation are in the middle drawer of my desk. We won't take or accept anything else. The good faith trade is in the lockbox in the upper right hand drawer of the desk. Give them what's in the box as a token that we believe in the relationship. Lastly don't report this to the Queen when you dock. If they asked why we were delayed there was a storm. I know she won't check on us but do not report anything." She said firmly, as she took off a necklace that was around her neck.

She held the necklace out to Jacob it was a silver chain holding a small key,

"This is the key to the lock box. Keep it on you." She said as she handed it to him.

"Aye captain, I will do my very best and we will be back to get you in no time." Jacob said and squeezed her shoulder.

"Aye I know you will. I doubt you would be able to go home without me. If Morgan saw you return without me; you probably wouldn't have a head." Claire chuckled.

"Allright shall we get going boys!" Jack yelled as he bounced the bag of coins up and down in the palm of his hand.

At the sound of his voice the men slowly began to back away from Claire's crew. Swords still drawn but they began to make their way back to their ghost ship, Claire sighed deeply.

"Take care of my ship Jacob and the crew. Adam, you are now first mate." She smiled.

Adam's eyes grew wide as she addressed him the situation settled in. He nodded slowly.

"Milady it's your turn now." Jack smiled as he extended his hand to her.

Claire grumbled and rolled her eyes at the sound of Jack's voice. This was going to be the longest few weeks of her life. Jack held his hand out to her as she offered to help her across the ladder. Claire glared at him. She did not need his help with anything. She spotted the rope he had used to get across as it still dangled in the wind. She smirked, as she stepped aside and ignored Jack. She grabbed a hold of the rope and without a second glance. Took several steps back. Jack smirked, his eyebrow raised as he watched her. She then swung herself across the gap and landed neatly on Jack's ship. Claire's smirk turned into a grin as she looked eyes with a wide-eyed Jack. She placed her

hand on her hip as if to say she was waiting. Jack shook his head as he hopped up onto the ladder and began to make his way across. A small laugh came from behind him as a voice rang out

"Good luck with her, Jack." Jacob called across the ships with a silly smile on his face, as if Jack didn't know what he was getting himself into.

"You best keep her safe or this whole ship and Gavin's ships will be after you. Never mind what Morgan will do." Jacob's voice was pleasant but held a deadly promise to it.

Jack shook his head slightly as he made his way back onto his ship. He knew what would happen if any harm came to Claire. He looked over at her. He would never let anything happen to her, regardless of the threat.

Chapter Four

Aboard

Claire stood aboard Jack's ship. She knew its name. It was on the tip of her tongue. Her eye caught the black sail The Evening Star. It had been Trevor's ship, Gavin's ex-partner. Betrayal, the one word she thought of them when she thought of the situation and the current. Her anger fumed off of her. She couldn't imagine this man being the boy she once knew. The boy who kept her safe aboard The Morning Star. The young man who would come back every month and visit her with Jason. Those weekends were the best. He would have fabulous tails for where he went and who he saw. What he ate and he always brought her a little something back. The presents were nice but the excitement and love she felt when he would rush to her and wrap his arms around her. Like he couldn't have bared to have been away from her. Her hand unknowingly went to her chest. Underneath her shirt hung a necklace. It was an aquamarine stone that hung off a simple silver chain. She smiled softly at the memory.

Claire's feet dangled off the dock, she had just turned fifteen that past summer. She dunked her toes into the ocean water. It had started to turn colder. The month was September and the days still held light longer as it clung to the last bit of summer and the sun was still warm. She had been eagerly counting the weekends till Jack would return. Claire had not seen him in four months. Her heart ached to see him. His bronze hair tousled about in the wind, the gold freckles that danced when he smiled, excited to see her again.

He had written to her and let her know that this journey was taking longer than normal. As long as he came back she didn't care. She would wait for him. Her bright blue eyes fixated on the entrance of the bay. The sun had now started to dip behind the ocean water and she could feel the dread tug of sleep. She didn't care, she knew he would come. She glanced up to the cliff side, Morgan had the candle lit since he had left. Morgan was waiting as well. A fish circled below her foot in the water and it took her eyes from the horizon. She watched it swim about and debated on if it should bite her foot. The sun was almost completely gone now and a sharp wind kicked up. It sent a cold chill down her back. The wind knocked her golden blond hair into her face. She frowned as she tried to move her hair out of the way. A warm chuckle that sent joy through her caught her ear. She instantly knew who it was. She didn't even take the time to get the rest of her hair out of her face as she jumped up and spun around. She went to take a step forward and bumped into his chest.

"Jackie!" Claire squeaked in excitement.

He couldn't help but laugh at the sight of her, he helped get her hair out of her face. As he swept her hair away from her face he was taken back by just how blue her eyes were. They did this to him every time. He smiled at her and then scooped her into the biggest bear hug.

"Oh how I've missed you Claire Bear!" He said as he picked her up off the ground in the hug.

She laughed at how happy he was to see her, her arms wrapped just as tight around him. He set her down, his hands still on her waist.

"Why didn't I see you come in? I have been sitting here for hours." She pouted.

"We docked on the other side; it was easier from the direction we were coming." He said with a grin.

"You've gotten so much taller!" Claire laughed as she took a small step back to look at him.

Four months had changed him a lot. Jack was now seventeen and in a few months time he slowly changed from young boy into a man.

"Yeah I thought you looked smaller for some reason." He teased her.

"Shut up! Are you hungry, I'm sure Morgan has put aside food for you and Jason." Claire grabbed his hand and started to pull him down the dock.

"Hang on." Jack said, his hand pulled her back.

"I have something for you." He smiled, his hand went to his back pocket.

Claire paused and tiled her head at him to ask what. He chuckled at the response.

"Turn around and close your eyes." Jack said a smile plastered on his lips.

"Ok." Claire chuckled, although she was secretly excited.

She turned around and shut her eyes. She felt Jack come up behind her and place something up over her head. Something with weight hit her chest and she felt him clip something behind her neck.

"I had to wrestle a mermaid for this." He whispered into her ear.

A small chill ran down her spine from his breath as it hit her ear. She laughed at his statement. She felt his hands on her arms as she turned her towards him.

"Ok you can open your eyes now. I wanted to see you look at it." He said excitedly as he waited for her to look.

Claire opened her eyes and her hand went to her chest. A necklace dangled there. It was the most beautiful stone she had ever seen. The bright blue ocean color of it made her smile brightly.

"Jack, it's beautiful." She whispered as she looked at it.

"You like it?" He asked, his voice sounded a little vulnerable.

"Like it? I love it!" She said and jumped into his arms.

He caught her his arms pulled her tight against him as he hugged. She fit perfectly in his arms like she was made to be his.

"Was the mermaid angry? Should I expect her to plot revenge against me?" She laughed as she set her back down on the dock.

"No but it is called the mermaid's treasure. It's called aquamarine. It means good luck, fearlessness, and protection to sailors." He whispered to her as he touched the stone.

"Oh then you should wear it." Claire said, her hand went to undo the necklace..

He caught her hand and shook his head no.

" I have all the good luck in the world." Jack said with a wink.

"Oh yeah." Claire said a smirk on her lips.

"Yup, I have the best good luck charm ever." He said mischief flashed in his eyes.

"Oh well it can't be as pretty as the one around my neck though." She said her voice teased him.

"Oh it's much much prettier." He said his voice dropped to a low serious tone.

"What's it look like then?" Claire said, as she wrinkled her nose at him.

"Well it's about this tall." He said as his hand hovered just above her head.

"You can't carry something that tall around with you." Claire said as she shook her head.

"Shhh. It's about this tall, has hair as gold as the summer sun, and has eyes bluer than any sky or ocean put together. And her laugh puts songbirds to shame." He said as he grabbed ahold of her hand.

Claire felt a chill rush through her as he took her hand in his. She watched his eyes soft but intense as he described her as his good luck charm. She felt her cheeks flush red as his eyes burned into hers.

"The only downside about my good luck charm is I can't take it with me. At least not yet anyways." He said his voice was now sad.

"Not yet?" She asked, confused.

When you turn eighteen come with me." He whispered to her, his hand squeezed her hand as he spoke.

"Claire, I know you love the sea, I know you love adventure. We could go anywhere you want, see or do anything." He said his voice was full of excitement.

"Morgan…."She whispered.

"I'm sure she'll understand. She has Gavin and they're a growing family." Jack said, his thumb brushed the side of her hand.

Claire thought for a moment her eyes flickered to the hillside where the candle glowed for Jack to come home. She then looked back to him, his mouth turned in a bright smile and his eyes danced with excitement. She felt her own stomach began to flip inside of her.
 She couldn't help but nod her head yes to his question. He scooped her up into his arms again and spun her in a circle. As her feet touched the dock. He brought his lips to hers and kissed her. Sparks went off inside of her

and she could see her future with him. Full of love and adventure. That was the last time she saw Jack.

Claire shook her head as she shook the memory from it. It always made her heart ache and she was left with so many questions. She frowned deeply.

"Frowning already, We haven't even introduced you to everyone." Jack's voice interrupted her.

"Don't worry, I don't need to know your band of hooligans. Just show me where I'll be staying, for the time being." She refused to look at him.

Every time she looked at him she felt a wrath burn through her. She knew deep down part of it was from the day he left her and never came back. No explanation, nothing. She felt betrayed and now she was missing out on her biggest adventure because of him. She could hit him, could throttle him. She turned slightly away from him. Her eyes scanned the ship; she watched the men from Jack's crew leave The Crown and come back to their ship. She saw Jacob frustrated as he paced back and forth on the helm. She frowned once more, she wanted to comfort him. She wanted to tell him everything was going to be ok. Jacob was family and she could only imagine what was running through his head.

Jack was studying the girl he used to know. She was different. The carefree Claire was gone. She was rigid, responsible, and almost pretentious. He shook his head at her. She was entitled. She thought she was better than him. He clenched his jaw and as he did he caught her glance. He didn't think the disappointed frown on her face could get any deeper but it did when he caught her glance.

"Well this is going to be lovely. This way, gorgeous." He grumbled as he walked towards the Stairs.

He didn't even look at her as he walked by her. If she wanted to be cold, so could he. As his foot hit the first step there was a bunch of commotion behind him. He followed the noise with his eyes. A man was on the lower deck with a circle of men around him. His blade was drawn and he yelled something about Claire not going anywhere. His men snickered at him as they closed in on him. Claire's eyes snapped from the man to Jack and without saying anything, she stepped towards Jack. His brows narrowed confused at her action and then in a blink of an eye her hand was on Jack's sword at his waist band. She yanked hard on it as it was released from the stealth.

Jack's hand dropped to where his sword was once and grabbed at the air. He looked from his waist band to where she was and she was gone. In a split second she was across the deck and to the circle of men that surrounded the man from her crew. Jack was stunned a bit as he watched Claire.

As she reached the circle she shoved her shoulder hard into one of the men. The men stumbled and fell to the ground and he took the man next to him with him. She moved quickly into the circle sword drawn and stood directly behind the man.

"Adam what in god's name do you think you're doing!?" She yelled at him as he joined him.

"Captain we can't let you go with these...these poor excuses for men." Adam said as he spat at them.

"I appreciate the sentiment Adam but I had given orders and you're disobeying them." Claire said, as she stared down at the men that were enclosed in one them.

Jack groaned as he stomped across the lower deck. He walked quickly to the circle. One of his men decided to lunge towards Claire. Jack's stomach twisted.

Claire's sword clashed against his as she shoved his strike back at him the man stumbled surprised. Another began to attack Adam. Adam blocked his strike. The men that attacked Claire looked at her and held his sword tight in his hand. Claire smiled at him, almost as if she begged him to try to attack her again. As he went for her she dropped down and swung her legs at his legs. Jack felt relief as he still had not made it to them as well as shock. A small smile came to his face. He should have known Morgan would have taught her how to fight. The man's legs connected with hers and he stumbled on to the ground, flat on his back.

Jack finally reached them as another man began a sword fight with Claire. He almost wanted to sit back and watch, he was very impressed. Adam held his own with two men. Jack paused for a second and something caught his eyes. A man crept up behind Claire with his sword raised. Jack's stomach dropped. She didn't see him coming with a cheap shot. Jack pushed past his men in a hurry. He didn't have a sword but he wasn't thinking. He needed to get to Claire. He raced towards her just as the man brought his sword down aimed for Claire's shoulder. Jack slammed into his man and threw his own shoulder in the place of Claire's. The blade sliced through Jack's shirt and skin. Jack let out a groan as he pushed his man away from Claire. Claire turned ready to fight but she stopped as she looked at Jack. Claire's eyes fixated on the blood that began to stain his shirt.

Jack's groan made the ship go silent; his men froze. Blood ran down Jack's arm and dripped off his hand. The drips began to form a small puddle on the ground. Jack gritted his teeth angrily as he saw his blood and pain seared in his shoulder.

"That's enough." Jack yelled, his voice sent chills through the men.

They moved back away from him. Cowarded underneath his yell. Jack turned his eyes on the man who started all this.

"You." Jack said as he stepped towards Adam.

Adam still had his sword drawn as Jack came towards him. The anger that fumed off Jack would terrify the bravest man. Adam pointed his sword at him and Jack didn't even seem phased.

"I suggest you get back on your own ship before I lose all my patiences." Jack growled.

"Claire-' Adam began to say.

"She's staying. Go back on your own ship and see her when you return with more coins. Or die now and never see her again. It's all the same to me." Jack said, through his teeth.

Claire blinked still in shock that Jack had injured himself to protect her. She didn't tell her feet to move but they were. She walked to Jack and stepped between him and Adam. Jack growled as he thought she went to defend Adam. Who was this man to her, anyways! Why did they care so much about each other! He thought a tinge of jealousy ran over him.

"Adam, I gave my orders, you're disobeying. Return to the ship now." Claire said her voice held so much authority in it.

Claire stepped closer to Jack and he seemed to freeze as she closed the space between them. She stood on her tippy toes, Her hand went to his shoulder as she pulled back the pieces of loose clothing. Jack felt his anger slip away as she touched him.

"Claire I-" Adam began to say.

"Adam! The ship now! " Claire said and turned on her heels to face Adam.

"Disobey another order of mine Adam and god help you." Claire said her hand in fist at her side.

Adam nodded and stepped back. The men around them didn't move away from Adam. He was not able to make his way back to The Crown even if he wanted to. Claire was becoming angrier and angrier.

"Well move!" She shouted at Jack's crew, who quickly cleared away for Adam.

Claire turned back to Jack who just stared at her, him and the rest of his crew. Adam made it back to her ship as she began to look at his wound again. She shook her head and sighed.

"There's too much blood right now. I need clean water and to get you to sit down. I can't stand like this and work on your shoulder." Claire grumbled,

Jack looked down at her confused, how was she annoyed with him? This wound would have been hers if he didn't step in the way. He thought as he looked down at her. Claire sighed loudly as she looked around at the crew who watched.

"I said I need clean water and some bandages. Bring them to the captain's cabin please." Claire ordered as she then glanced to the upper deck.

She didn't say another word and began to walk to the captain's quarters. Jack stood there dumbfounded. She basically just scolded him and then gave his crew orders. The crew nearly jumped to do what she yelled at them. You wouldn't believe she was captive on his ship. He watched one man headed off to get clean water. He smirked a little bit as he shook his head. This was going to be a long two weeks. He then saw the man who sliced his shoulder. Anger bubbled up from inside him as he approached the man. The man slowly backed himself into a corner and shrank down into it. He was angry he injured him but even more

angry that it was meant to hurt Claire.

"Captain, I swear I didn't mean it. Captain I…, it wasn't meant for you. I am so sorry." He said as he shook.

Jack debated throwing him overboard but instead he took out his dagger and pointed it at the man, he motioned for him to stand.

"Get up." Jack growled as the man continued to try to shrink away,

"Captain, I would never hurt you." He pleaded.

Jack gritted his teeth before he motioned for him once more to stand. The man stood shaking. Jack looked him over quickly as he debated on how bad he was going to injure him. He twirled his dagger in his hand.

"Right handed or Left." Jack sneered at him, he didn't need anyone useless on his ship either.

"Rrrright." The man whispered.

Jack nodded and snapped his hand at the man's left hand. The man held his hand out like a misbehaved child. Jack rolled his eyes at his response. He took the man's hand and placed it against the ship's side.

"Don't move." Jack said in a whisper.

The man nodded and closed his eyes. Jack in one swift motion pinned the man's hand to the ship with his dagger. The man let out a painful yell as Jack turned and walked away. Claire's head snapped over to the direction of the yell as she reached the stairs of the upper deck. Jack was headed to the opposite stairs. She sighed irritated as she turned to follow him. He paused and lingered at the stairs as if he knew she was coming. As she reached him she raised an eyebrow to ask what that was all about but Jack ignored her. He walked up the stairs. Red little droplets of blood followed behind him. Claire clenched her jaw as she followed.

Chapter Five

Wounded

Jack pushed open his cabin door holding it open slightly for Claire who was mumbled under her breath behind them. Claire paused in the doorway and turned slightly. Her eyes watched The Crown pull away along with her long awaited dream. Claire took a deep breath in as her stomach knotted up. She told herself that this was for the best and she saved her crew by doing this, which any good captain would do.

"You make a lot of breathing noises." Jack stated as he cleared his throat from the other side of the doorway.

"Happens when I'm annoyed." Claire grumbled.

Claire did not say another word to him, even though the look on his face taunted her to explain. She walked over to his desk and cleared things out of the way. Jack was about to fuss at her but his arm started to bother him. He sat in the chair next to it. A sudden uneasy feeling rushed through him. He felt light headed. Concerned he glanced down at the puddle of blood on the floor, he couldn't be losing that much blood from this wound. He shut his eyes and told himself he was ok as he let the moment pass. A knock at the door drew his attention.

"Come in." He shouted as the door opened.

Two of his men came in; one held a bowl of water and the other held clean rags. They stood there unsure of what to do. Claire tapped the desk as she rolled her eyes at them. Was every man on this ship helpless? She thought. She nodded to them as they set them down and quickly retreated.

"Benji." Jack yelled to the taller man's back.

"Aye Captain? " Benji answered as he turned around.

"If I die, kill that fool Greg." Jack said no emotion in his voice.

"Will do captain, he is still stuck to the ship. Where you left him." Benji chuckled as he walked out.

"Leave him there a little longer then help him." Jack yelled at him again.

Benji nodded, his chuckle had turned into a laugh as he shut the door. Claire raised an eyebrow to Jack at the exchange but decided she could care less. She almost wanted to tell him she was not going to let him die but she bit her tongue. He could use something to worry about. She dunked a clean rag into the water. She turned to look at Jack. She paused as if really seeing him. He was becoming paler by the minute as the blood dripped down his shoulder and off his hand dropped on the floor. Shit she thought in her mind as a frown appeared on her face. He did have something to worry about. She needed to move quickly.

She grabbed a hold of her bag and rapidly searched through it. Her extra clothing fell all over the desk as she searched for it. She smiled seeing it.

"Thank you Jacob." She muttered as relief washed through her.

She pulled out a rolled up soft cloth brown bag. She unrolled it quickly. Surgical tools sprawled across the desk. Jack shifted in his chair as he saw it unroll.

"What exactly do you have there?" He said his voice was weaker but he sounded nervous.

She ignored his statement and grabbed a pair of scissors. She walked towards him. Jack backed up further into the chair.

"Gorgeous, you're going to have to at least explain to me what you think you're doing." He said as he put his good hand up to stop her.

She sighed like he was the most annoyingest thing in the world.

"Look if you would like to live, I suggest you let me fix you. The scissors are just to cut your sleeve off so I can see what exactly is going on. If you can't tell already you're losing a decent amount of blood." Claire said as she moved the scissors around as she talked.

"Fine." Jack muttered as he gave in to her, he was getting way too tired to keep fighting her.

Claire approached him in the chair, she carefully cut away the upper part of the sleeve from the shirt where it connected at the torso. She easily slid it down over the wound and down his hand to the floor. She grabbed a hold of the rag she had sitting in the clean water and ran it out. She pressed it into the wound on his shoulder. He winced slightly but didn't make a sound. She applied pressure for a minute and then removed it. Her eyes quickly studied the wound. She watched the blood pool and filled up the wound. She spotted it, the little blood vessel that caused all the bleeding. She placed the rag back over the wound. She grabbed Jack's other hand and placed it on top of it.

"Apply pressure." She said as she went back to the desk.

She studied her tools, she grabbed a pair of hemostats, needle holders, and thumb forceps. She grabbed some suture as she turned back to Jack tools in hand.

"Explain." He said as he closed his eyes softly.

"The sword has cut through your flesh; it's mostly surface bleeders. Which you're lucky. However there is one blood vessel which is causing this mess. I need to tie it off to stop the bleeding. Then you could really use most of the wound sewn up." She said to him and waited for him to acknowledge her.

"Ok do what you need to." He said eyes were still closed

She looked at him and she felt a small flutter inside of her stomach. The best angle to work on the wound would be if she straddled his leg. She pushed back the thoughts of how close she would be to him and moved and she straddled his leg. The moment her legs straddled his thigh, Jack's eyes shot open. His hazel eyes locked on to her bright blue ones. He swallowed the lump in his throat as he tried to quiet his mind, that screamed how close his leg was to her center and how if she moved her leg, at all she would brush his groin. As if she had the same thoughts, Claire's cheeks turned a shade of red as she cleared her throat

"This position will give me the best angle to do this." Claire said her voice cracked a tiny bit as she explained

He nodded and took a deep breath in as he shut his eyes. His plan was to zone out.Claire felt better now that he wasn't staring at her.

"This is probably going to hurt….alot." Claire said apologetically.

He didn't say anything, just nodded. She pushed the thought of how it was going to hurt and she didn't want to hurt him from her mind. She strung the suture through the needle holders and had the hemostats ready to clamp the bleeder.

She tapped Jack's hand and he slowly brought it down holding the rag. Claire studied the wound again and quickly spotted the bleeder.

"Ok be still."Claire said quietly as she grabbed the hemostats and clamped the bleeder.

To her surprise Jack didn't move. She quickly looped the suture underneath the bleeder and began tying it off. She removed the clamp and was happily surprised as the wound stopped filling with blood. She leaned over and grabbed another clean rag and dabbed at the wound. She smiled to herself.

"Ok I am going to start suturing. It's definitely going to hurt." Claire said to him, she looked at his expressionless face and waited.

He just nodded and remained still. She grabbed the thumb forceps and pinched the left side of the wound. She held it up and fed the needle and suture through the skin. She repeated this on the opposite side and then pulled the skin together before she tied it off. She waited for some type of response from Jack but he remained lifeless. If it wasn't for his chest that rose and fell she would have thought he did die. She continued to sow the rest of the wound up until everything was neatly sealed. Just before she completely closed. She took a small package of powder and sprinkled it into the opening. She then closed up the last bit of opening. She took another clear rag and wiped down the surface of the wound. She smiled at how neatly everything looked. She looked at Jack who still sat with her eyes shut completely still.

"Jack?" She asked quietly.

He didn't respond. Her eyes immediately shot to his chest. She watched it raise and fall again. Was he sleeping? She shifted slightly in his lap. He nodded out.

She looked at him for a second, a small smile crept on to her slips, he wasn't annoying while he was asleep. Jack had turned into a very handsome man. Her eyes wandered over his defined cheekbones and down his chiseled jaw. They looked down his neck and a small pink mark that was on the bottom of his neck peeked out of his shirt caught her eyes. A scar? She thought. Without thinking her hand went to the collar of his shirt and she pulled it out slightly so she could look down. It looked like a long scar traveled down from his chest.

"If you wanted to look, I would have just taken my shirt off for you." Jack said playfully as a smirk appeared on his lips.

She nearly jumped off of him. His good arm slipped around her back and stopped her from falling backwards. She placed her hand on his good shoulder steading herself.

"No. I… Um I wasn't sure if you had another wound." Claire said, as she tried to recover from being caught.

He straightened up slightly, his arm still held her in place. He glanced at his shoulder, a look of surprise came over his face. He looked at her and then back at the wound.

"That's amazing. I haven't seen anything like that. Where did you learn this? And where did that stuff come from?" Jack said genuinely.

"A monk." Claire smiled brightly.

"A monk? Seriously?" Jack asked, chuckling.

"Aye a monk." Claire said sharply.

"You're amazing." Jack said as he looked like the boy she once knew.

"Thank you." Claire smiled, she could feel her cheeks turn a deep shade of red.

"You're going to need to not do much with that arm for two weeks and you really should rest right now. You didn't lose enough blood to kill you but it was a decent amount." Claire said as she tried to shift back more to place distance between them.

She pushed back against his arm that held her in place and he reluctantly let go of her. She walked over to the other side of the desk. She needed more space between them.

"Who's your first mate?" Claire asked as she started to clean her instruments.

"Jonah." Jack said shortly as he watched her.

"I'll let him know that is going to need to give out whatever orders are needed for the remainder of the day while you rest." Claire said.

Jack laughed at her comment. Who did this woman think she was?

"Something funny?" Claire said as she turned sharply to face him.

"I will be just fine." Jack said as he matched her stare.

"No, you will rest." Claire said as she folded her arms across her chest and dared him with her eyes.

"If you rip those sutures open or fall out today. I am not resuturing or helping you at all." Claire continued before he could answer.

She began to put her stuff away in her bag as she did so she waited for Jack's argument but it never came. She turned and looked at him, her face questioned if he understood. He smiled softly but you could tell that he was in fact really tired. She frowned and then put her stuff down.

"Jack. come lets get you over to your bed. Just take a nap and I won't hound you about anything else." Claire said as she went to him and picked up his good

arm.

"You promise?" Jack asked with a playful smile on his face.

"Promise." Claire whispered and then helped him stand.

She felt him about to protest about her helping him but changed his mind. They walked slowly across the cabin and to his bed.

Claire helped him sit on his bed. She watched him steady himself before he laid back. She looked at him, a small urge pulled at her heart. She wanted to stay with him. It had been buried and crept up from her deepest wants. She remembers the disappointment she felt when he never returned to take her away on the many adventures he promised.

"Claire?" Jack asked her, as he watched the emotions flash across her face.

"What did you want me to tell Jonah?" Claire asked as she dismissed how nice her name sounded coming out of his mouth.

"Tell him we need to find another source of income before we meet Rowling." Jack said not pursuing her look.

She nodded, questions forming in her mind. She dismissed them; she didn't need to make herself anymore invested in him or his crew. She started to the door.

"Just step out and tell the nearest man to tell Jonah to come up." He said his voice was more of a warning.

Claire narrowed her brows at him. She had planned to just leave but he now acted like she was meant to stay.

"Just tell the nearest man to send Jonah up and you can get settled in the chair for now." Jack said, his voice suggested not to argue.

Claire rolled her eyes as she opened the door of the cabin. A man leaned against the top rail as she looked out.

"You! Have Jonah come to your Captain's cabin immediately." Claire said her voice full of authority.

Jack listened to her and fought back the proud smile that wanted to stretch across his lips. She was definitely a captain. He thought as he shut his eyes softly and listened for the sound of her coming back into the room. He counted her steps as she sunk down into the chair near the desk. She let out a loud sigh and mumbled to herself. She wasn't not at all happy about being shut in here.

Jack did not have the energy to bicker with her. Sleep tugged at him. He heard Jonah enter and he shifted slightly.

"Aye Captain." Jonah asked, his voice a little worried.

"We need to find another ship or something to attack before Rowling meets us...it won't be pretty if we don't have at least a little bit more. Then I might be able to swing him on the fact we have more on the way." Jack said as he kept his eyes closed.

Claire listened closely to the conversation. She was about to protest about them attacking another ship but she heard that there was another person involved. Rowling...what did he have on Jack? She thought about waiting to hear more.

"Aye captain, we will make our way out by another dock. Maybe we will get lucky." Jonah said his eyebrows seem to frown, he was concerned as well.

"Good." Jack said softly.

Jonah began to walk to the cabin door when Jack's voice stopped him.

"Another thing Jonah." Jack called,

"Aye captain?" Jonah asked as paused in the doorway.

"No one is allowed to mention that there is a female on board and no one is going to touch her either. Let them know that if they think they've seen my worse. They haven't." He said as he shifted slightly in pain.

"Aye captain, I will make sure the men know." Jonah said as he walked out the door.

"Jack?" Claire went to ask one of the several questions that was now formed in her mind from that conversation.

The sound of snores was the only response she got. She grumbled as she leaned back in the chair. This was going to be wonderful. She wanted adventure now she was stuck looking at the wooden walls inside Jack's cabin.

Chapter Six

Impossible

She rolled over, she was so comfortable. She stretched outwards and yawned. Her eyes fluttered open and she looked around confused at first. Her mood instantly turned sour. This was not her ship. She sat up slowly. She dozed off and she was no longer in the chair. She glanced to the side of the bed and there was no Jack. She gritted his teeth, he did not listen. She got off the bed, her eyes locked on the cabin door as she stormed towards it. She could not wait until she was back on her ship. Her ship, she gritted her teeth as she realized that it would take Jacob even longer to reach their destination and then to get back to her. Three weeks at least. She sighed deeply, she might as well make herself at home. As she reached the door handle she paused. Jack had made it clear for her to stay in the cabin. Did he not trust his own crew? What kind of person did he become? She gripped the handle and began to turn the knob. She was not afraid of any man and she was not going to spend three weeks trapped inside his cabin. She would go crazy. She turned the handle the rest of the way and yanked it out.

She had expected for the sun to still be shining but when she walked out of the cabin the sun had set and stars speckled across the deep blue sky. She heard male voices by the helm as she looked about the vacant ship. In the far corner of the ship a small group of men were playing cards and drinking by candle light. Cliare smirked as she thought that it was almost romantic. The cool breeze from the sea ran through her hair. She shut her eyes and enjoyed it. She was made to be on the open water. She never felt more safe or at home then

when she was on a ship.

She made her way quietly through the ship. She was excited to explore without anyone to bother her. The moonlight reflected off the tiny silver details of the ship and it played into the ghost feel of it all. She crossed the lower deck careful not to wake anyone and instinctively she headed towards the helm. Before she knew it she was up the stairs and faced the helm. She frowned and shook her head as her eyes spotted Jack as he attempted to steer. He had not seen her yet but his brow had sweat beads across it and his face looked painful. She sighed, his shoulder was never going to heal. She walked over to him and cleared her throat.

"Minimum usage of your shoulder is what I said. Sure looks like your following orders real well." Claire said her voice held disappointment.

"I don't follow orders real well. That's why I became captain." Jack said as he flashed her a forced grin.

"You're supposed to be in my cabin." Jack said his tone matched hers.

"I don't follow orders." Claire mimicked.

"I see that." Jack said as his hand began to shake.

"Where's your first mate or second in command? They should be steering for you." Claire said as she looked about the ship.

"Jonah is the only one who knows how to steer besides me. He needs to in the morning." Jack said annoyed.

"You only have two people who know how to steer on your whole ship." Claire said, shocked.

"The more people who know how to steer, the easier you are at being replaced. I die and Jonah dies, they sink." Jack explained his logic.

"Seriously! Move!" She stated as she walked over to the wheel.

"You are not steering my ship." He growled and gripped the wheel tighter.

"When your shoulder becomes more painful then you're not going to have an option. Hell you could have made yourself bleed already." Claire said bitterly as she stood her ground.

He frowned and ignored her. He kept his eyes on the ocean in front of him and tried to push the pain and her presence from his mind.

"Jackie! Seriously. You have turned into an impossible man." Claire yelled at him, her hands in fist at her side.

"Impossible. Well you're not a peach either." He grumbled to her.

Claire folded her arms across her chest and moved to the railing. She leaned her back against it and stared him down. She could count the sweat beads on his forehead. He was going to cave at some point. She just had to wait him out.

"So you're going to stand there all night and stare at me?" He asked, his voice grew tired.

She didn't answer and chose to look up to the star. A memory of her and Jack laying out under the stars on The Morning Star flashed through her mind. Jason steered and told them stories about the stars and their patterns. She followed the stars till she found Ursa Major and then the north star just as Jason and Jack had taught her. It had stayed with her all these years.She learned much about the stars and the night sky sailing on many trips with Gavin but this memory was one of her favorite memories.

Jack watched her face as she looked at the stars. He wondered what she could possibly be thinking of. The pain in his shoulder radiated down his back now and caused an awful cramp in his neck. His opposite arm ached from trying to compensate. Claire pretended not to notice as he struggled. She shifted her gaze to the men below. The card game from earlier was done and their romantic candle blown out. She smiled softly. She missed her crew, she missed her ship, and she was angry for missing out on her one opportunity. She hated dwelling on it but she kept thinking about it.

The ship swayed one way and then quickly back to the right. She stumbled but kept her footing. A man walking across the low deck wasn't so lucky and fell over. She looked at Jack who looked like he was about to topple over. She turned to him, putting her hands on her hips. She watched him, watched her and took a deep breath.

"Don't say a bloody word. Just come take over for now." Jack said as he gave into Claire finally.

Claire smiled triumphantly and started over to him. She took the wheel and then went to gloat but as she saw the pain streak across the face and how pale he looked she decided not to rub it in. He leaned up against the first mate's cabin watching her.

"Just stay the course, we're sailing close to the next docking area." Jack said and then lowered himself to the floor to sit.

"I know so you can go raid another poor helpless ship." Claire said out loud, irritated.

"Aye Gorgeous." Jack said as he flashed her a small smile before he closed his eyes.

He irritated her so much. She gripped the wheel tightly as she clenched her jar. She glanced back at him to see what he was doing. Her eyes scolded him..

"Gorgeous, I can feel the daggers you're shooting at me. If you're any good of a captain you know when steering you keep your eyes on the horizon." He said with a smirk on his lips.

"Why?' She shouted at him as she fought the urge to let go of the wheel and shake him.

"So we don't crash? You have steered before?" He asked as he opened his eyes slowly.

"No thats-" She started to say but he was up on his feet trying to walk to her.

"For the love of god you can't sail!" He said nearly falling over.

"Shut up!" Claire screamed at him, her frustration and anger rolled off of her in waves.

Jack stopped short and almost stumbled back, as if she hit him physically. He paused and waited for her to continue. Claire took several deep breaths in and out before she could even respond to him.

"That is not what I was saying. Now go sit down before you fall down." Claire said not looking his way.

Jack put his hands up defensively and walked back to the spot where he once sat. He sat down completely confused about what just happened. Even his own actions confused him. If she had been anyone else, she would not have been able to yell at him. He would have cut her down where she stood. He sat silently as he watched her.

She could feel his eyes on her as he watched her. He wanted her to continue or to explain and she debated asking her questions again. She was torn for one he had turned into this arrogant, irritating man and she would much rather ignore him completely but she had this nagging need to know what happened, what turned her Jack into this Jack.

"Why...I meant why are you doing this? " Claire asked softly, almost sad.

"I'm a pir-

"Jack, don't give me no smart ass answer. I know you're a pirate but why turn into this?" Claire said sharply as she cut him off.

"Don't worry yourself with it. It doesn't concern you. When your men get back you'll be free and back on whatever path you were heading down." Jack answered short and cold.

"Fine." Claire said in the same short tone he had used.

Claire tried to focus on anything but the thought of Jack sitting behind her. She stared up at the night sky as she tried to get her mind off of him. She steered silently. The whole ship was quiet, the only sound was the soft whoosh of the ship as it sliced through the ocean. She gritted her teeth and she couldn't help herself, she glanced back and his eyes were closed again. A small noise escaped out of his lips as his breathing deepened. Claire rolled his eyes, that's all she needed was him snoring away.She stared at the horizon, her thoughts drifted to home. She began to hum quietly to herself.

"Keep this candle lit for my love's at sea. Keep it bright so my love can see." She sang quietly in between humming.

"The sea is rough and the days are long. My love is gone. I'll keep this candle lit for me, so my love comes back to me." Claire sang softly.

Hours past and every so often she found herself glancing over her shoulder to steal a glance at Jack. she sighed softly as she shook her head. She could feel the change around her and just as she predicted the sun began to peek over the horizon. She could always

sense dawn. The shimmers of gold touched the tops of the waves. The sunlight dancing on them. Claire's eyes were heavy and she slowly began to nod in and out. The men below started to wake as the sunlight began to slowly spread over the deck and seeped into the deepest cracks on the ship. The men that fell asleep on the deck groaned and stretched.

"What's your name Lady Captain?" A voice said from behind her.

Claire snapped her head up as she realized it had slumped forward. She glanced over their shoulder to see a tall man. He stood just beside Jack who was still sleeping. His hair was the color of the raven's wings and his eyes almost golden. She straightened up and looked forward again.

"It's Claire." She said firmly.

"Ah...Claire." He said as if he had heard of her.

She glanced back at him and narrowed her eyebrows at him, a small frown developed on her face as she did so.

"And you are?" She questioned him.

"Jonah. I'm the Captain's first mate." He said as he walked up to the wheel.

"Nice to meet you." She said but she did not pay him any more attention to him.

"Where did you learn to sail?" Jonah asked, as he moved to lean against the upper rail that faced her.

"My cousin." Claire answered shortly.

"Don't like to talk much?" Jonah asked with a small smile on his lips.

"Did you want to take over?" Claire asked him with a sweet smile.

"Tired?" Jonah asked, his smile grew.

"I could go back and forth with you, with whatever silly nonsense this is but aye I am tired. So if you wish to take over please do so and if not then it would be much appreciated if you took your mindless chatter elsewhere or get to the point of whatever it is you're trying to ask me." Claire said bluntly, was every man on this ship annoying.

Jonah's smile quickly turned into laughter. Claire was a bit taken back by it but his laughter was a little contagious and she began to smile but shook her head at him.

"What?" Claire asked with a smile on her face.

"Nothing." Jonah said through another laugh.

"No seriously you're laughing at me." Claire said, trying to frown at him.

"You're just different….it's nice. Here let me take over." Jonah said as he walked over and held his hand out to take the wheel.

"Thank you." Claire responded and let him take the wheel and step back.

"Welcome. Go get some rest. You can sleep in my cabin behind us. No one will bother you and I'll be right out here to make sure." Jonah said protectively.

Claire smiled at him. She decided that maybe everyone on this ship wasn't so annoying. She might just like Jonah.

"Thank you." Claire said softly as she nodded at him headed towards his cabin.

She stepped past Jack. She frowned slightly as she squatted down to look at his shoulder. The sutures were still intact. It was very swollen from his ignoring her after care instructions. She shook her head and went away from him and into the cabin.

Chapter Seven

Trap

Claire jolted up right in the small cabin bed, her hands clenched as she tried to figure out why she felt threatened. She swung her legs out quickly and placed them on the cool wooden floor. She stood still and listened. She was confused because she thought she heard something. She then heard it again. Shouts echoed from outside the door. She stood and walked to the door. She could the men as they ran about the deck in a hurry. A loud noise that sounded like soft thunder rolled from underneath the floor and Claire knew right away it was cannons. What was going on? She flung open the door and marched out. Men raced to their post. Everyone's sword was on them. Claire's eyes spotted Jonah still steering. She frowned and quickly walked to him. What more could happen, she thought. As she reached Jonah her eyes searched for Jack. A small tinge of worry rushed through her. Jack stood tall in the midst of the chaos giving orders.

"What the hell is going on?" Claire asked as she reached Jonah's side.

"Have a nice nap?" Jonah asked as he tried to keep his voice light and playful but his eyes were fixated on something in the distance.

She ignored his comment and followed his eyes. An incoming ship. She looked at the ship and her stomach sank. It was one of the Queen's ships. Her eyes shot across to Jack. He didn't notice her; he was too busy preparing his men for battle.

"Is he crazy! That's one of the actual Queen's ships! It's not just some pruny ship that has one or two cannons." Claire shouted at Jonah.

He inhaled slightly and nodded saying he knew. Claire eyes ran over the incoming ship. She knew this style of ship. It wasn't the best but it could be deadly if you didn't know it. She grabbed Jonah's forearm.

"Don't you dare pull this ship up on an angle!" Claire said and pulled on his forearm more to have him move the wheel.

Jonah pulled back and tried to get her arms off of his so he could steer. It was better to angle your ship to ensure your cannons could fire.

"Jonah, listen to me! Don't go to the left side of it, it has more cannons on the left side. You need to pull the ship right up on it. If you could get right up on it, the crew won't fire for fear of sinking themself. The cannons they carry have a huge back fire risk. It's been drilled into those men to never fire when they are right up against any other ship." Claire said as quickly as she could.

Jonah paused for a second, his eyes searched her face and she watched his jaw twitch. He nodded to her and then began to slowly approach the ship still on an angle.

"Once I get close enough I'll straighten us out side by side. You better pray for this work." Jonah said to her, his voice nervous.

Jack's eyes shot up to the helm as he felt Jonah change the plan. He saw her stand next to him and he let out a frustrated grunt. He knew she had something to do with it. He began to walk across the lower deck. His face twisted in annoyance which worsened with each step he took. Before no time he was across the deck, up the stairs and at the helm. His hands clenched into fist at his sides. His eyes locked on both Claire and Jonah, he could feel his nostril as they flared with each moment he watched them. Jonah dropped his gaze to

the ground. Jonah wanted Jack to know he was not challenging him. Claire on the other hand met him halfway, her hands in fist at her side as she stomped up to him.

"What-" Jack began to ask.

""Are you crazy? Have you lost your bloody mind? Maybe you can't see what flag hangs off the starboard side but let me tell you. That's the Queen's Colors and it's not just under her protection. See the second flag! This is one of her personal ships! Do you like where your neck is!" She yelled at him, her body shook as she yelled.

The men on the lower deck stopped in amazement as they watched Claire scream at Jack. Jack growled his left hand caught the back of her head and his right hand captured her mouth and covered it.

"Do you have any idea who you're yelling at! Shut your mouth and know your place! You are my prisoner and if you like to be able to walk about then keep your pretty little mouth shut!" Jack bellowed at her.

Claire's eyes narrowed and fire burned in them. That's it, this is enough. She moved her head slightly as she opened her mouth, his hand slipped into it and she bit down. She then slammed her foot down on top of his. Jack let out a small groan as she sank teeth into him. He dropped his hands from her head. She smiled triumphantly.

"If you would just listen you might not die." Claire said to him.

He growled and squared his shoulders at her. She narrowed her eyebrows at him as he tried to intimidate her. She just shook her head at him as she went to open her mouth to finish what she had started to say. Jack in one swift movement grabbed her by her waist and flung her over his shoulders. Claire let out a small shriek and then began to pound on his back with her fist. Jack hung on to her with one hand and let his injured shoulder hang to decrease risk of injury. He walked to Jonah's cabin and kicked the door open. He in long strides reached the bed in no time.

"Jack put me down at this very moment!" Claire yelled at him.

"You bastard!" Claire yelled as she flopped on the bed.

She tried to get up but got tangled in the cover. Jack didn't say a word and turned as he stormed out of the cabin without a word to her. He slammed the door and turned towards it. He knew any second she would be back out here acting like this ship was not his but hers. He felt his eye twitch. He felt around in his pocket for his knife and pulled it out. He slammed the tip into the key hole of the door and snapped it. That should hold her, he thought.

"Seriously, how am I supposed to get into my cabin now?" Jonah said, frustrated slightly.

"Want to explain the change in plans?" Jack said to him with anger in his voice.

"Look, you should listen to her, she knows what she's talking about." Jonah said confidently.

"Seriously, not now Jonah." Jack grumbled.

"Look, she knows that ship. She said if we get right up on it then they can't fire their cannons. Jack, I trust her." Jonah said with a shrug.

Several loud bangs came from behind them as the cabin door rattled. Jack smirked a little at the sound but then heard Jonah's statement and Jack groaned.

"Fine it will just make it easier to board them anyways." Jack said as he turned away from Jonah and went to the rail.

"Jack let me out now!" Claire yelled from inside the cabin, her fist pounded on the door.

He has no idea what he is doing, he is going to get himself hung. She thought as she became even more angry that she was locked in. She slammed her shoulder into the door, whatever he had done she wasn't getting out by force. She turned away from the door, her eyes scanned the dark cabin. She headed towards the desk in the back of the room. She pulled opened the drawers and searched frantically through them. She could not waste any time. She needed something sharp and heavy. She could not see anything in dark drawers, her hands fumbled over objects. She needed a light, this was taking way too long. She shook her head at herself as she spotted a candle on the table and next to it a box of matches. She quickly lit the candle. The amber glow filled the cabin. The glow bounced off something shiny in the drawer. Claire grinned as she saw it. Her fingers wrapped around the metal handle of the long blade. She turned quickly and started towards the door. She paused and she needed something to hit the end of the blade with.

She could feel her heart as it pounded in her chest, her blood pumped through her body as she tried to move quickly. The longer she took, the closer they came to doom. She let out a small breath as her eyes locked on a small hammer and she quickly grabbed ahold of it.

She rushed over to the door and tried to fit the blade into the keyhole to push whatever was held the door in place out. She held the blade tightly in place and then with the hammer began to hit the end of the handle of the blade. Nothing happened. She frowned as she tried again. Still nothing. She groaned. She needed to get out of this cabin and stop Jack before he goes too far. She slammed her fist into the door. She needed to think, she pushed the anger aside and began to look at the door. There had to be a way out, she thought, she ran her hand over the door and fingers tips brushed the metal hinges. Hinges! The hinges! If she can't get through the door, she would just take it down! She grabbed the long blade and anchored it at the bottom of the hinge, she used the hammer to hit the bottom of the handle of the blade. After a few quick hits the bottom bolt was up through the hinge. She grabbed a hold of the bolt and pulled it out. She then stood and did the same to the top hinge. She grinned widely as she took a step back and kicked the door.

Jonah's stomach twisted inside of him as he watched Jack board the Queen's ship. The ladders were across and without the use of the cannons the ship quickly fell to them. Jack walked across the deck of the Queen's ship with a grin on his face. The men quickly rounded up the sailors. They didn't even fight them. They just allowed themselves to be boarded. Jack was uncertain about this but he didn't care.

"All right lads, we will be taking your gold and coins. The quicker you hand them over the quicker we will be off the ship and out of your hair." Jack announced his sword drawn.

No one moved. Jack groaned. His eyes searched the men that stood in front of him for some that was in charge. A tall man caught his eye and Jack

walked over, placing his sword under his chin and smiled at him.

"I will not repeat myself." Jack said his smile threatened as he locked eyes with this man.

"I suggest you put your sword down sir. Did you not see what colors are flying on this ship?" The tall thin man asked Jack.

"I don't care about the colors and if you value the ability to keep speaking then I would suggest you stop and do what I said." Jack said as he pressed the tip into the man's throat.

The man smiled at him, nodded and then whistled. Jack titled his head slightly at the sound of the whistle, confused. At the sound of the whistle armed men began to pour out of the lower deck, they even came out of both cabins. Jack's sword dropped slightly as his crew was surrounded by these new men. Jack looked back at the thin man who smiled from ear to ear.

"If you value your life as a pirate...well that's a funny statement. If you care to not end it now then drop your sword." The thin men chuckled

Jack gritted his teeth as he slowly put his sword down. Jack's men looked around confused, not sure what had just happened. They still held their swords up.

𝒶loud bang behind Jonah nearly made him let go of the wheel. Claire smiled brightly as she stepped over the cabin door that now laid on the ground. Jonah blinked a few times as he watched her. Claire walked over to him and patted him on the shoulder.

"Sorry about your door." She said to him with a silly grin on her face.

Jonah went to respond but a whistle caught his ear. His eyes turned to the Queen's ship. Claire stomach

71

dropped because she knew what the whistle meant. Armed men came flooding out of every hidden space of the ship. Jonah's stomach twisted in on himself and he felt sick.

   "It's a bait ship." Claire said her voice panicked.

   "Bait ship?" Jonah asked as he watched Jack drop his sword.

   "The Queen has armed ships with her colors posted daring pirates to attack them. When they do, they are overrun with hidden men. They bring in all the pirates, hang them and take their belongings to the Queen." Claire said heading back to the cabin.

   "What? Where are you going?" Jonah yelled to her.

   Claire came back out her hat on her head, hair back in a ponytail and her bag slung over her shoulder.

   "Well yeah I guess this would be your rescue. Nice knowing you." Jonah said a little upset.

   Claire nodded her head at him as she headed down the stairs to the lower deck. She walked across the lower deck head held high. Her eyes fixated on Jack. He looked calm and collected but she could tell he panicked underneath it all. He was trying to come up with some sort of plan to get him and his crew out of this. Claire pulled herself up onto the ladder and began to climb across it. Jack's eyes spotted her confused at first and then the same look of betrayal that Jonah had spread over his face, however there was a touch of sadness there. The other men of both crews stopped and watched her curiously. Claire jumped down onto the lower deck of the Queen's ship. She stood there for a moment and then smiled brightly. She then began to clap. Every man looked at her like she was mad.

“Well done gentlemen! Well done! The Queen will be very happy to hear you passed!” Claire announced her voice echoed the silent ship.

“Um, excuse me?” The tall thin man who now had his sword at Jack's throat.

“Captain correct?” Claire asked as she walked to him.

“Aye Captain Wells and you are?” Wells said, looking at her confused.

“Captain Abner.” Claire said as she set her hand on his sword and pushed it down away from Jack's throat.

“Abner...as in the Abner's that run the Queens trading business?” Captain Wells asked, confused but he let Claire push his sword down.

“That's right. We are on our way to settle an old contract however the Queen asked us personally; to see how well her bait ships were doing. She informed us there would be one in the area that we would be traveling through. Hence why the very pirate looking ship we took.” Claire smiled brightly at him.

“A trick pirate ship?” Captain Wells said out loud while he processed.

“Aye trick but more of a training exercise. And you pass! I mean it wasn't exactly fair that I knew that you had less cannons on one side. That they have a horrible back fire risk and you wouldn't fire if we pulled right up on you but still you were triumphant!” Claire smiled.

“Oh and for formalities.” Claire said, opening her bag and pulled out a piece of paper.

“The Queen's seal just so you can be certain we are who we say we are.” Claire smiled and showed him the piece of paper.

Captain Wells looked down at the paper and his expression changed. He nodded and turned to his men.

"Well done gentlemen, we have made the Queen proud and passed her test!" Captain Wells said to his men with a big smile on his face.

Claire clapped as the men began to cheer for themselves. Claire glanced over to Jack whose mouth hung open at the scene in front of him. Claire smirked and pinched his side. His mouth closed quickly.

"Well we have much to do and in a bit of a time crunch since we stopped to help the Queen in this task. I will have my men back on our ship and we will be on our way." Claire said as she held her hand out to shake Captain Well's hand.

"Aye Captain Abner. We have heard much about your family and my youngest wants to be like you and your cousin. Scares me to death but unlike most men I am proud my daughter has ambition." Captain Wells said as he shook Claire's hand.

"That is wonderful to hear. If you're ever in our area and your daughter wants a tour of our ships you stop by our office. I will personally show her the ships." Claire said with a big smile.

"Aye we will do that!" Captain Wells said, returning the smile.

"Alright boys back to the ship we have a lot to do!" Claire yelled as she turned on her heels back towards the rail of the ship.

She hopped onto the rail and climbed across the ladder to The Evening Star. Jack stood still as he watched his men follow her over to the ship. He was beyond baffled at what exactly just happened. Captain Wells clapped Jack on the back.

"Aye sir, women like that are one of a kind. Not for the light hearted. I would put your eyes back in your head, lad, and make your way back to your ship." Captain Wells chuckled.

Jack smiled back at him and then walked over to the rail and crossed to his ship.

Chapter Eight

Torment

Claire had a big grin as she walked up the stairs to the helm. Jonah stared at her, his face riddled with confusion. She laughed at him and shook her head.

"Once all the men are on board Mr. Jonah, you may set sail." Claire chuckled more.

"Care to explain how the hell you just did, whatever it is you just did?" Jonah said as he continued to stare at her like he couldn't believe his eyes.

"I-

Claire went to explain but her elbow was caught by someone's hand. The hand gripped it and led her away from the helm. She groaned and rolled her eyes. She knew who it was without even looking at him.

"Jonah set sail." Jack muttered as he walked by him and led Claire to the cabin.

He stopped short in front of Joanh's cabin as he stared at the door on the floor. He glanced down at Claire who had the silliest grin on her face. He shook his head as he stepped over it and into the cabin as he tugged her along. Once inside he dropped her elbow.

"What you want to thank me for saving your neck in private. Too embarrassed to say it in front of your men. That's fine, I don't need to hear it. Pretend it didn't happen." Claire said as she waved her hand at him as she went to walk by him.

He caught her arm again and stopped her from walking past him. She became angry with being handled. He was so ungrateful.

"You know Jack, you have an awfully weird way of saying thank you." She said as she spun around to him about to give him a piece of her mind.

Jack's hand quickly went to her cheek and Claire froze as his hand touched her skin. He pulled her towards him and pressed his lips against hers. Sparks shot through her the minute his lips touched hers. This intoxicating feeling wrapped around her and she couldn't stop herself as she stepped closer to him. Her mouth began to move with his. His arm wrapped around her waist and pulled her even closer to him. He pulled back for a second and looked down at her. She was absolutely stunning, brave and fearless. He thought. The glossy look in her eyes left and fire was replaced. Jack raised an eyebrow confused. Claire pulled back and in one quick motion slapped him across the face. She turned on her heels and walked out of the cabin. She paused in the doorway to glance back at Jack who still held his face.

"Don't ever Thank me again!" She said as she turned back around and stepped over the fallen door.

She stomped over to Jonah who was still steering. He glanced sideways at her, a question lingered on his lips.

"Don't ask." Claire said firmly as she looked out over the horizon.

"That back there was pretty amazing. Thank you. I'm sorry I thought you were leaving us. I mean I wouldn't have blamed you." Jonah said quietly.

"Thank you." Claire said a small smile came to her lips.

"Where are we off too now?" Claire said as she settled herself on the rail.

"Skull cavern, well just outside of it. We're not docking." Jack interrupted the conversation.

Claire frowned as she heardJack's voice. Jonah nodded to Jack but then spotted his red cheek and a silly smirk appeared on his face.

"Something funny about the skull cavern?" Jack asked Jonah through gritted teeth,

"Not at all Captain ... .although we keep going from one horrible situation to the next so maybe we need to find the humor in it. We just escaped death to head for it again." Jonah said, beginning to rant.

Claire squinted at Jonah wondering about his statement as she went to ask Jack but he spoke before her.

"You talk and think too much Jonah just steer the ship; we should be there by sunrise. " Jack ordered as he made his way towards the stairs.

"Explain now." Claire said to Jonah as Jack disappeared to the lower deck.

"I really shouldn't be saying anything to you but since you just saved all of our lives. I'll give you the super short version. We're going to meet a dangerous man to give him what little we made and hope he doesn't get mad and kill us." Jonah said and shrugged his shoulders.

"Well that sounds silly, why would a bunch of pirates give away their loot or whatever you guys call it to someone else?" Claire asked as she turned around to face him.

Jonah shrugged again. Claire narrowed her eyes at him and flooded her arms across her chest to let him know she wasn't going to budge on this.

"Ugh ok. There is this insane man who wants to be king of the pirates and now you have to pay him to use the ocean. No payment and you're caught on the ocean, you're dead." Jonah said like it was nothing.

"So Jack's going to pay him?" Claire asked, confused.

"Yup or hell hunt us down. He's got a thing for Jack." Jonah said with a wink to Claire.

“Why would Jack even agree to this? Why not just ignore him, the ocean is so big? Who does this guy think he is claiming he owns something that he has no right to.” Claire said as she became mad.

“Simple Jack has seen what happens when you don't pay him.” Jonah said his voice cracked a little.

“What happened?” Claire asked quietly.

“The former Captain everyone loved. He was fair and got things done. We weren't really pirates, more treasure hunters. We went on all these adventures and made a good living doing it. Jack was like a son to him. Jason had stepped down from Captain and was letting Jack take the reins. We were out at sea and we were trapped by ships. We were quickly boarded and even though we fought hard there were too many of them. Rowling is his name. He had a proposition for Jack, he wanted him to join his fleet of pirate ships. Jack wanted nothing to do with this man. Just by looking at him you got a bad feeling. He then ordered Jack to pay him seventy five percent of what he had on board. Jack laughed in his face. Rowling went to slice Jack's throat and Jason stepped in. Jason tried his best to smooth things over but Jack had insulted him. He gutted Jason in front of Jack. Left Jack on the floor of the deck holding Jason with Jason's guts sprawled about him. I've never seen so much blood. I've never seen Jack like that. He was so frantic and in so...so much pain as he tried to save Jason. He even tried to get his guts back inside of him. It's a slow painful death to die that way. Jack had to put Jason out of his misery.” Jonah's voice cracked several times while he spoke, it was too painful still to talk about.

Tears fell down Claire's cheek as she realized what had happened to her friend. She felt sick like she was going to vomit. Her eyes searched and found Jack and she couldn't imagine dealing with all of that.

"Jason." Claire said softly as another tear slipped down her cheek.

"You knew Jason?" Jonah asked her, surprised.

"Aye when I was a little girl." Claire said as she let out a small breath to calm herself.

"I'm sorry. I didn't know." Jonah said softly.

"I had just assumed he retired. Or something." Claire said as she wiped her eyes quickly.

"I am so sorry. I didn't know, I would have told you differently. Now you know why Jack is the way he is." Jonah said softly.

Claire watched Jack walk about the lower deck as he inspected things. She tried to pull herself together. As if he sensed her eyes on him, he looked up locking eyes with her. She felt so much pain for him. She couldn't imagine having to go through that and she herself had been through a lot. He looked up at her confused and then concerned. He began to cross the lower deck to get to her. She shook her head to let him know she was ok. He paused for a second confused. She smiled at him and then stepped back from the rail.

"Strange woman." Jack muttered to himself as he went back to inspecting the rest of the ship.

Claire began to think of how she could help Jack. She glanced at Jonah.

"What do you mean he has a thing for Jack?" Claire asked curiously.

"Well he enjoyed seeing Jack in so much pain that he now looks for Jack to make his life even more hell. Jack had told him to his face on their second encounter that he was going to run his blade through him and cut him from end to end. So Rowling cut Jack after killing the cabin boy. He sliced Jack from his chin down his throat, over his chest and to his belly button. He had Jack pinned up and did it with one slow cut so that he wouldn't kill him. He enjoys tormenting him." Jonah said with disgust.

"How much is he wanting tomorrow?" Claire asked, feeling sick.

"It doesn't really matter, it won't be enough and we don't have anywhere to get anymore." Jonah said defeated.

"You know for someone's fate hanging in the balance here you're ever bla about." Claire said to Jonah as she frowned at him.

"I've been waiting for this day for years now." Jonah said with another small shrug.

"Stop shrugging about everything. And why stay?" Claire asked him confused.

"Most of us this is all we know. That and Jack. He might be mean and difficult or impossible." He said impossible and threw a wink at her.

"But he's a good man." Jonah said with a nod.

Claire didn't say anything but looked down at the crew. Tomorrow will be here in no time. Her stomach sank. She left Jonah and headed into his cabin. She headed to the desk lighting the candle once more and began to try to come up with some plan.

Claire frowned, she had nothing. She didn't have any jewelry on her, she had nothing at all. The sad pouch of coins Jack had taken from The Crown would not be enough. She sat at the desk and folded her

head into her arms. She had to double check, maybe
something in her bag would make her think of
something. She began emptying her bag. Clothing,
journal, maps, the Queen's contract, the seal, and then
a box came thumping out. Claire tilted her head. The
box was a deep velvet color and a maroon color ribbon.
Her eyes widened. The Queen had a gift for the people:
the trade agreement. Claire took a deep breath.

"Please, please, please! Be something good."
Claire whispered to the box.

She pulled the maroon ribbon and slowly lifted
the lid to the box. She squealed as she looked inside the
box. She stood up happily. Inside the box was the
biggest ruby she had ever seen. She was ecstatic this
surely would hold the asshole over. She was so excited
she did a little dance. She needed to tell Jack they
would be ok. She closed the velvet box and tied the
ribbon back around it. She held onto it like it was the
most precious thing in the world and started to make her
way to Jack's cabin.

She walked out of the cabin as she tried to
contain her happiness. Jonah steered and his demeanor
seemed to have gotten gloomy. He glanced at her and
she smiled brightly at him. He raised an eyebrow at her
asking without words.

"Oh just off to save your lives again!" She smiled
at him.

"Claire. What do you mean?" He yelled at her
back as he watched her bounce happily down the stairs.

"You'll see don't worry anymore today!" Claire
chuckled as she yelled up to him and made her way
across the lower deck.

"You're crazy!" He yelled to her several of the
men looked up and wondered about the exchange.

Claire ignored him and nodded to the men who had watched as she continued on her mission.

Chapter Nine

Talks

$\mathcal{J}$ack paced the floor in his cabin. He had been
for hours, the last time they came up short he killed one
of his men. There were no docking sites along the way
so no ships to rob. He sank to the ground in front of his
desk as he leaned into it. He wanted to kill him. The
thought plagued his dreams. He had thought of every
way possible. Drowning him, hanging him, gutting him
and leaving him on the floor of his own ship like he
deserved. He wanted to watch the life fade from his
eyes like he had to watch Jason. He leaned his head
back into the desk. Maybe he could just kill him
tomorrow, he smirked. Get close enough to him just to
run his knife through him. He smiled. He felt like if he
could kill Rowling and maybe his first mate, everything
would fall apart and it would go back to the way it was.
This was his only option. He needed to end it all, he
needed to kill Rowling and if he died doing it then so be
it.

He frowned thinking of Claire. He needed to hide
her. If Rowling knew she was on board it would be
worse then what happened to Jason. He couldn't think
of the things that he would do to a woman, especially a
woman that meant something to him. His crew would
fight to protect her. He saw it in their eyes the moment
that she saved them all. The way they didn't hesitate to
follow her on to his ship. They all immediately admired
her. He ran his hand down this face and covered them.
Rowling would die tomorrow. He'll save his crew and
Claire.

Jack stared at the bottle in his hand. He had opened it only a few minutes ago and had three long swigs out of it. The whiskey hit the back of his throat and was warm going down. He didn't have much of a life to celebrate but while Jason was alive he had seen many amazing things. So it wasn't all that bad. He took another sip as there was a loud knock on the door.

"Aye?" He yelled slightly annoyed.

Whoever it was did not respond but turned the knob and walked in. Claire came in and shut the door behind her. Seeing her, he took another shot from the bottle, this woman would be the death of him if he wasn't already planning on dying tomorrow. God she was gorgeous he thought. She walked towards him, her hair flowed down around her in soft curls. Her hair was always so golden. It reminded him of the gold that hit the tops of the waves and scooted across the ocean tops as the sun came up. His eyes ran up her legs that went on for days and lingered on her hips that begged for someone to grab on to. His eyes traveled the rest of her another moment lingering on her breast that even her white loose button shirt couldn't hide. They stopped at her face that was now filled with annoyance.

"You know you're really pretty when you're not making that face all the time." Jack chuckled a little bit, his voice a little slurred.

"And we're all about to die in the morning and your plan is to drink." Claire groaned as she sat on the floor next to him.

"I have a plan and it's a good one. No worries gorgeous we'll be out of this mess in no time. After tomorrow I'll have Jonah set sail towards your previous destination and you will be back commanding your ship in no time." Jack grinned and nudged her with his arm.

"You really are the most exhausting person I know." Claire sighed.

"And your the most annoying, aggravating, thorn in my side-

"Hey! Alright-" Claire began to cut him off.

"You didn't let me finish." Jack smirked.

"Gorgeous, stubborn, admirable, and smart woman I've met." Jack said with a silly grin on his face.

"Well Thank you ...I guess." Claire chuckled.

"You're welcome." Jack said as he took another sip of his whiskey.

"Alright that's enough of this." Claire said and took the bottle from him.

"Hey I wasn't finished with that." Jack pouted.

"Now tell me exactly what is this master plan of yours." Claire said as she put the cap on the bottle and placed it off to the side of her.

"Nope." Jack said, shaking his head.

"Really, we're going to be a child right now." Claire said, as she rolled her eyes at him.

"You won't like it and you're not a part of it. I still have to figure out where I am hiding you." He said, his eyes wandered around the room.

"Even dressed as a man you're a very pretty man. You draw way too much attention." Jack said, his eyes coming back to her.

"Anyways, I have another plan." Claire said as she ignored his drunken statement and pulled out the velvet box.

"What's that?" Jack asked as he looked down at the neatly tied ribbon that sat on top of the box.

"Open it. I think it will give us some time to figure out in the long run what to do about this Pirate King." Claire said as she handed him the box.

"Holy shit Claire! Where did you get this?" Jack asked as he looked down into the box.

A large ruby sat inside of the velvet box. Jack's eyes kept looking from her to the ruby. A smile grew on his face.

"It was supposed to go with Jacob as a present to renew the contract. The contract will be renewed with or without the ruby." Claire said with a smile on her face.

"This will differently please that bastard." Jack said as he closed the box.

Jack tried to reach around her to get the bottle. She scooted it further away and shook her head no at him. He chuckled lightly before he realized just how close they were to each other. His face inches from hers. She could feel her stomach tight up with excitement. She caught his eyes as they stared at her lips and she subconsciously pulled in her bottom lip wetting it. Desire flashed in his eyes as he studied her face. She could feel her cheeks flush.

"Jack?" Claire whispered.

"Claire." He answered her back as he began to lean in closer.

She began to panic as he came closer to her. So many thoughts flooded her mind. So many questions.

"Why didn't you come back?" Claire whispered, as she leaned back away from him. She felt like she had just cracked her chest open to let the sentence escape. She shut her eyes as she waited for him to answer.

Jack froze, why didn't he come back? Her sentence echoed in his head. His eyes studied her face, there was so much hurt there. Something shiny caught his eye at the base of her collar. He moved his hand slowly to it and hooked his index finger around it. As he pulled it slowly out from under her shirt. The silver chain holding the aquamarine stone fell through his fingers. He pulled back slightly amazed that she still had it and still wore it. Claire's hand came up and grasped the stone, her eyes still shut.

"Jackie, why didn't you come back? Do you know how much time I spent waiting for you? I would go to that stupid dock waiting to see you. Knowing that you would eventually come back one day and then when you didn't. I thought you most likely died. Because my Jack always came back to me." Claire said her voice shook more as she fought back the tears that begged to escape.

She thought she was tougher than this. She had promised herself that she was done with these silly emotions about him. She had promised to strangle him if he wasn't dead and she saw him again. She smiled a little at herself with the last thought.

"Claire, I wanted to. Believe me, I thought about it every day. I couldn't. " He said his hand went to her cheek as he moved himself more in front of her.

"You said you would. You said that you would come back and get me; we have all these silly adventures." Claire said as she opened her watery eyes.

Jack stroked her cheek with his thumb. His chest tightened, it ached to see her like this. It felt like something had grabbed ahold of his heart and was squeezed it

"Silly. I guess that was the right word." Claire laughed at herself and went to move her face away from his hand.

"Claire, I wanted to. Everything happened so fast. Jason got…. sick. I had to take over and then when everything was looking better and I thought about going back to get you...Rowling appeared. I couldn't bring you out here, not with him." Jack said as he stopped her from , capturing her other cheek.

Claire's eyes searched his, she understood but was still so hurtful. She didn't want to bring up Jason and Rowling. She knew he worded it the way he did to avoid telling her. She didn't want to cause anymore pain for Jack, especially when he would be seeing Rowling in a few short hours. She nodded slightly.

"I thought about leaving. I thought about going back and maybe starting a new life." Jack said, leaning forward and rested his forehead against her.

"I could see the whole thing. I had plans for us. I had happily ever drawn up. I did, I swear I did Claire. I swear I was coming back to you." Jack said his voice sounded painful.

A tear slipped out of Claire's eye and ran down her cheek. Hearing Jack her heart knotted up on itself. She put her hand to his cheek and nodded that she understood.

"Then Rowling happened. I made one hell of an enemy. If I went back to you, he would find me. He would find us. I would lead him right to you. I couldn't let him be anywhere near you." He said quietly.

Then he chuckled softly. He placed his lips to her forehead and kissed her like she was the most precious thing in his world. Warmth spread through her as his lips touched her skin. She leaned into the kiss. It felt so right.

"And then you showed up. Just like the first time but instead of my ship, it was yours I was on." He laughed as he sat back on his heels.

Claire chuckled softly and wiped her eyes. The world had a funny way of working.

"Jack, we'll figure out a plan to get rid of Rowling." Claire said as she took his hand in hers and squeezed.

"No right now I need to figure out how to hide you." Jack said almost like he was talking to himself.

He could hide her below deck. He wouldn't go down there...or would he. Jack wasn't sure what he would do. He sat back and ran his hands down his face. The alcohol started to wear off. Claire leaned forward and placed her hands on his. She slowly pulled them down from his worried face. She scooted closer to him, her hand slipped around to the back of his neck and she curled her fingers into his bronze hair. His face showed confusion at her actions but he didn't stop her. She slowly pulled him forward, her mouth going to his.

She gently placed her soft lips against his and kissed him. He blinked at the realization of what was happening all of a sudden click. He wrapped his arm around her and pulled her body up against his as he swept her into his lap. His hand wrapped around the back of her neck as he kissed her back hungerly. He had been waiting years to kiss her like this. He had dreamt about her lips, her touch and what it would be like to hold her in his arms. Shivers went through her body as she felt his mouth capture her lower lip. She kissed him back as she matched his own want. She felt his mouth open against hers and she mimicked his motion. His tongue slipped into her mouth and teased hers. Another wave of shivers went through her as she felt his tongue explore her mouth. She grew brave and

began to follow his motions. His hands ran down her spine, a trail of tingles following wherever his hands went. He pulled her closer to him if at all possible, her breast pressed up against his chest made him grow even more eager. His hands slipped around the front of her and began to explore under her shirt.

An ache grew in her core and began to grow as she felt his hands on her bare flesh. His hand traveled up over her stomach, Claire trembled against him. His hand didn't stop, it traveled to her full breast and cupped it firmly in his hand. Claire let out a small moan from her lips as her breast begged to be touched and squeezed more. Her moan brushed across his lips and he groaned in response. The nose made him want her more.

He broke their kiss and began to place kisses down her neck. As he reached the curve of her neck he grazed her skin with his teeth. She inhaled sharply at the sensation as she grabbed a hold of him to steady herself. He brushed his thumb over her nipple and teased it and another sweet noise escaped her mouth. He pulled the skin of her neck slightly into her mouth and sucked on it. Claire melted into him another whimper of pleasure passed from her mouth. The ache that had formed between her legs deepened. All these sensations were new to her and she was losing her mind. She wanted him in ways she didn't understand but her body did.

"Captain." The cabin door flew open as Jonah all but ran in.

Jack quickly pulled Claire's shirt back down as he removed his hand from underneath. He didn't move her from his lap but turned his gaze to Jonah with daggers shooting from his eyes. Claire was still in a trance.

"Jonah I swear to god-

"Jack he's here." Jonah cut him off, he did not even acknowledge what was going on in front of him.

Chapter Ten

Rowling

The words he's here shook him to the core. He glanced down at everything he wanted in life sitting in his lap and he panicked. He grabbed a hold of Claire as he stood up and lifted her to her feet as well.

"What does he's here mean exactly?" He asked Jonah his eyes frantically looked about the cabin as he still held on to Claire.

"Wait what?" Claire asked as she snapped out of it.

"As in he's boarding the ship now." Jonah said his own worries came out in his voice.

"Fuck..Fuck..Fuck" Jack said he almost turned in a full circle as he looked about.

"Ok so we're fine. We'll give him the coins and the ruby. Tell him we'll get more and everything's fine." Claire said as she grabbed ahold of Jack who looked like a dog chasing his tail.

"No, we're not fine, you're out in plain sight." Jack said, gritting his teeth.

"Jack its-

"No Claire, it's not ok. He'll hurt you. He'll hurt you in horrible ways." Jonah said as he leaned against the door blocking it from anyone coming in.

Claire eye's shot to Jack and understood his panic, he was freaked out not because the big bad wolf was here but because he didn't want her to get hurt. She glanced around the room and there was no way out other than the front door. She tried to come up with some plan as Jack pulled her across the way. She followed behind him, her mind caught up in her thoughts of what she could do to hide herself. Jack opened a small closet door. It was big enough to fit a few coats. He grabbed a coat out of it and tossed it off to the side and then grabbed a hold of Claire.

"Thank god you're tiny." He muttered as he grabbed her by the waist and placed her inside the closet.

"Look at me, look at me!" Jack said and grabbed her face in his hands.

"Don't you dare come out of here. You hear me? Don't come out. No matter what you hear. When everything is ok Jonah or I will get you." Jack said forcefully at her.

Claire nodded. Everything happened so fast, she almost couldn't keep up. Her brain felt scattered.

"Say it. Say you understand!" Jack said as he felt the clock ticking.

"I understand." Claire nodded.

"Good girl." He said with relief as he brought his lips to her forehead.

He kissed her on the forehead and pulled away like it might be the last time he touched her. Claire's stomach dropped as he shut the door. He left in the darkness of the closest. Jack placed his hand against the closet door as he took a deep breath in. He then stood tall and walked over to his desk and leaned casual against. He gathered his emotions and got himself in check, he glanced at Jonah and nodded to his as if to

say it's going to be fine. Jonah walked over to join him
at the desk.

"Jack my boy! Ahead of schedule!" The cabin
door pushed open as Rowling walked in followed by
three of his men.

"Rowl-" Jack went to greet him but that stood
behind Rowling cleared his throat.

"King Rowling." Jack said as he changed his
tone, he tried his hardest not to show irritation.

"Jack, I'm excited to see what you have for me
this month! Surely I won't be disappointed. I hate being
disappointed." Rowling said as he walked around Jack
and took a seat at the desk.

Two loud thuds rippled across the desk as
Rowling propped his feet up. Jack turned to the
so-called king. He wasn't much of a man, he had broad
shoulders but a thin build. No muscles at all. He had
plain mossy brown hair and shark eyes. They were so
dark you could not see the center of them. A silly
mustache danced upon his lips that he played with while
he waited.

"Jonah go retrieve the coins we have collected."
Jack said to Jonah who nodded.

Jonah nodded and walked over to the chest in
the corner and pulled out a small pathetic bag. Jonah
walked over to the desk and placed it down on it. He
then stepped back behind Jack. Jack glanced around
quickly...the ruby. His eyes shot over to the closet. Claire
still had it. It was too late now, he couldn't go retrieve it.
He inhaled and prepared himself for whatever would
happen next. He didn't have any weapon on him so his
original plan of killing him did not look too good. Rowling
picked up the bag and bounced it in his hand lightly.
Anger came across his face.

"This...This is what you have for me." Rowling said, dropping the bag on to the desk as he stood.

"You know Jack, this is unacceptable." Rowling said as he slammed his fist on the desk which made the bag bounce.

"We were on our way to get more. We had a run in with one of the Queen's ships and managed to bullshit our way out of it. We would have had more." Jack said he did not let Rowling's anger phase him.

"It sounds like you think this is no big deal." Rowling yelled as spit flew out of his mouth.

Jack stayed quiet, if he opened his mouth right now the wrong thing would slip out and he knew someone would get hurt.

Claire heard the yelling and glanced down at her hand, she could barely see in the dark closet but she could make out the ribbon on the box. How did she still have it? She thought as the urge to throw up overcame her.

"Jack, I am talking to you." Rowling yelled.

Rowling snapped his fingers and the two men came up behind Jack and brought him forward to the desk. Jonah went to move but Jack shot him a look telling him to stay put. Jack's face was slammed into the desk.

"Jack, you would think by now you would understand that I am not someone to make unhappy. I mean first your friend Jay, then the cabin boy, then umm..I'm not sure it's hard to keep count but how many times do I have to hurt you and those around you. Soon you won't have a crew left if we keep going this route." Rowling said as he walked about talking with his hands.

"Jason." Jack said with anger in his voice.

"What was that?" Rowling asked as he took a step forward and leaned down to look at Jack.

"His name was Jason." Jack said through gritted teeth.

"Kenton….Knife." Rowling said and snapped his finger.

Jonah went to move again and Jack narrowed his eyes at him. Jonah reluctantly stepped back. Claire fidgeted in the closet, she had to get the ruby to him. She froze as she heard the word knife. She turned the handle of the closet slowly and a stream of light came in. Claire peeked out of it. Her heart sank as she saw Jack being held by two large men on his desk. She knew right away which man was Rowling he was pranced about as he talked. In his hand he twirled a knife. Jonah saw her and his eyes widen as if to tell her to shut the door. She shook her head and although it was a small crack she knew she was still hidden. Jonah began to cross to her, Rowling and his men were too caught up with Jack to notice him move.

"Now now Jack, what should I do with you?" Rowling snickered.

Jack did everything he could to stop himself from rolling his eyes. This man was all about the dramatics. He wanted to ask him to stab him in the ear so he didn't have to hear his voice anymore. A smile crept across his lips at his own thoughts.

"Something funny." Kenton, Rowling's first mate asked.

Jack went to shrug but the wound on his shoulder hurt. He winced from the pain. The way they held him down put too much pressure on it. Rowling caught the action and came over to investigate.

"Hurt, are we Jack?" Rowling asked, sounding too happy about it.

"Here?" Rowling asked as he pressed the knife to his shoulder.

Jack clenched his jaw shut in an attempt to not give into Rowling. The mere movement was enough to get Rowling to giggle.

"Oh I must see what has Mr. Tough guy in pain." Rowling giggled again.

He took the knife and sliced through Jack's shirt exposing the sew up wound. Rowling studied it curiously.

"Who sewed you up? I didn't know any of your men were talented." Rowling asked.

"It wasn't my men. An island woman did." Jack said shortly.

"Ahh I see." Rowling said a sinister grin on his face.

He ran his blade over the sutures popping them open one by one. It didn't phase Jack, he was unsure why Rowling would think that would hurt. The wound spread open again. It had enough time to start the healing process so less of his inner meat was exposed. Rowling then pressed the blade into the open wound Jack clenched his jaw shut again as he blocked out the pain. He felt the blade dig deeper into his flesh as blood began to flow from it. Rowling slowly dragged the knife back and forth through the wound in almost a sawing method. Jack didn't budge or make a sound. Claire watched in horror, something told her this was only the beginning. She had to do something. Jonah had made his way across the room and leaned back into the closet door as he tried to shut it. Claire wedged her knee in it slightly trying to keep it open a crack. She realized all she had to do was drop the box outside of the door.

"Jonah, I'm going to drop a small box outside the door. It will save Jack." She whispered as he still tried to push the door shut.

Jonah stopped as he heard what she said. Claire squeezed the velvet box out of the crack and let it fall to the ground. Jonah quickly bent over and picked it up.He then pressed the closet door shut.

"You know Jack, I recently discovered that I am fascinated with ears. Maybe it's because I like the sound of my own voice. Anywho do you think your Island girl could reattach your ear?" Rowling said wickedly.

Rowling leaned over Jack, his hot sour breath hit Jack in the side of his face as he grabbed a hold of Jack's ear. He placed the knife to the back of it and began to press.

"Wait! Stop!" Jonah yelled as he stepped forward.

Rowling let the blade drag down behind Jack's ear before he stopped and looked up. The look of annoyance plastered on his face.

"Well get on with it before I cut something off of you as well." Rowling held up his knife that had Jack's blood on it.

"This fell out of the coin bag, you thought it was just coins but here." Jonah said as he walked over and placed the box on the desk.

Rowling looked over at the velvet box, his eyes filled with wonder as he picked it up.

"Did you wrap this for me?" He laughed as he pulled the ribbon and took the top off the box.

His eyes widened as he looked into the box. A chuckle escaped his mouth as he turned to Jack. He snapped letting the men know to let him up. They pulled him up off the desk and upright. Jack had blood that ran down his neck from the cut he had behind his ear. Blood also ran down his arm. Rowling walked over to Jack and slapped him on his bad shoulder, like they were friends.

"Why didn't you say something! This makes me very happy!" Rowling laughed as he took out the ruby and held it in the air.

"It's beautiful! You fool, you almost lost an ear!" Rowling said as he hit him in the shoulder again.

Jack was biting a hole in his tongue to stop himself from saying anything.The men on the side of him loosen up a bit with their captain happy.

"And you, why did you take so long to bring it forward?" Rowling turned as he asked Jonah.

Jonah looked unsure of how to answer but Jack stepped in answering for him.

"I ordered him not to speak unless spoken to." Jack said quickly.

"Ah I see." Rowling said not questioning the silly statement Jack just made.

"Nevertheless you, you put your hand on the desk. Making me waste my time when this could have been a quick meet and greet." Rowling said, looking at Jonah as he twirled the knife in his hand again.

Jack stiffened up unsure of what exactly Rowling was going to do to Jonah but he knew it wasn't going to be good. Jack shook off one of the guys that held him and stepped forward and placed his own hand on the desk.

"It was my order, I wasted your time not Jonah. I knew the box was in there as well." Jack said his eyes narrowed at Jonah telling him not to move.

"Jack, you always surprise me. It seems that your love of pain is never ending." Rowling chuckled and walked over to the desk.

"Very well. Kenton give me a knife I don't like." Rowling said, snapped again.

Kenton smirked, reaching inside his inner pocket and pulling out an old knife. He pulled the blade out of the sleeve. It didn't look sharp at all. Jack rolled his eyes at the dramatics going on again. Rowling whistled lightly as he took the knife from Kenton and went to Jack. He looked at Jack and studied his hand as he debated on what he wanted to do. Then without warning he impaled Jack's hand to the desk. Jack shut his eyes as the pain washed over him, not one gasp or sound escaped his lips. Rowling laughed at Jack's reaction.

"Jack, I love how strong you are! I was debating cutting a finger off but seeing how you got me some coins and a lovely ruby I figured that would be too much. Well I shall show myself out. It was a pleasure as always. See you next month Jack my boy." Rowling said as he waved his men off to leave.

Rowling walked happily out of Jack's cabin with a hum and a whistle as he went. His entourage followed behind him. Jonah rushed over to Jack to look at his hand. Jonah's hand going to the knife.

"Leave it for a second!" Jack yelled.

"Go make sure he's gone." Jack ordered Jonah.

"I'm fine, just go watch him leave." Jack yelled at him this time.

Jonah nodded and headed to the cabin door and looked back at Jack once more before left. As the cabin door shut again, he heard the closet door creek.

"Don't you dare come out here yet. Doesn't anyone listen around here! I said we would come get you when it was safe." Jack said to the closet door becoming frustrated.

The creaking stopped for a second, it took everything in Claire not to rush out and run to Jack. She didn't want to cause anymore trouble so she listened for once.

"Tell me how bad you are?" Claire asked through the door.

"Nothing happened, he's all talk." Jack responded, his free hand touched the blade and he debated if he could pull it out himself.

"He asked for a knife and threatened to cut your ear off. Just because I couldn't see doesn't mean I couldn't hear. Don't lie to me Jack or I'll come out right now." Claire said firmly.

Jack shook his head. He was bleeding, he needed to be sewn back up again, he didn't know what the back of his ear looked like, he was literally stuck to his desk and now he was being harassed by Claire through the closest. And she said he was impossible, he shook his head.

"Cut me some slack Claire, just stay quiet until Jonah comes back just to make sure you're safe. I'm injured but fine." Jack pleaded with her.

He heard a fine mutter from the closet as he touched the knife again and winced. He didn't know if he could get the right angle or have enough strength to pull it out. He sighed he would have to wait for Jonah.

Chapter Eleven

Want

The door of the cabin opened up and he could hear footsteps. He let out a sigh of frustration. The minutes felt like hours as he waited for Jonah to come back. His stomach twisted, all he wanted to know was that they were off his ship.

"What in the hell took so long? Is he off my fucking ship yet?" Jack said as he tried to see Jonah.

A low chuckle echoed through the cabin. Jack gritted his teeth, he hated this man just as much as Rowling. Jack balled his free hand into a fist as he tried to control his anger.

"Now Jack, that kind of hurts my feelings. Rushing us out like that. We didn't even get to chit chat." Kenton chuckled as he walked closer to Jack.

"Rowling has everything I got." Jack said almost mono toned.

"Oh well he sent me back up here to let you know he's taking half of your food rations as well." Kenton chuckled again as he now stood next to the desk and sat down on it.

"Fine." Jack growled.

Kenton's eyes lit up as he studied Jack, he looked him over and smirked. He reached over and tapped the blade held him in place. Jack clenched his jaw and shut his eyes and blocked out the pain.

"You know Jack, I don't understand you...these men of yours are replaceable. Here you are stuck to a desk, bleeding, in pain and all because you didn't want someone else to get hurt." Kenton said he tilted the blade slightly one way.

"Someone like you wouldn't." Jack said his eyes snapped open and locked with Kentons.

The threat in Jack's eyes told Kenton that the only reason he and Rowling were still alive was because of all the people Jack cared about. If there was nothing left, they would be dead. Jack's eyes were full of rage and made Kenton pause for a moment. Kenton smiled slightly and leaned into Jack's ear.

"It's never going to happen and you're gonna end up dead trying to be the hero." Kenton chuckled.

Kenton leaned back and looked at the blade once more. He stood and then just as Jack thought he was heading out Kenton slammed his fist down on the blade and pushed it further into the desk. Jack fell forward slightly to brace himself with his other hand. He clenched his jaw as he squeezed his eyes shut and waited for the pain to pass. Kenton laughed at him.

"Jack, someone like you I would love to break. See just how long you could really last in this tough guy role." Kenton said with a sinister grin on his face.

Jack ignored him and focused on the desk in front of him. He knew Kenton was trying to bait him but he would block him out until he went away. If he focused on him any longer he was going to rip the blade through his own hand and use it to slit his throat. He didn't need war right now. Kenton stepped back and slid his hand over Jack's ass. He squeezed Jack's ass cheek tightly in his hand.

"Don't fucking touching me." Jack said through gritted teeth as he instantly yanked back on the blade as he tried to get his hand free.

"I would enjoy breaking you…in every way Jack." Kenton whispered to him as turned, his hand slid from Jack's ass to his hip and he pressed his pelvis against Jack's ass.

Jack tugged hard on the blade. Images of using it to slit his throat flashed through his head. The more he pulled the more blood seeped out. Kenton laughed and backed away from Jack. His slow footsteps echoed through the cabin as he walked to the door. He lingered in the doorway and looked back at Jack with an evil smile on his face.

"It's only a matter of time Jack until Rowling figures out you're useless. Your crew will be slaughtered and I'll be able to have my fun." Kenton laughed, pulled the door open.

"You look good bent over a desk Jack. Sweet dreams." He chuckled even more as he slammed the door behind him.

Jack let the breath he was held in out and a small groan escaped. The pain from his hand was coming in waves now.

"Don't you dare." He growled and looked at the closet door.

He took several deep breaths as he tried to calm his rage. He would kill them all. Rowling, Kenton, and anyone that tried to stop him. He slammed his free fist into the desk and even though the ripple caused him more pain he didn't care. The door opened a second time and he shut his eyes. If this was anyone other then Jonah he was going to lose.

"God Jack are you alright?" Jonah said as he appeared at Jack's side.

"I'm fine. If you don't get this knife out of my hand you might not be." Jack growled at him.

"Ok...ok...I...uh how do we do this?" Jonah shuttered out.

"Are they gone?" Jack asked impatiently.

"Yes, I made sure they started to sail away before I came back." Jonah said with a nod as he looked at Jack's hand.

Before Jack could say anything the closet door busted open and Claire all but ran to the desk. She stopped short as she looked at Jack. He was a bloody mess. Blood dripped down the side of his neck and over his collar bone coming from a long wound behind his ear. His shoulder was now bleeding again and she couldn't take her eyes off the knife that impaled him to the desk.

"Shit Jack." Was all she could manage to say.

"Yeah I know. I'm fine." He grumbled.

"Ok hand first." Claire said as she gathered herself and let out a deep breath. She stepped closer and leaned down to study the blade.

"It's straight so that's a plus There's no way to really do it other than pulling it straight back out." Claire said her voice became pitchy with the thought of having to hurt Jack more.

"Aye I know just yank it out Jonah." Jack ordered him.

Jonah's hands shook as he gripped the blade handle. His rattling hands caused the blade itself to shake. Jack reached over and slugged him in the shoulder.

"Damn it Jonah." Jack said through his teeth at him.

"I know, I'm sorry." Jonah said and tried to steady himself.

"Oh move!" Claire yelled as she pushed Joanh out of the way.

Jack raised an eyebrow at her, not sure of how to take this. He looked at her. She took a deep breath in and rubbed her hands together to try to work her nerves out.

"You got this?" Jack said his voice steady as he locked eyes with her.

"I got this, I'm going to count to three." Claire said gently and placed her hands around the blade handle.

"Wait..wait..on three or one two go?" Jack's voice asked nervously.

"On three..ready?" Claire asked as she moved her fingers slightly.

Jack inhaled quickly to prepare himself, this was going to hurt. It was going to hurt badly. He clenched his jaw and nodded.

"Ok one!" Claire screamed and yanked as hard as she could upwards.

Jack let out a yell as the blade ripped up out of his skin. He grabbed his injured hand with his free one, putting pressure on the wound as blood seeped out. Claire was on the floor from pulling so hard. Jack glanced down at her and flexed his jaw as he looked at her. Before he could stop himself another yell of anger escaped him and he knocked everything off the desk.

"I am going to kill Rowling and that bastard Kenton if it's the last thing I ever do. I am going to gut them both alive and strangle them with their entrails." He yelled and slammed his bloody fist onto the desk.

Jonah backed up away from him and waited for the storm to settle while Claire quickly got off the ground and stepped forward. She put her hand on his shoulder. Her touch instantly calmed him. He dropped his head and shook it.

"You're getting blood everywhere." She smirked as she teased him

"Do you not know how to count?" He growled.

"Sorry, if I had waited until three you would have tensed up." Claire said as she tossed the blade to the side.

Jonah stood there and watched the back and forth at them, his mouth hung open a little bit. Claire straightened herself up and walked over to Jonah and closed his mouth for him,

"Jonah, I need my bag, water, and clean rags." Claire tapped his shoulder to make him focus as she spoke.

He nodded and headed out without saying anything as if he was still stunned by what he just saw. Claire grabbed a hold of a chair and slid it to Jack. She motioned for him to sit down. He gladly sat without any protest. He cradled his hand in his other. Claire squatted down next to him and held out her hand for his injured one. He narrowed his brows slightly before he handed his hand over. Blood splashed into Claire's hand as she looked at the wound.

"It's gonna need to stay open to heal. We'll wrap it and I have some powder we can use to stop the bleeding but it will need to heal on its own." Claire said her face scowled as she handed him his hand back.

She then stood quickly, she leaned over him as she studied his shoulder. She frowned deeply as she saw all her work gone and it all had to be redone. She then grabbed his chin and tilted his head. Jack let out a small scuff as she man handled him to see the wound. She touched it slightly and he winced. The cut was long but wouldn't cause any damage to his actual ear.

"Ok so I need to sew your shoulder back up again, good news the ear is not affected and should heal quickly on its own. There's a lot of blood but ears like to bleed." Claire said very matter of fact.

"Are you always so forced with your patients?" Jack asked the very end of his lips turned up in a half smile.

"Hush." Claire lectured him as she looked to the door as Jonah came in with her things.

Jack didn't say anything. A fire of rage burned inside of him. He hated having to sit by and seem weak. If he didn't have people he needed to look out for he would have already killed them. He sighed so wrapped up his thoughts. He didn't even notice that Claire had sunk his hand in a water bowl. The water stung but he ignored it. If he had more ships, if he had help he could ambush and over run Rowling. His men could fight and they would gladly die fighting but against Rowling and his men they would perish alone.

He glanced down and watched his golden hair angel work on his hand. She was truly amazing. He smiled at her. He wanted to know what she had seen, where she had been and how she knew so much. He watches her take a small envelope out of her medical kit and look at him.

"What?" She all but whispered.

"Nothing." He smiled softly.

"Well this is gonna burn so get ready." Claire said as she looked.

"Are we counting again or you just going to -" Jack was cut off as the powder hit his skin.

"Damn it Claire!" " He groaned as he glared down at her, a silly smile on her face which softened his anger.

The bleeding slowly began to stop as did the burning. She took some gauze wrap and began to wrap his hand securely. She then wrapped bandage material over the gauze. She nodded at her work as if she had approved it and then stood. She sighed as she grabbed her scissors.

"For the time being why don't you just wear shirts without sleeves." She grumbled as she stepped into his lap.

She tried to get in a position where she could reach his shoulder best. There was no way, she frowned and then straddled his thigh not even thinking of the position she put herself in again. Jack stiffened slightly. She didn't notice. She reached across and dunked a rag in the water and brought it up to his shoulder. She began to clean the wound. Sighed as she saw the damage was worse than before.

"You keep acting like I did this on purpose." He muttered in response to her sigh.

"Hush." Claire dismissed his comment.

She reached over once more and grabbed her tools. She glanced at Jack's face, His expression was almost hardened as if he tried hard not to focus on her. She brought her eyebrows together in a form of a question but she was not going to voice it.

"Ready?" She asked quietly.

"Yeah I'll be fine." Jack said quietly his eyes focused on the wall behind her.

She nodded and began to work. Jack tried hard to not focus on the fact that she straddled his leg, that every moment she made her breast move and they were practically in his face. As she worked she moved and her thighs brushed against his and then her leg would rub against his groin. The pain was no longer in his mind. He felt himself grow behind his pants. He swallowed hard, he needed to put distance between his member and her leg.

"Can you just sit still? I swear I'm almost done." Claire said firmly but with an understanding tone.

He clenched his jaw and shut his eyes as he hoped that it would help shut out her presence. She moved again and that hope was shattered.

"Claire." Jack said calmly.

"I'm done with your shoulder, just let me look at the ear." Claire said as she pushed herself closer to him.

She leaned up to inspect his ear, her breast pushed into his chest as she did. She placed the cold wet rag to the blood on the back of his ear and a chill shot through him.

"It's not that bad." She said her warm breath hit his ear.

He couldn't take any more. In one quick motion with his good arm and hand he picked her up as he stood and set her down on his desk.

"Jack!" She yelled as she was set down.

Jack placed his arms on either side of her, locking her in that position. He took a deep breath in. Claire studied his face confused by his reaction but then noticed a bulge that had grown in his pants; she quickly became embarrassed. She nervously bit her lip and pulled her lower lip inwards not sure how to respond. Jack watched her become nervous and embarrassed and it made her that much more irresistible. He quickly thought of how her breast felt in his hand, the small sweet noise that escaped her mouth. He wanted to make her make all sorts of noise. His hand went from the desk to her hip as his good hand captured her chin. His thumb ran over her bottom lip and tugged it softly. Her eyes filled with desire at his mere touch.

He leaned forward and captured her bottom lip with his mouth. He pulled her bottom lip into his mouth and sucked on it. Shivers passed over Claire's body as the shock of his action took over her. She moved closer to him, his arm wrapped around her waist as he released her lip. She slipped her hand up to her cheek and pulled him back into her lips for a kiss. She met his mouth eagerly and pressed her lips against his. He smiled at her response and kissed her back deepening it. His tongue slipped into her mouth rubbing against hers. His grip on her tightening. Claire's hand began to travel from his cheek down his neck and over his chest. She ran her fingers over his abs and stopped at his pants line as she looped her finger in it and kissed him just as fiercely back. He let out a soft groan as her finger began to run along his pant line. He pulled back from the kisses and placed small ones along her neck. Her hand still exploring, He bit down softly on her shoulder.

"Claire." He growled against her skin.

A soft chuckle escaped her lips as she tucked another finger in between his pants and his skin. In one swift motion Jack grabbed the bottom of her shirt on either side and pulled. All the buttons of her shirt popped off. Her shirt split open down the middle and her bare breast completely exposed. She withdrew her hand and went to cover herself but he caught her hands. He let out a sharp grunt.

"Don't." He muttered to her before he buried his face into her collar bone.

He began to place small kisses down her collar bone and over the tops of her breast. She let out a small moan of pleasure as he reached the tops of her breast. He kissed down them, her skin begged to be touched wherever his mouth traveled. Jack's mouth captured her nipple. He pulled into his warm mouth and sucked. Claire arched into him as she let out another moan. Her hand tangled into his bronze locks and begged him not to stop. A moan as he sucked hard on her nipple, he twisted his tongue around them and she felt her body throb with need. A moan escaped her as she shut her eyes. With each sound she made his desire for her increased. His mouth left her breast and continued down her stomach. He reached up and carefully pushed on her chest to have her lay back as his mouth made his way down.

He stopped at her pants line. He placed teasing kisses there as he ran his mouth along it, He undid her pants button glancing up to take a look at her. She arched her hips into him. He smiled to himself as he undid them and began sliding them off. Her pants slid to the floor. He ran his hand over her core which was still covered by thin underwear. She pressed up against his hand. She was shivering with pleasure, her mind empty and her body filled with every new sensation that she craved more of. He lowered his face down to her core and placed teasing kisses over the top of her underwear. Another wave of shivers passed through her. She found herself anticipating each kiss, her body arched to greet them. He bit the top of her under with his teeth. He began to pull the underwear slowly down. His nose brushed against her and his warmth breath against her made her in hale sharply as she raised her hips to help take them off completely.

Jack ran his hands up her legs and then slowly pushed them apart. She shivered with the cold air as it her center. Jack stared down at her, her body ached for him. Her eyes closed, her mouth hung open just slightly. He looked down at her center and could see wetness there. Her body wanted him as much as every part of him wanted her. Jack settled himself between her legs. He wanted to taste her. Claire inhaled sharply as she felt his tongue slide down the middle of her crease. She tasted as sweet as she looked. His tongue moved over her bead and rubbed against. Claire let out a low moan and he felt hand weave through his hair.

Her body had never felt anything like this before. She couldn't describe the feeling. The ache and need that grew from inside of her. Her mind and body

screamed for more. Jack pressed a finger against her entrance and felt Claire stiffen. The amount of wetness there made him know she was almost ready. He gently sucked on her bead and she let out a loud moan. Her head titled backwards and she was instantly lost in desire. Jack slid his finger inside her. Her body tightened around him. He began to move his finger in and out of her in a slow motion so she would get used to the feeling. When he knew she was used to it he slipped another finger in and repeated the motion. She arched into him. He moved his face away from her center.

       "Claire, I want you." He groaned into her stomach.

       "Please." She whispered breathlessly,

       That was all he needed to her, he undid his belt with one hand and his pants hit the floor. He almost questioned himself again as he stepped towards her. She sensed his hesitation and sat up, her hand reached for him. He moved towards her and she slipped her arm around his neck and pulled him into a kiss. Her mouth met his hungry. Jack kissed her back just as fiercely as Claire pulled him closer, her legs wrapped around him. As she pulled him toward her his member brushed against her core. Jack broke the kiss and moved his mouth to her neck. Claire hesitated for a second and then began to relax. Jack eased himself inside of her. Claire stiffened up at the sharp pain at first. Jack's hand moved down in between them and gently began to rub her bead. The sensation sent her back into bliss. Claire relaxed as Jack began to slowly move in and out. The way her body clamped down around his member he almost lost himself. Claire began to mimic him, as

she followed his movements. The heat in her core rose as pleasure rippled through her. She clung to Jack as the feeling overwhelmed her. Jack began to move faster and harder. Claire moved with him, her hips arched to meet him each thrust. Her soft cries of pleasure pleaded for a release. She felt the tension in her whole body as it contracted. She was headed over the edge and a rush of warmth spread over her as she hit her release. Jack groaned as he felt her release. He couldn't contain himself and he filed her. He pulled her closer and rested his forehead against hers as he tried to catch his breath. Claire was just as breathless as him. She ran her hand over his cheek. He pulled back and placed a kiss on her forehead.

"You are so fucking gorgeous." He whispered before he scooped her into his arms.

"Jack!" She let out a small yell as he carried her to the bed.

He grunted in response to her yell.

"Jack your shoulder! I'll kill you if you rip it open again." She said as she glared at him and he ignored it.

"You'll have to get in line, there's a list now." Jack smirked.

He placed her down on his bed and then crawled in next to her. He was still half naked as he slid in. He tapped the bed and motioned for her to lay down. She grumbled softly but didn't fight it. He captured her with his arm and pulled her against him. She sighed happily, as she settled against him as he threw the covers over both of them.

"What if someone comes in?" She whispered sleepily.

"No one is coming in." He said just as tired back.

Within seconds Claire was out cold. Jack watched her chest rise and fall, feeling happy for the first time in a long time. He was also terrified, terrified of losing the woman he held in his arms. He kissed her forehead once more before giving into the nagging call of sleep.

Chapter Twelve

Plans

It was dark and raining...no not raining she was
falling. Wait no not falling, sinking. Sinking down into the
dark cold emptiness, her skin burned as water started to
flood her lungs. Momma was what she tried to say. She
felt warmness and reached out towards it. Warm arms
captured her and pulled her out of the darkness. Hitting
the surface she saw her haunting eyes as she sank
back into the ice. Momma was what echoed the
surrounding shore line. She was running, running hard
and fast. He was coming. Arms picked her up holding
her close to her. The warmness she clung to. Red hair
flying out behind them as they ran through the dark
trees. Run. Falling, falling onto the ground her body felt
shattered. He was there again. She stood loud banging
echoing in her ears. She glanced around her heart
sinking, their old room. The banging coming from the
door. A bloody bleed morgan standing between here
and the door. Morgan telling her to go, to run. The door
crashes in. He was reaching for them, his hand
capturing her hair as she fought to get away. A voice
calling out to her as she fought for her life.

"Claire. Claire" It called to her as she was being
shaken.

"Claire."

Claire shot up, her chest pounded, her heart
raced as she quickly went to defend herself. Her eyes
scan the room wide with fear. Jack shifted away from
her and waited for the attack. She froze as she saw him,
the realization of where she was hit her. Jack carefully
pulled her against his chest cradling her.

"You still get them." He whispered to the top of her head.

She didn't say anything but just nodded. Jack remembers many nights when they were younger the trauma haunted her in her sleep. Jack had cradled her several times back then letting her know she was safe and that everything would be ok. Claire curled up closer to enjoy his warmth and the feeling of safety.

"What was it this time? " Jack asked quietly.

"Now the dreams are more like someone flipping through pages of a book, random scenes that were the worst to go through." Claire said as she nestled into his chest.

He began to run his finger through her hair. She let out a sigh of contentment as she closed her eyes. Jack smiled as he watched her go from terrified to instantly happy just from his touch.

"So what is the plan?" She whispered into his chest.

"Stay like this forever? See how many times I can make you make those sweet little noises from earlier?" Jack said with a wicked smile on his face.

Claire's heart sped up in her chest, her stomach flickered with excitement and she turned instantly a shade of red, as she cleared her throat slightly as she ignored him.

"I don't think that's the best plan for the situation right now." She said as she shifted slightly in his grasp.

"Oh but I disagree this is the perfect plan." He said as his hand went to capture her chin.

She leaned into his touch, her body craved it. He pulled her in for a short kiss as he then buried his face into her neck and kissed it softly. She inhaled slightly tingles spreading through her. His arm captured her waist and pulled her up against him as his kisses began to trail. She lost herself again with his touch. She ran her hand up into his hair and pulled his head again from her skin.

"No, no, no." She said as she pulled him away.

He growled and began to fight back. He quickly flipped his left leg over her and straddled her. Her hand is still woven into his hair. His intense gaze stared down at her. She bit her lip nervously as she tried to find her voice.

"Jack, we need to think of something." She said as she still held on to his head, afraid to let go in case he decided to go back to kissing her skin. She didn't know if she could stop him again.

He sighed and buried his face into her chest. He groaned before he gave up. She saw that he gave up and she let go of his hair and he rolled back to the side of her.

"I don't know. He always has two ships with him. He has more elsewhere." Jack said as he sat up and placed his feet on the ground.

Claire pulled the blanket around her and sat up with him. She scooted to the edge of bed and watched Jack. He placed his elbows on his knees and dragged his hands over his face, sighing as he did so.

"If we could just take Rowling and Kenton out the rest will crumble or give up, No one wants to follow them." He said into his hands.

"Ok so let's get rid of them." Claire shrugged.

Jack moved his hand from his face and stared at her like she had just said the most annoying thing in the world.

" I feel like I am talking to a seven year old you right now and we're about to prove Morgan didn't try to poison Gavin." Jack laughed.

Claire smiled as he brought up the memory. He looked over to her as straighten up and grinned. The word poison set off a thought in her head.

"So two plans, one we could invite him back saying we have something big for him, offer him drinks to celebrate and boom poison or two we find more ships and ambush him," Claire said like it was the easiest thing in the world.

Jack looked at her shocked and full of questions. She giggled as she looked at his face and tapped him on his thigh like he was a pet.

"Questions, How do you think we are going to get either of those options?" Jack frowned at her.

"Someone is bound to sell poison at any sleazy sailor bar and you're looking at a captain who also has a ship and has a family with more ships." Claire said and rolled her eyes at him.

Jack made a face at her as he thought over the options. He didn't want to drag Morgan and Gavin into this. He didn't even like that Claire was here. Poison might work. It wasn't the most honorable thing but then again they were not the most honorable people.

"Fine poison it is." Jack said as he got up and walked to the desk.

Claire watched a pantless Jack walk across the floor, her eyes scanned over his naked bottom half. She blushed deeply and quickly looked away. She cleared her throat a little bit as she went to speak as she stared at the floor.

"Do you have any maps over there?" She asked quietly.

Jack scooped his pants up off the floor, not slipping them on quickly. He glanced back at Claire who had her eyes glued to the floor. He smirked a little bit, seeing her embarrassed.

"Aye over here." He said as he picked up the different pieces of paper he had thrown to the ground when he was angry.

Claire wrapped the blanket around herself and headed to the desk. Jack rolled out a map and looked it over as she got to his side. She studied it quickly and realized where they were. She leaned over the desk. She tightened her hand around the blanket and used her free hand to trace along the map. She found where they were and then looked along the route Jacob was traveling, he should be starting to leave the port now. She wondered if she could meet up with the Crown as a backup plan. She knew the Crown with the Evening Star could take down Rowling's ship. She sighed and then looked over the map for ports nearby. There was not one far away. If they could get there, maybe find some poisons and then meet up with Jacob before inviting Rowling onto the ship, this could end very well.

Jack watched her work with a smile on his face. She began to map the route in which she thought they should take to the destination. His smile grew and he was proud of her. She went from this young girl who was unsure of herself to this strong brave woman, who could hold her own.

"What?" She asked as she caught his look. She hugged the blanket closer to her.

"Nothing." He chuckled.

"Mhmm." She muttered at him.

"So I guess you have a plan?" Jack asked and leaned against the desk with his arms folded across his chest.

"Yeah, I've been to this port before. It's a little stretchy and there is definitely the type of people that would have what we are looking for" Clarie said and circled the point on the map where she wanted to go with her finger.

Jack turned looking at the map, a smirk formed on his lips. He knew this port as well, he raised an eyebrow at Claire. Stretchy wasn't the word to describe this place.

"What exactly were you doing there?" Jack said his smirk grew as he turned to her.

"Errands, now we should get headed there." Claire said dismissively.

Jack smirked as he stood up away from the desk. He began to walk toward the door as he grabbed a hold of the blanket while Claire looked at the map. She was so deep in focus that she didn't even notice his action. He tugged real hard on the blanket and the blanket fell away from her. Claire let out a small shriek. She grabbed the map and used it to cover herself.

"Jack!" She yelled at him as her eyes narrowed in anger.

"Better get dressed, gorgeous adventure awaits. I wouldn't want someone to stumble in on you." Jack laughed as he took in the sight of her before heading out the door.

Shutting the door behind him, he heard something hard hit the door. He laughed harder as he walked away from the door and shook his head. He spotted Jonah at the helm. They awaited orders from Jack since Rowling had left. The ship sat idle in the water. He walked across the lower deck, the men shifted out of his way as he did. He knew he looked like he was in rough shape but he did not take notice of the glances his men gave him. He walked up the stairs and onto the upper deck.

"Jonah." He said firmly as he called to him,

Jonah looked out over the ocean, a look of worry on his face as he watched the sun sink beyond the horizon.

"Captain." He said looking at him, Jonah's eyes immediately looked over his wounds.

"I'm fine Jonah." Jack shook his head.

"That's it, I'm done. Jack, how much longer can we keep this up? Look at you! Next time what will it be, a missing limb?" Jonah said as he became upset.

"We should just give this life up or join him." Jonah said as he started to pace and flap his arms about as he talked.

Jack leaned up against the rail and let his friend vent. Jonah caught sight of him and began to settle down.

"I'm serious Jack, he's going to kill you one day." Jonah said softly.

"Ya done being an angry seagull?" Jack said with a grin formed on his face.

"Jack, this isn't a joke. I'm serious. I don't want that for you." Jonah said as he tossed his hands down to his side.

"Jonah I have a plan, this is all going to be over with soon and Rolwing and his thugs will be gone." Jack said confidently.

"Ugh, fine Jack, I hope they kill me first so I don't have to watch you die." Jonah grumbled as he came to his side and leaned up against the rail next to him.

"No one's dying Jonah." Jack said as he nudged him.

"Aye so what's the plan captain?" Jonah groaned.

"To the bearded lady." Jack smirked and waited for his friend's reaction.

"Seriously Jack, that's where we're going? Port Sin? The bearded lady at the bar? " Jonah nearly yelled at him.

"Aye Port Sin, Give the orders get us going." Jack ordered as he tried to bite back the laughter Jonah's fed up face caused him.

"Fine, I guess it will be great fun before we die. I seriously don't understand you sometimes." Jonah muttered to himself.

"Aye but you would follow me into hell and I love ya for it." Jack said and slapped Jonah on the back.

Jonah rolled his eyes at him as he shouted out the orders to the crew. The confusion from the crew was almost as bad as Jonah's seagull impression however some were very excited. A cheer rose up from the few scandalous men on board and Jack grinned, shook his head.

"Well the orders made some of them happy. I hope you know what you're doing Jackie." Jonah said to the wheel as he began to stir the ship.

Chapter Thirteen

Port Sin

Claire leaned over Jack's desk and focused on the map. She looked for the perfect spot. They needed back up in case everything went south or they didn't find the poison they looked for. She was deep in thought she didn't hear the door open behind her. She fumbled around with different routes but her mind kept taking her to one spot over and over again. It was a cove but it had a secret passage that seemed to be hidden. She traced her finger along the route of the hidden passage. If she could get Rowling's ship in the cove and block off the exit with another ship; they could somehow ambush him using the hidden passage. She ran her finger from the hidden passage to the cover. It would work perfectly. Her finger tapped the cove as she thought.

Warm hands wrapped around her waist as she was pulled back against a hard chest. A familiar groan echoed in her ear as Jack buried his face into her neck, his lips moved over her skin softly. She leaned back and enjoyed the feel of him.

"What are you doing gorgeous?" He mumbled into her skin.

"Coming up with a very solid back up plan." She sighed happily and melted into him.

"Back up plan? No faith?" Jack said and moved his face from her neck and looked over at the map,

"Hang man's cove?" He asked curiously.

"Aye look here." Claire said as she tapped her finger on the hidden passage.

Jack leaned over her, his eyes squinted at where she was pointed. A hidden passage that opened up to the open sea. It leads right to the cover. He looked down at Claire who traced the route with her finger.

"You could have Rowling meet you here and then I could bring the Crown down this passage and we could ambush him." Claire said excitedly.

Jack studied the map knowing that what she said was true, if they had three ships it would work even better: one to block the exit, one to bait Rowling and one to ambush him. Jack sighed as he thought about how it meant more people involved, more people he cared about at risk.

"Jack the Crown has many cannons, more than your average ship. I could sink his ship so quickly. This will work." Claire said and reached down to his good hand on her hip and squeezed it.

"Let's see how plan number one works first." Jack said softly.

"Well I like to be prepared. Can we at least invite him to drink poison near this cover just in case?" Claire grumbled.

Jack chuckled lightly as he leaned down and kissed the top of her head. He squeezed her against him once more before he stepped back from her but not dropping her hand.

"We're here. I came to let you know. Also to tell you to stay close to me. I was going to order you to stay on the ship but I figured you wouldn't listen and go off on your own. So. Stay close and near me." He said strongly.

Claire rolled her eyes at him but nodded. She didn't want to be left behind. She wanted to go see what she could help with. Jack ignored the eye roll and took her hand and led her towards the door.

Jonah was still muttering to himself about how this was a bad idea as he pulled the ship up to the dock. The men below secured the ship and let the anchor go. He sighed as he looked out over the dock. Before you even got into the city it was already a complete mess. Drunken men sprawled out on the docks. Women who were in the business giggled and waited for payment.

"This place is trash." Jonah groaned, as he stepped away from the wheel.

"Oh come on Jonah it's not that bad. You need to let some steam off anyways." A man chuckled behind him.

"Me and a few of the guys are going to check out one of those houses." He continued with a grin on his face.

"Enjoy yourself Greg." Jonah said and waved him off.

Jack made his way out of the cabin with Claire. Jonah spotted them and headed to him. They met on the lower deck and Jack turned to the crew who were eager to get off the ship.

"Greg, Tim, and Leo. We need you to get supplies, I don't care what you do after that, be on this ship in an hour or we leave without you." Jack said as he dismissed those men.

"Sam, Dean and Kyle, I need you to get me information on Rowling. I know he frequents here. Keep a low profile." He nodded to them and they left.

"Jonah, you're coming with me. The rest of you clean up the ship and get her ready to set sail in an hour. If you finish your duties before the hour is up, you can explore the port. Everyone has an hour to complete their task and have their fun." Jack yelled out over the ship.

"Logan, you are in charge of the ship while Jonah and I are gone." He said to a young man with chestnut hair.

He nodded to Jack and went towards the helm. Jack looped his hand through Claire and walked off towards the exit.

"An hour doesn't seem like a very long captain." A voice perked up as Jack stepped up onto the walkway to leave.

"Tim, take all the time you want. I leave in an hour." Jack said his voice sent chills through the men around him.

The tone set for all of them and Jack made it known not to question him. The man nodded fiercely and stepped back. Jack turned to Claire and offered to help her up but she was already behind him. She looked at him with a small smirk on her lips, as if to tell him she's got this. Jonah had a frown plaster on his face and occasionally shook his head as he kept telling himself that this was a bad idea.

"Lighten up Jonah." Jack said and walked across the walkway.

Jonah snorted in response which caused Claire to chuckle. They made their way away from the dock into the small port town. The streets were lined with bottles and trash. Men walked around as they fell and fumbled all over themselves. Women dressed in the most revealing clothing they could. Several homes were set up for these women to entertain guests. Claire looked around and took everything in. She had been here once before but didn't remember it being this bad. Jack glanced back at her to see her response and a small smile came to his lips.

"Do we have a destination captain?" Jonah asked as he swerved to avoid a drunk man who fell towards him.

"Watch it." Jonah growled as he shoved the man away from him.

The men fell over as Jonah stepped over him disgustedly. He glanced back to Jack who found Jonah's annoyance amusing.

"Shark Baits." Jack said and tossed a wink at him.

"Wonderful." Jonah groaned as they rounded a street corner.

Claire was too busy wrapped up in the environment to keep up with the banter. A symbol on a sign caught her eye. It was an R but the ends swirled up, it was fresh and burned onto the sign of the little shop. She looked around at the other signs and random ones throughout the street seem to have them on it. She thought that it was strange and wondered what it meant.

Jack stopped in front of a tavern, it was the color of the moss growing on the outside of it. Claire glanced up to the sign. Shark bait was engraved on a copper metal and here too was another one of those R's.

"So what are we going to find here?" Claire said, as she looked at the sign confused.

"Information and maybe what we are looking for." Jack said, as he grabbed ahold of the door and opened it for Claire to pass through.

Claire stepped in and the smell hit her first. It was a sweet rotten smell. She placed her hand over her nose to block the smell.The tavern was dimly lit with the only light from the bar. Men were passed out about the room. Some propped up in corners. Scandalously dressed women sat on top of tables, they giggled as they lured the drunk men in. Claire moved aside to let Jack and Jonah led the way. Jack started to make his way to the bar Claire followed with Jonah. A loud squeal was heard as an auburned hair woman jumped down from the bar and ran towards Jack. Claired stepped back as she watched the women run towards them. Her breast bounced around in her low cut shirt. Claire wondered how they did not break free. She saw Jack's shoulder tense as the woman bloated in his arms and wrapped her arms around his neck.

"Jay! You're here!" She smiled brightly, she made sure to press her breast into him before she pulled back.

"Oh my Jayie what happened to you." She pouted

Claire stood still, her eyes could not believe what they saw in front of her. A rage formed in the pit of her stomach. She glanced at Jonah who looked quickly at the ground. The woman now looked him over like she meant something to him. She gushed over Jack's wounds and then pulled him in for another hug. Claire gritted her teeth slightly. She took a deep breath. She didn't know who this woman was but she wasn't going to sit around and watch this scene any longer.
 They had a mission and she was going to get on with it. Claire pushed past them and as she did she threw her shoulder into Jack. Jack stumbled forward and nearly knocked over the woman that clung to him. Jonah smirked as he followed Claire.

"Claire." He called to her as he took the woman's arms off of him.

Claire ignored him and walked over to the bar. She sat down and began to assess the patrons. Someone here must have some type of poison.

"Jay whose that?" The woman asked as she pouted her mouth more.

"Maria...she's...she's mine....she's my...I...She's important." He stumbled over his words, the realization hit him that he did not know what he was to Claire right. He had all these thoughts of what he wanted her to be to him but they didn't get that far in conversations.

"Important?" Maria frowned.

" Nevermind I'm here on business." Jack dismissed her.

Maria narrowed her deep olive eyes at Claire from across the room. A frown settled on her lips as she watched Jack walk over to her. Jack reached out and touched Claire's shoulder, Maria felt acid rise in her throat as she watched the exchange. The word no rang in her head. He was supposed to be hers.

"Claire, stop ignoring me." Jack said as he touched her shoulder.

"Jay don't touch me." Claire said bitterly as she mimicked the name the woman had called him, Claire's eyes full of anger as she looked at Jack.

"Seriously Claire, we don't have time for this." Jack muttered.

"Oh I agree, if we split up we might find what we're looking for quicker." Claire said her tone was snotty.

Claire stood and Jack caught her arm. His eyes narrowed at her, Claire matched his stare and ripped her arm away from him. She spotted a man in the dark corner and he looked like the type that would have or know where to get poison.

"Come Jonah." Claire said as she walked away from Jack.

Jonah shrugged as he held back the smile on his face. He walked by Jack and followed after Claire. Jack shook his head confused as he watched Jonah follow Claire. He was about to mumble something about loyalty but he much rather have Jonah with Claire. Jack sat down at the bar as he watched Claire walk over to the shadiest looking men in the whole bar. He turned and was about to go to her but decided to see how it played out. As she sat down the men smiled at her. Jack clenched his jaw, he didn't like the way he smiled at her, only he could smile at her like that. He shifted again trying his hardest to not rush over there.

"Jay, did you need something? Where have you've been?" Maria said as she rounded the bar.

He sighed as he looked at her. They had a history; a one night history. That only happened because of way too many ale and poor judgment. Ever since then Maria had been obsessed with him.

"Poison, you wouldn't happen to have any? " He smiled charmingly at her.

"Maybe….why?" She smiled as leaned seductively across the bar top.

"Do you have some or not Maria? I don't have time or patience for games." Jack said as he rubbed his forehead.

"What kind do you want darling?" She said as she brushed her fingers across his forearm.

"The kind that kills." He said and moved his arm from her touch.

"Maybe, I'll have to look. Jay you better be nice to me or i wont-

"Maria it was once and that's all it was and will ever be. I've told you this." Jack snapped.

"Because of her?" Maria nodded towards Claire, fire in her eyes.

"No, because we wouldn't be anything even if she wasn't around." Jack spoke very slowly so she would understand.

"I saw the way you looked at her, Jay. It is her." Maria cried as she back away from the bar.

"I'm not discussing this anymore. If you have what I need I gladly pay for it otherwise I believe we're done here." Jack said and then leaned back into his chair.

Maria stomped off into the back kitchen area and disappeared from sight. Jack flagged down another girl and asked the same question as well as ordered an ale. She nodded and quickly got him his drink. He sighed about to take a sip when he heard a loud noise coming from the corner. His head quickly snapped over in the direction the noise came from.

"I said no!" Claire said as she ripped her hand away from the man.

"Money is the payment and that is it." Claire said as she slammed her fist down on the man's hand holding her own.

The sleazy man grinned at her and snatched her hand again.

"Let her go." Jonah said, his voice calm.

"Listen lad I suggest you shut up or I won't share with you." He grinned and went to pull Claire towards him.

In one quick motion Jonah grabbed a hold of the man's face and slammed it into the table. As he pushed the man's face further into the table his free hand grabbed a hold of his glass mug and smashed it over his head. The man let go of Claire's hand. Claire, who was stunned, slowly pulled it back. Jonah then grabbed the man by the hair and slammed his face once more into the table. The man's nose broke on the second impact as he was knocked out cold. Jonah glanced at Claire who didn't even have time to blink. He realized she was free and nodded to her.

"Excuse me Claire." Jonah said sweetly to her as he got up from his chair.

He walked over to the man and slumped him back. He fell to the ground as Jonah began to search his pockets. He patted him down as he did so. No one in the bar looked up or even cared. Jonah grabbed a pouch full of coins from one pocket, a knife from another and then at last the small pocket of his shirt contained a blue vial. Jonah looked at it and knew it was the poison. He tucked everything into his own pockets and then walked over to Claire. He held his arm out for her as she took it and he walked over to the bar.

"Jonah, I didn't even know you could move that fast." Claire said as he led her over to the bar.

"Thanks lass." He chuckled.

He pulled a chair out next to Jack. Jack who had stood and was about to make his way to them when he realized Jonah had. He clenched a knife still in his hand. It took a second but once Claire sat down Jack put his blade away and sat down. He nodded his thanks to Jonah.

"Welcome, we have what we came for now, can we leave this shit hole?" Jonah said as he went back to his charming self.

"I understand the appealingness of this whole place but why do you hate it so much Jonah?" Claire asked him softly.

"Aye we can leave." Jack said as a drink was placed in front of Claire and Jonah.

Jack shrugged as he picked up his drink and drank it. Claire raised a brow at the drink and then looked back to Jonah waiting for him to answer. He inhaled sharply and shook his head. Claire picked up the glass in front of her and took a long sip.

"Short version: I grew up here. Lovely childhood, mother was a call girl and didn't know who my father was. Lots of fun family memories." Jonah said as he pushed his glass away from him.

"Oh Jonah, I'm so sorry." Claire said and reached out and squeezed his hand.

"It was a long time ago but it's still not a place I like to go to ." Jonah said quietly.

"How did you meet Jackie?" Claire said as she took another sip.

"On one of his trips here, he was looking for men promising riches and adventure. I would do anything to get out of this place." Jonah said with a nod of thanks to Jack.

Claire began to feel light headed. She glanced down at her cup. She swirled the liquid a little bit. She didn't drink often but two sips shouldn't make her feel like this.

"Jack...ie what's ss in this." Claire said as she pushed the cup to him as her words started to come out slurred.

"Claire?" Jack said alarmed as he held his arm out to steady her.

The whole world rocked back and forth. Claire gripped on to Jack as she tried to steady herself. Jack shot a panicked look at Jonah. Jonah snatched the mug and smelled it. Jack looked at him for an answer. Jonah dunked his fingers in it and rubbed them together, there was something in the drink. He could feel a trace amount of grit. Jonah picked the glass up and took a sip. He swished it around his mouth and then spit it back into the cup. He then took a sip of his own drink and did the same. He rinsed whatever was left from Claire's out of his mouth. Jack looked at him, his eyes demanded an answer.

"Poison." Jonah whispered to Jack.

Claire heard the word poison and she tried to look at Jack. By the look on his face she knew she was in trouble. Jack's heart sank to his stomach. The world spun out of control and then went black. She crashed into Jack.

Chapter Fourteen

Poison

Claire's body collapsed forward and Jack wrapped his arms around her. Her head fell backwards as her body limped in his arms. Panic rushed through him as he tried to think of anything to save her.

"Claire!" He yelled as he shook her lightly, her head flopped back and forth as he did.

Jack lowered her to the floor. His hand still cradled her head. He watched her chest rise and fall. A small bit of relief washed over him as he saw that she was still breathing.

Jonah's eyes scanned the bar as he looked for some one who may be behind this. He needed to know what was given. The girl who brought them the drinks passed in front of them. Jonah reached across the bar and grabbed her by the shirt and pulled her into him.

"You! Where did those drinks come from!" His voice echoed off the walls in the bar.

The anger in his voice and rage made the whole bar silent. The girl was too afraid to speak as she pointed across the way. As Jonah raised his voice Jack saw a red cloaked figure bail out the back.

"Jonah….Claire." He said as he placed Claire's head gently on the ground and took off after the hooded figure.

Jonah kneeled down and cradled Claire's head. His eyes searched her face for any clues. His stomach twisted as he looked at her lips started to become outlined in blue. Her breathing remained normal but he had seen poison work and any second now that could change. He needed to do something. Claire needed help now.

"Girl! When he gets back you tell him we went to the Frisky Kitten! You hear me!" Jonah yelled at her as he scooped Claire up in his arms and rushed out the door.

---

*J*ack busted out the back door after the red cloak. The person was light and quick on their feet. They jumped over a small stack of boxes and pushed them back so they toppled at Jack. It didn't phase him. He quickly jumped over them and did not miss a step. Claire's life hung in the balance and he wasn't going to let her die. He couldn't even stomach the thought. He ran around the corner and stumbled over a broken bottle. Jack gained his footing and then looked up. He smiled. The red cloak figured was stood in the back of the alley and faced a brick wall. It as a dead end. The person was stuck and had nowhere to go. Jack stopped in front of them and pulled out his sword. The red figure pushed itself back against the brick wall as Jack moved closer.

"If you want to live, I suggest you tell me what was in her drink now." He yelled his voice deadly.

The hooded figure turned slowly to face Jack. The alley was dark but the light from the moon lit it. The figure remained silent and still as the darkness of the alley crept around them.

"I'm not going to ask again, tell me now, If she dies I will hurt you in ways where you wish you were dead." He promised through his teeth as he stepped towards the person.

The person put their hands up and slowly pulled the hood back. Auburn hair cascaded down out from under the hood and Maria's tearful eyes stared back at him. He paused for a second confused and then became angry. He trapped her against the wall, his sword at her throat.

"Tell me now. I swear Maria I haven't hurt a woman before. I have never thought about killing one but if you don't tell me what poison that was I swear I will." Jack said as he pressed the blade hard against her throat to let her know the threat was real.

"I don't know." Maria said as a soft sob escaped her.

"What do you mean!" He yelled in her face as he slammed his fist into the wall beside her head.

"My arm, look at my wrist." Maria pleaded.

Her plea got to him and he looked at her confused. Jack stepped back as she rolled up her sleeve. A brand was burned into her arm. The letter R was pressed into her flesh. Jack shook his head, he didn't understand.

"What does that have to do with Claire and poison?" He yelled at her as he slapped the wall with an open hand.

"He said his name was Rowling. He's claiming business around here and people. I bumped into one of his men in the alley after I stormed out upset with you. The man asked me what was wrong and I told him about you and how you loved the golden hair girl. He told me to put this in her drink or else he would kill me." Maria sobbed.

"I don't know what kind of poison it was." Maria continued to cry.

"You're pathetic." He yelled at her as he slammed his fist in the wall once more before he turned to leave.

Jack ran to the end of the alley, his stomach in knots up as he felt like he was going to be sick. He just wasted more time. Just as he was almost out of sight. Maria's voice stopped him.

"He's coming. He knows your here and now about the girl. If the poison doesn't kill her. He's planning on taking her." Maria yelled, her voice shook.

Jack felt his blood run cold. He did not say another word, his body took off into a run before he could even tell it too. He couldn't let him have Claire, he couldn't even begin to think of what he would do to her.

Jonah stopped short in front of the Frisky Kitten. His lungs burned in his chest as he went to the bright red door. He didn't even hesitate as he kicked it open. He rushed in with Claire held tightly to him. The noise hit him as he walked into the building. The sound of laughter, giggles, and pleasure noise echoed down from the rooms above. The door he kicked crashed into the wall behind him. The loud noise echoed in the building as he entered. A girl who welcomed guests stood behind a table and jumped back, Her eyes grew wide as she stared.

"Sonya, now!" Jonah yelled at her.

The young girl jumped up, one hand went to her chest as if she held her heart and the other hand pointed up the stairs as her hand shook. Jonah didn't blink and stormed up the stairs.

"First door on the left." He heard the same girl yell up the stairs.

He got to the door and tried it, it was locked. Jonah took a step back and kicked the door. It flung open as he walked into the room. He looked about the room and his eyes landed on Sonya. She was an older woman with warm colored hair and deep chocolate eyes. Her mouth was outlined in wrinkles from the frown that was on her face. Sonya stood over another blonde hair girl who looked like she was dead. Jonah didn't say anything but went over and laid Claire down on the wine colored couch.

"Poison, do something." Jonah yelled at the older woman.

Sonya went over to Claire and began to assess her. She put her ear against her chest and listened to her chest. She opened her mouth and looked for blisters. The blue ring around her lips gave her an incline of what type of poison. She pressed on her fingernails to see how quickly the color returned to them.

"She drank it?" Sonya asked.

"Aye it was a gritty textured, sour smell but a sweet taste." Jonah said as she shifted his stance, the adrenaline that still pumped through him made him jittery.

"Ah yes." Sonya said quietly and walked to the back of her room.

A maroon curtain was hung up in the back of the room. She pulled it open and behind the curtain was all sorts of herbs, vials, and potions. She grabbed several vials and some herbs, she crushed the herbs and then dumped them into a cup. She took liquid from a blue vial and then one from a purple and mixed them in the cup. She stirred it lightly before she brought the cup over to Claire.

"Jonah come here and lift the head. She needs to drink this." Sonya said as she knelt next to Claire.

Jonah went to Claire's side and held her head so Sonya could pour the liquid into her. Claire coughed a little but the liquid went down. Jonah looked up at Sonya with questions. Sonya smiled.

"She will wake shortly. She's going to have an awful headache but she will be good. Did you have some of it too?" Sonya asked him.

"I tried it to determine what it was, I didn't swallow any of it." Jonah said as he put his hand on Claire's forehead.

Sonya nodded, " Drink a little just to be safe."

She handed Jonah the little that was left in the cup. Jonah drank it making a face. It tasted like dirt. He sighed and looked back at Claire. Jonah ran his hand over his face.

"Is she yours Jonah?" Sonya asked as she got up and brought the cup back to her shelf.

"No, she's a friend. Jack loves her." Jonah said quietly as he sat on the floor next to Claire.

"Ahh how is Jack?" Sonya asked, as she went back to look at the other blond girl.

"He's fine." Jonah said shortly and then stood going over to look at the dead girl.

"Is she?" Jonah asked but knew the answer, the girl was blue.

"Dead..Aye, same deal. Someone is going around poisoning people. This girl waited too long. Your's will be fine." Sonya said as she rubbed his shoulder lightly.

"Thank you." Jonah said quietly to her as he started to feel relief.

Sonya's door rattled as someone pounded on it from the outside. Sonya went to the door slowly, the look on her face said she wasn't expecting anymore visitors. Jonah drew his sword not sure what to expect. The door busted open and Jonah's stomach clenched. Sonya stood in the way of two of the people he hated most.

"No, no more visitors tonight, come back in the morning." Sonya said as she started to shut the door.

Kenton smiled brightly at her and shoved his sword through her stomach. He didn't even blink as he impaled her. He pulled the sword out and Sonya let out a deep horrible sound as she crashed to the floor on her knees. Jonah dropped to the ground next to her. The look of pain on his face as he knew the wound was fatal. Sonya smiled at him as he scooped her close to him. Her hand went up to his face and held his cheek lightly.

"I'm glad I saw you again. I'm sorry. I tried but it wasn't good enough. I wish I would have done better." Sonya whispered to him, blood began to seep out of mouth as she tried to talk to him.

"No, it's ok. Don't shh." Jonah said as he grabbed a hold of her hand and squeezed it gently.

"I love you Jonah." Sonya coughed as her breathing began to slow.

"I love you too mom." He whispered, the words caused his eyes to get glossy.

She smiled at him as she let out one long breath and was gone. Jonah shook with anger as he stared up at Kenton and Rowling.

"Well that was one of the saddest things I've seen today. Well getting on with it. Jack here? Where's the girl?" Rowling said as he looked around.

"Well which one is Jack's?" Rowling asked Jonah.

Jonah couldn't control himself any longer. He quickly stood and lunged for Kenton. He lowered himself as he ran at him. He threw his shoulder into his chest and slammed him against the wall behind him. He drew his fist back and brought it towards Kenton's face, a loud crack noise echoed in the room as Jonah's fist connected with Kenton's jaw. He brought his fist back again Kenton saw it as it came for his face again and moved his head as Jonah's fist connected with the wall. Kenton brought his knee up and used it to wedge space between him and Jonah. Kenton brought his fist forward as he did, it connected with Jonah's eyes. It instantly swelled. Jonah smirked and threw his face forward; he smashed it into Kentons. Kenton grabbed ahold of Jonah's hair as he brought his fist back. A sword tapped Jonah on the side of his neck. Kenton and Jonah stopped.

"Well that was spirited. Now enough of this nonsense. Which girl is Jack's" Rowling said, annoyed.

Jonah didn't answer and Kenton grabbed him by the hair. Jonah ignored him and Rowling waved Kenton off. Jonah didn't say anything. Rowling glanced at the two blond girls confused. He walked over to the dead girl. He picked up her hand and dropped it. He made a small noise as he walked over to Claire. Jonah stiffened up but continued to ignore them. He did the same with Claire. Jonah prayed that he wouldn't notice Claire was still alive, her breathing was shallow and she was cold.

"Well Kenton there goes that plan and you're having fun. They're both dead." Rowling said with a shrug.

Kenton growled and then looked down at Jonah, a smile coming to his lips. He grabbed Jonah by the hair and began to yank him upwards.

"Isn't he Jack's first mate?" Kenton said to Rowling.

"I don't know, he must be." Rowling said his eyes searched the room.

"So let's take him. Then his whole world will be slowly perishing. The father figure, his love and now his best friend." Kenton smiled wickedly.

"All right all right, Leave Jack a note saying we have him and to meet us with double what we normally ask." Rowling stated as he walked to the door.

He paused and glanced back at the girls. Jonah felt his chest tighten once more. Did he notice?

"A shame they were pretty whichever one was his." He shrugged and continued out the door.

Kenton let go of Jonah and shoved him forward. Anger coursed through him and he was fighting himself not to attack Kenton again. He knew they had to leave before Claire woke up so he sucked it up. He gritted his teeth as he stepped over his mother's body. Her blood pooled around her, the horrible feeling in his stomach grew. Jonah looked back at Claire once more before he followed Rowling out the door. Kenton found some paper in the room and scribbled a note. He walked over and tossed it on the dead girl's body. He snickered as he strolled out the door.

Chapter Fifteen

The Frisky Kitten

*J*ack stepped back into the bar breathless. The smell of blood and burning flesh hit his nose. He had an uneasy feeling balled up in his stomach; His eyes scanned the scene. Several men were on the floor bleeding. A bar maiden cried as she held her arm. He scanned the room, his eyes frantically looked for Jonah and Claire. His stomach knotted up as he didn't see them. He stepped over the dead men in his way as he walked to the bar. As he reached the bar he locked eyes with the bar maiden. He didn't have to speak.

"The Frisky Kitten." She cried as she held a cold cloth to her arm.

Jack paused for a moment as he reached forward and slowly pulled back the cloth. The letter R was burned into her flesh. He looked at her and then glanced around the bar. A man laid in his own blood had the same R branded on the side of his cheek. He looked at the rest of patrons, many of them now had R's seared into their skin. Jack was confused and looked back at the bar maiden, his eyes asking for an explanation.

"Rowling, he's now calming people." The girl sniffled as she placed the rag back on her skin.

"Jack, right?" She asked as she winced at the pain in her forearm.

Jack's eyes shot to her as he nodded, he could feel the acid in his stomach as it burned a hole in it as he waited for the girl to explain.

"He's about fifteen minutes ahead of you and on his way to where your friends are. You better hurry." She said, her voice scattered as she spoke.

Jack nodded as he bolted to the front door of the tavern, the door slammed behind him as he took off. He ran as fast as his feet could carry him down running the cobblestone street. Jonah was quick on his feet and taking Claire to Sonya was the safest bet. He was happy Jonah had his wits about him during this whole mess. He rounded the corner, the sound of his feet as they hit the pavement echoed in his head. He saw the candle glow that was from The Frisky Kitten as he rushed towards it. He barreled through the wooden front door. Ashe hit the door with such force it burst open and he stumbled forward. The girl behind the desk cowarded and simply pointed up the stairs. Jack didn't take a minute to ask her anything. He was up the stairs in no time. He paused slightly, almost scared to see what he would find. He walked towards the only open door.

As he reached the room he felt weak in his joints as he saw the blood that seeped out from the room. It stained the white title floor. He swallowed hard, he wasn't one to pray to god but he was now silently begged him to not let the blood belong to Claire. He slowly walked into the room, stiffening at the sight. Sonya laid in a lake of her own blood, a single stab wound to her stomach. He quickly looked about the room. A blonde girl laid on a cot.

He could see the tinge of blue to her skin from the doorway. His eyes scanned the rest of the room. Seeing Claire on the cot his heart sank into his stomach. His body felt shook as he crossed the room to her. With his body shaking he made himself cross the room to her. He kneeled next to the couch, hand shaking he reached out to touch her. He grazed her skin with his finger tips, almost frightened to confirm if she was alive or not. He stopped breathing himself as he waited to see if he could tell if her chest was rising and falling. The seconds seemed to drag. His eyes stared dead locked with her chest. His mind screamed, it commanded her chest to move. Seconds seem to be minutes. His own chest burned inside of him, his lungs reminded him that he had yet to take a breath. He inhaled and laid his forehead on her arm. His world slowly cracked and shattered.

"I'm so sorry." He whispered, his voice just as broken as he felt, she was gone.

He tried to control himself, his body betrayed him as his eyes stung. His stomach twisted and turned and begged for him to let loose its contents. He was on the edge of breaking completely down. He should have let her go with her own crew. He didn't take her hostage; she would still be alive. He balled his fist up and brought it down on the cot.

"I'm so sorry." He said louder, as his voice cracked and his body fought back a tremble.

His thoughts wandered to how he would have to tell Morgan and Gavin. How he could have to bring her body back home to them. He could see Morgan breaking down in his mind. She had fought so hard for them to survive, to help Claire grow into this amazing woman. Now she was gone. It was all his fault. He squeezed his fist shut fighting hard to keep himself together.

"Jackie?" Claire's voice broke the silence in the room.

Jack bolted up right and leaned over her, his face frantically cupped hers.

"Claire?" He nearly shouted in her face.

"Aye Jackie." She whispered her head killing her as she tried to figure out where they were and what was going on.

"Oh Thank God." Jack said as he leaned forward and kissed her forehead.

"Fuck Claire you scared the crap out of me." He said, as he placed several more kisses across her face.

"Jackie, where are we?" Claire whispered, as she pulled back from his kiss.

She could barely focus on anything going on. Her vision was blurry and the world rocked. She shut her eyes to shield from the light. It made everything hurt more. She grabbed a hold of head with both of her hands as she tried to fight through the pain.

"Were at Jonah's mom ... .um The Frisky Kitten. It doesn't matter, we need to get you back to the ship. Jonah..." Jack said and as Jonah's name came out of his mouth, he realized Jonah was gone.

When his eyes landed on Claire, passed out and slightly blue, he forgot about everything else.He looked around the room. His eyes spotted the dead girl across the way. A piece of paper laid across her body. Jack rubbed Claire's shoulder before he moved away from her and over to the girl. He reached out and took the piece of paper in his hand. He unfolded it slowly. In chicken scratch was written:

Jack, sorry about your girl. We would have had great fun with her. It's a shame. Now meet us at Raven's Peak. If you want your friend alive, bring double what we normally ask. The longer you take the longer he's stuck with us.

Jack gritted his teeth as he crumbled the piece of paper in his hand. He chucked it across the room as an angry groan escaped his mouth. Claire lifted her head up and went to ask what was wrong. She inhaled sharply as her eyes focused on the woman in a pool of her own blood. She glanced at Jack and covered her mouth as she saw the other blonde girl dead.

"Jack, where are we, what the heck is going on?" She said, confused.

"They have Jonah." Jack said anger shook through him.

"Who?" Claire said her mind was still boggled as tried to connect the dots.

"Rowling and Kenton. They have Jonah, they killed Sonya." He said as he pointed to the woman on the ground.

"They poisoned you and thought you were dead so they took Jonah." Jack blurted out quickly as he tried to control the anger in his voice.

"What did the note say?" She asked as she tried to sit up.

"I need to meet him at Ravens Peak if I want to see Joah alive and I need double what they normally ask." Jack said to Claire as he ran his hand over his face.

Worried crossed his face, he didn't know how he was going to pull that off. Double, they couldn't even get what they needed the first time.

"Alright then let's get to the ship." Claire said as stood unsteady on her feet.

The world began to swirl and she stumbled. She had to shut her eyes and steady herself as her legs began to fight her. Jack was by her side in an instant.

"Easy." He said to her as he put his arm around her.

"I can walk, let's just get back, we need to get to Jonah." She said as she tried to fight the anxiety that was in her chest.

The thought that Jonah was with those monsters and what they might do to him made her chest hurt. She moved away from Jack. She would walk.

Jack shook his head as Claire stumbled again. The sound in the room began to fade in and out as Claire tried to take another step. A strange sensation traveled up the back of her neck. She felt wobbly. She heard Jack sigh as she felt him come up behind her and sweep her into his arms. He cradled her against his chest. She gave in and leaned into him. The warmth of him felt good. She leaned her head into him and shut her eyes. The world did not rock as much. Jack frowned slightly as he stepped over Sonya's body and made his way out of the room. He carefully carried Claire down the stairs. A small smile came to his face as he heard her sigh as she nuzzled into him not realizing she was doing it. He walked down the stairs and paused at the girl behind the desk.

"I want a burial for Sonya. In my right pocket there are coins, take them and I will be back to ensure it's done right. If it isn't, it will be worse than what happened here tonight. I will be holding you responsible." Jack threatened.

"Sonya...she's..dead?" The girl said in horror as she reached into his pocket and took the coins.

The coins rattled and jingled as the girl's hand shook from the new.

"Aye can you make sure this gets done." Jack said as he softened his tone.

"I will she was like a mother to me." The girl said her voice cracked as tears fell from her eyes.

She slowly lowered herself into the chair behind the table, as she blankly stared at the coins, tears falling down her porcelain face. Jack frowned and he wanted to take care of it himself but Jonah needed him.

"I'm sorry." Jack said his voice filled with kindness and then he turned to head out the door.

The cold air hit Claire's face as she shivered into Jack. It was cold but felt nice and made her head feel better. Jack felt her shiver and tightened his grip to try to bring her more warmth. She sighed happily again. Jack smiled again hearing the small noise as it came so naturally from her. He could get used to hearing that all the time. He carried her down the cobblestone road and headed towards the docks.

"Jack, you should let me down. Let me try walking. You can't carry me all the way to the ship." Claire said sluggishly.

He didn't respond to her, just simply grunted his protest and continued to walk. Claire frowned but didn't have the energy to fight him on the matter. They passed the small business and bars along the way. This town was nothing but bars and call houses. Jack noted the randomly placed food merchants. The town made its money on liquor and women.

A commotion to the right of him caught his attention. A man was thrown out of a bar. His face skidded across the ground.

"Hey, watch it!" One of the men yelled as he helped his buddy up off the ground. Another man stumbled out behind him, in his hand was a mug of ale.

"I told you not to touch her!" The men said, as the ale spilt out of the mug.

"They wouldn't have cared if I paid." The man who was on the ground chuckled.

Jack groaned, his chest vibrated and it stirred Claire and she looked over to what caused Jack to become upset. Greg, Tim and Leo were across the street and they stumbled over each other. Claire could feel Jack becoming more and more annoyed. Claire glanced up at his face although she didn't have to, she already knew his face was scrunched up with anger and he looked like he was going to throttle them.

"Lads!" Claire yelled before Jack could, she then instantly regretted it.

Their heads snapped towards the sound and then like bad children all shrinked at the sight of Jack.

"Ship now and I swear if you didn't get supplies you're staying in this shit hole!" Jack yelled at them and walked away.

Claire squeezed her eyes shut tight at the sound of Jack's yell vibrated through his chest. The movement made her head hurt worse. She could hear Greg, Tim and Leo scamper behind them as they try to keep up but keep enough distance from Jack. They all walked silently back to the ship.

Jack's feet hit the deck and the shout of "Captain on deck." echoed throughout the ship as men stood at attention. Logan came down from the helm and met him on the lower deck.

"Jonah-

"Can you stir, I know Jonah has been secretly teaching you?" Jack said shortly at him.

Logan nodded and then looked down at a very pale and sickly looking Claire he raised his eyebrow at Jack. Jack didn't respond. Claire could feel the yell coming as Jack's chest tightened.

"Jack, can you let me go to the cabin before you yell?" Claire whispered weakly.

Jack titled his head down looking at her and then felt bad he did not realize how bad her head must hurt. Jack looked at Logan and calmed himself.

"I will be addressing the men as soon as I have Claire settled. I need you to start stirring us out of the harbor now. Any men that are not on board were leaving. They've had longer than the time I allotted to begin with." Jack said so softly Logan had to lean in to hear him.

Jack glanced down at Claire and then locked eyes with Logan letting him know to not be loud. Logan nodded and walked over to one man and whispered the instructions to him. The game of telephone began as the orders were given in whisper form throughout the ship. Logan made his way to the helm as Jack made his way to his cabin.

Chapter Sixteen

Torture

 *J*onah was dragged into the bottom of Rowling's ship. The darkness overwhelmed him as his eyes adjusted. Kenton shoved Jonah along as he had this place memorized. He pushed him to the back corner of the ship and the smell of iron, feces, and ammonia hit him in the face. The smell made his stomach curl. Rowling put a hand onto his face to cover his nose but the smell didn't phase Kenton. He stumbled around looking as he looked for something. He struck a match and lit a candle. The amber glow crept into the cracks of this place. As it creeped across the small area of the ship they were in, the source of the smell was uncovered. Rowling and Kenton had designed their own personal tortured corner. Blood was scattered about the floor and all over a table that had chains and shackles attached to it. Jonah heard a small moan of pain to the right of him. His eyes followed the noise to see a man covered in his own excrements, beaten, and bloody. He was in the far corner chained to the wall. A table to left had instruments sprawled out. Rowling chuckled a little bit as Kenton waited for Jonah to have some type of response. Jonah remained expressionless. He had been preparing for something like this since Rowling popped up. Inside his stomach turned in on itself but he wasn't going to give them any pleasure. Kenton grinned and the man in the corner groaned again this time the noise caught Kenton's attention.

"He's still alive?" Rowling asked, more annoyed than anything.

"I was debating on if we should send him back to his crew like this, or send him back in pieces." Kenton shrugged.

"I wasn't sure which one would get our message across." Kenton said as he walked over to the poor soul and kicked him in the face.

"How much did he owe?" Rowling asked with a sigh.

It was clear that this part of their operation was mostly Kenton. Rowling was in charge but Kenton was like a rabid dog that Rowling kept chained up and he let loose every now and again to prove his points. Jonah stood there silent as he waited for the big dramatic scene.

"He missed two payments but there were also rumors he wanted to rise up against us." Kenton said, as he leaned down toward the man.

He grabbed a hold of the man's hand that was mangled. His hand looked although it had been repeatedly smashed with a hammer. The man cried out in pain but his cry was soft. He had no energy or much life left in him. Kenton smirked and grabbed his pinky finger that was barely attached. The man whimpered. Kenton's smirk grew into a sadistic grin. In one swift motion he snapped the finger back. The noise of the bone snapping echoed through the empty ship hull. The man let out a loud yell as Kenton then twisted. The ligaments popped and ripped. With one quick tug the finger came loose. Kenton laughed as he looked down at it in his hand. Jonah kept his face blank and emotionless as it happened. The scene, it was horrific as the poor man tried to scoot away as he cradled his hand in pain.

"We hadn't decided that yet, Kenton, " Rowling said as if reprimanded a bad dog.

"I know but either way he didn't need that finger. He doesn't even need his hand. You should just let me take it." Kenton said the rush of enjoyment spread over him.

"Leave him be for now. I need to think. Before the missed payments he was actually one of the overachievers. He might be more motivated now. " Rowling said as he thought out loud.

Kenton frowned as he walked away from the man. Kenton held on to the detached finger. Kenton made his way over to a small ledge that looked like it was built into the ship for him. There were several glass jars on the ledge. He opened one of them and dropped the finger into it. Only after seeing that action Jonah realized that each jar on the shelf held body parts. Kenton collected pieces of his victims. Jonah wanted to throw up.

Kenton turned and walked towards Jonah with a sinister grin on his face.

"I almost forgot about you." Kenton said and booped Jonah in the nose.

It took everything in Jonah not to hit him. Jonah stood there acting unimpressed. Kenton smiled brightly and then slammed his fist into Jonah's stomach. The sharp pain made the air rush out of his lungs and he doubled over. Kenton grabbed Jonah by his hair and pulled him to the blood soaked table. Rowling sat and looked like he was debating something. Kenton pushed Jonah's face down on the table. Old blood smeared across his face. Kenton reached over to his tool beside the table and grabbed a long thin knife.

"Ear, nose, lip. Oo eye." Kenton said and brought the knife closer to his face.

Although Jonah felt like he was going to be sick and inside his mind screamed that this could not be happening. He remained calm on the outside. Kenton pushed the blade into his cheek and ran it down the side of it, the blade separated his skin and left a long cut as it made its way. Jonah gritted his teeth but did not let out a sound, blood dripped down over his cheek and across his lower lip.

"Kenton." Rowling said softly behind them. Kenton grumbled and pulled the knife away. He stared at Rowling clearly upset that he wasn't being allowed to have his fun.

"String him up and let him dangle for a while. Do not do anymore. I'm still wanting Jack to join our team and if we kill the last person that matters to him. We might as well kill him." Rowling said as he waved his hand as he talked.

"Fine, I don't know why you care so much about him joining us anyways; he's a nobody." Kenton grumbled like an upset teenager.

"It's none of your business why. All you need to know it's what I want and what I said. So follow orders or you can sit next to no finger over there." Rowling said, and then paused his eyes to look at the poor man that coward in the corner.

"As for him. Take care of him and chuck the body." Rowling said, annoyed.

Kenton's eyes lit up as he was told he could do away with the man in the corner. Kenton quickly yanked Jonah to his feet. He grabbed a rope and began to bind his hands together. Kenton then pulled him over to a low hanging rafter. A hook was dangled from it. Kenton tugged on it, and the hook released. He brought it down to Jonah's hands and looped the rope through it. Kenton then stepped back and tugged on the rope. Jonah began to be lifted upwards. His arms stretched up over his head and his feet barely touched the ground. If he strained he could have stood tippy toes.

"I'm going up to the helm. Finish up down here, do not touch him any more and meet me on the upper deck. Kenton follow my orders or you'll regret." Rowling said his voice was deadly.

Kenton groaned his response and nodded. He watched Rowling walk out of the ship's hull before turning back to Jonah. He still had the knife in his hand as he approached him.

"Soon, soon he'll forget about Jack." Kenton said, as he tapped with the knife Jonah once more on the nose.

Jonah just inhaled as he tried to focus on anything else beside Kenton and the pain in his arms. Kenton turned to walk away but then remembered about the man and the corner. He grinned as he walked over to him. He leaned down with the long thin knife as the man tried his best to scoot away from him. Kenton smiled and then rammed the knife into the man's eye. The man didn't even make a sound as he let out a long breath. Kenton stood up and dusted off his hands. Leaving the man's dead body stuck to the wall of the ship. Kenton didn't say another word as he followed where Rowling went. Jonah hung in silence, he needed to come up with some type of plan. He remembered

something he had in his pocket, the poison. Now if he could only find a way to use it. With that one thought in his mind he smiled slightly. He would make sure he would end one of them if not both.

$\mathcal{J}$ack brought Claire to his bed and placed her down gently. He sat next to her and covered her with the blanket. She smiled weakly. Her stomach still felt sick and her head pounded. Jack leaned down and kissed her forehead. Claire's smile grew and then she frowned.

"Jonah." She said upset.

"I know we need to meet Rowling in Raven peak with double or else. We need to get there quickly. I'm afraid for him." Jack said as he let his fear slip out in his voice.

"We'll save him, don't worry." Claire said and reached over and squeezed his hand.

"I know, for now you need to rest." Jack said, he brushed her cheek with his hand and then stood.

"Jack, can I have some water?" Claire asked, as she closed her eyes.

"Aye Gorgeous, I'll have one of the guys bring it to you. I need to meet with Logan and figure out a plan." He said as he headed to the door.

Once he left the room, Claire sat up and quickly stumbled to the desk. She found a piece of paper and scrambled something on it. She rolled it up. She then fumbled through Jack's desk finding a ribbon to tie it together. She held tightly onto the desk as the world rocked. Dean walked through the door and quickly went to her side. He caught her by the arm and helped lower her into the chair next to the desk. He set the water down on the desk and turned to her with a questioning look.

"Dean, we don't have time. I need you to get this message to Abner's trading company asap. I don't care what you need to do to get it there. In my bag there's a few coins. If you want to help save Jonah, get off this ship and get this note delivered. They'll help Jonah and they have more than one ship. We can take down Rowling." Claire blurted out to him.

Dean listened to everything Claire said, he debated for only a fraction of a second before taking the letter. He glanced at her and then the door.

"Go quickly. Don't tell Jack, tell him you don't want to risk your life anymore and go. Send my love to my family too." Claire smiled at him.

He grabbed the coins from Claire's bag before quickly ducking out the door. Dean tucked the letter and pouch of coins into his pants pocket. He took a deep breath in as he began to walk down the stairs. They hadn't pulled away from the dock just yet. Jack on the lower deck instructing the men. He could hear the frustration in his voice because they were not out at sea yet. Dean ignored him as he walked across the lower deck, hoping maybe he could just walk off the ship without Jack noticing. He got to the walk way when Jack spotted him.

"Dean!" Jack yelled to Dean's back.

Dean froze and took a deep breath in. Here we go he thought as he turned around to face him.

"What are you doing?" Jack yelled as he stepped in front of the walkway and blocked.

"Leaving." Dean said short and sweet.

"Leaving? Leaving!" Jack scoffed angrily.

"Aye Leaving, getting off this ship before we all end up dead." Dean said as he played his role.

"You're a coward, Jonah is captured by Rowling and you're going to just leave." Jack screamed at him on the tops of his lungs.

Dean didn't say anything the words Jack said stung, especially since they weren't true. It hurt that his captain would think those thoughts about him. He didn't react though. He needed Jack to believe he was done.

"Don't you remember who saved your ass when those debt collectors had you. Jonah stepped in, settled everything and then gave you a position on my ship. He saved your life and now when he needs you, you're leaving him!" Jack continued to yell.

"Aye, I'm not risking my life anymore." Dean snapped and pushed past Jack.

"Go! You Coward. You're Worthless!" Jack yelled and then spun on his heels facing his crew who had stopped working and watched silently.

"Anyone else?" Jack yelled at them, they all jumped and went back to their task.

Jack kicked the walk way and it tumbled onto the ship. His anger rose in him as he watched Dean walk across the dock and out of sight. He stomped up to the helm to find out what was taking Logan so long.

$\mathcal{A}$ few seconds after the door shut, she could hear Jack, his voice echoed like thunder throughout the ship. She heard the words coward and worthless, her heart hurt for Dean. It had to be this way. Claire knew Jack would not accept any help. He did not want to risk anyone else.

Claire glanced down at the map. Her eyes searched as she tried to find Raven's Peak. The world rocked as she squinted more at the map. It was so hard to focus. She braced herself with her elbows on the desk. She pushed through the pain and focused back onto the map. She sighed in relief as she found Hang man's cove. Why couldn't it be there? She became annoyed and it caused her head to hurt worse. She ran her finger over the hidden passage and traced it out to the ocean. A high peaked cliff was hiding the passage. She squinted at the small writing next to it. Raven's Peak. Claire nearly jumped up and down. Everything would be perfect. They could meet at Raven's Peak and act like they were going to escape through the passage. Rowling would follow suit and they'll trap him in Hangman's Cover. It was perfect.

Chapter Seventeen

Calling for Backup

Claire hovered over the map a little longer. She heard the cabin door open and she smiled, knowing who it was by the way he walked. He came up behind her and pulled her close to him.

"This doesn't look like you're resting." Jack said firmly.

"What's the plan?" Claire said as she ignored his comment.

"We're going to meet him. We'll fight and pray everything goes well." Jack said quietly.

Claire groaned and shook her head. Jac couldn't help but smile at her frustration. The way her cheeks turned red and her eyes narrowed. She was beautiful even when she was annoyed. It also meant she felt better. She leaned back into him.

"That's not a good plan." She grumbled.

"Well it's really our only option." He said as he kissed the side of her cheek.

"I have a plan." Claire said as a shiver passed through her as Jack's warm lips inched closer to her ear.

"Aye? Of course you do." He whispered into her ear.

"Jack, can you be serious and focused?" Claire said and jabbed him lightly with her elbow.

He responded by playfully biting her earlobe. Tingles ran through her as she inhaled sharply.

"I can't focus much with you around." He growled, his voice coated in lust.

His strong muscular arm wrapped around her stomach and pulled her closer to him. His lips moved down her ear and over her neck. She couldn't help but react as she leaned back against him and moved her head to the side to give him better access. He reached the crook of her neck and bit softly with his teeth. She made a small noise of pleasure. He grinned against her skin.

"You're much too distracting." He told her his voice went deeper.

She spun in his arms face to face with him. She placed her hand on his firm hard chest. A thought of wanting to run her hand down his chest and over his abs ran through her mind. She wanted him just as much as he did her. She cleared her throat as she tried to control herself.

"Jack. We need to come up with a better plan." She said to him, it was meant to come out firm but it came out in a whisper.

Absent-mindedly her hand began to travel as she waited for his reply. Her hand had a mind of its own as it ran down his abs, lingering at his pant line. His shirt was slightly short and exposed a hard v line that peeked out from under his pants. She tucked a finger into his belt and pulled him closer. She could see his bulge as it grew. Her heart began to race and her mind wandered with images of kissing parts of him. Jack smirked.

"I think your mind and body have two different opinions on what plan we should be discussing." He said as he backed her up against the desk.

His hand captured her cheek as his mouth went to capture hers. Claire realized what her hand was doing and pulled it away. She couldn't help herself. She saw the kisses coming and moved her head slightly. Jack's mouth placed a kiss on her cheek.

166

"Claire." He groaned.

"Jack, I want you too. But we need to save Jonah." She said and placed her hand back on his chest and pushed him slightly away.

He groaned again and stepped back. His face was waiting for her explanation.

"Now don't get mad." Claire said softly to him.

"Tell me what you did." Jack said his tone changed from lust to frustration.

"Promise you won't get mad." Claire said, sounding almost child-like.

"I can't promise what I don't know." He said, as he crossed his arms.

"Fine you can be mad but don't throw a fit." Claire said as she stood up and placed her hands on her hips.

"Oh god fine Claire I promise, just tell me now." He said annoyed.

"Dean didn't leave because he's a coward. He left to deliver a message to Gavin and Morgan-

"Claire-"

"Hush, they will be meeting us at Raven's Peak but we're going to ambush Rowling. Come here." Claire said, as she held a finger up to him when she told him to hush.

Jack inhaled as he tried to bite back his annoyance and anger. He walked over to the map. Claire pointed to Raven's Peak.

"Jackie, look where this passage leads. Hang man's cove. We get Rowling to chase us down the hidden passage but we will have more ships waiting. Gavin and Morgan will bring at least two. One to block the exit and another to block his side. There's no way he won't surrender or sink." Claire said very proud of herself.

Jack looked over the plan and it was full proof. He was annoyed Claire went behind his back, proud that she thought of all this, worried because now more people he cared about may possibly be in danger, and angry because he was worried. Claire watched several emotions pass across Jack's face. Claire placed a hand to his cheek, he leaned into her touch.

"Jackie I know you didn't want to get more people involved. I know you think we can do this alone but why risk it. This is going to save Jonah, the rest of the people Rowling is terrorizing, and it's going to save you. I do anything to make sure you don't have to go through this torment any longer. " Claire said as she rubbed his cheek lightly with her thumb.

It was amazing what her touch did to him. He had been with other women and felt their touch. But Claire's it kept his demons at bay, put out any rage that burned in him and made him feel at peace, whole. He looked at her and couldn't help but love her. His hand moved to the back of her neck, his fingers entwined into her hair as he pulled her closer to him. His nose brushed against hers.

"I love you." He whispered to her lips as his mouth claimed hers.

Claire kissed him back and wondered if she really heard him. He lifted her up on the desk as he kissed her. His lips began to wander again down her throat and across her collar bone. She let out a small noise of pleasure as his fingers began to brush against her breast. He began to undo her shirt, almost breaking the buttons as he tried to quickly get the shirt off of her. As he undid each button his mouth trail behind. Claire wove her fingers in his bronze colored hair as his mouth traveled over her stomach. Chills and tingles pulsed through her. Her core wanted and waited for him.

She glanced down at him as he met her waist line. She mustered up the courage, she wanted to please him the way he did her their first time. She bit her lower lip and tugged on his hair, asking for him to stop. He groaned against her stomach as he pulled back.

"I know, I know we need to-

Claire's finger stopped him from talking. She put her finger under his chin and pushed up lightly wanting him to stand. He raised an eyebrow at her but did what she wanted. As he stood she grabbed his hand and scooted off the desk. She began walking him over towards the bed. Her stomach flipped inside itself the excitement of what she wanted to try leading her but at the same time she was a little nervous. As they got to the bed Claire placed him in front of it. A confused look on his face but he let her lead the way. Claire brought her lips to his and began to kiss him. The want and need for him displayed in her kiss. He quickly began responding back. Her hands tugged at the bottom of his shirt as she kissed him. He lifted his arms and let her pull it up over his head, only breaking the kiss when it was time for the shirt to come off. She pulled back and ran her hands down over his perfect chest, his rock hard abs, and then lingered on his belt.

He watched her and the desire in her eyes made him want to take her now. Her hand tugged his belt loose and he watched her eagerly. She quickly began placing kisses down over his stomach. He had never had anyone do this to him before. Getting to his pant line she undid them just as her mouth reached them. Her hands slipped his pants and underwear down to his ankles.

"Claire-"

Claire smirked, liking the feeling of being in control. She looked down at his erect member and hestatied not sure how she was going about this. She kissed her way to it and then slowly placed him inside her mouth. Jack let out a loud groan as she did his hand moving to her head. She began to move her head up and down. Her tongue brushed against him as she did.

"Fuck." He stuttered out with another groan.

Hearing him make noises excited her even more, she could feel herself growing with need as she moved. Jack's pelvis began to move with her head. He groaned again as she flicked her tongue across the top of it. She liked the noise. She wanted him to make it again. She swirled her tongue around the head and back down before placing him back in her mouth. He let out another groan as he twitched slightly. She went to do it again but his hands captured her. In a swift motion she was on the bed next to him. He then moved over her, straddling her. She arched against him pulling his face to hers as she captured it with her mouth. His hand ran down the length of her finding her bead. His fingers began to rub it, her mound pushing against his hand begging to be touched. Her body twitched with pleasure as she was getting close. He could sense it and placed himself between her legs. He pushed himself inside of her, filling her.

She felt no pain this time, if anything it was like he was meant to be inside her. He began moving, thrusting in and out of her. As the pressure building at her core continued to climb. She clung to his board, strong shoulders moving with him. Every move of in and out brought her closer and closer. All of her muscles began to contract. Her toes curled as she felt a release coming. She closed her eyes, her nails digging into his shoulder blades. Her body arching into him. He felt

her organ pulse around him, tightening as he felt her build up. He couldn't take any more. He released at the same time she climaxed. Her body was shivering and quaking. He pulled out burying his face into her chest. His breathing is short and heavy. Claire brushed her fingers through his hair and enjoyed the aftermath.

       Morgan stared out the kitchen window as she tried to make out the ship that was docked in the harbor. She didn't recognize it but the ship next to it she did. Claire was back. She smiled brightly as her heart bounced in her chest. She had been worried since the moment she left. Not because she didn't think she could handle it but because Claire was like her own and a mother worries. She glanced over her shoulder, Gavin was on the floor and playing with the babies.

"Claire's back." Morgan smiled at them.

"Auntie!"

"She made good timing. I'm impressed." Gavin said as he stood.

"They must have just got here and there's another ship I don't know." Morgan said with confusion in her voice.

"Hmm." Gavin muttered as she got up to see, his eyes squinted as he looked out the kitchen window.

As they tried together to look at the ship. A loud bang echoed through the kitchen as the front door was pushed open. A man stood in the doorway.The front Gavin grabbed a knife from the kitchen counter and stepped in front of his children. Morgan scooped up her two little ones and quickly put them in the other room.

"Explain yourself quickly." Gavin said his voice deadly as he pointed the knife at him.

Morgan returned with a pistol in her hand, she stood next to Gavin and blocked the way to her children. The man got shoved forward again and Jacob walked in behind him. Morgan slowly dropped the pistol down. Gavin wasn't ready to let up his guard.

"Where's Claire?" Morgan asked as she tried her best to hide the panic in her voice.

"Tell her." Jacob said and then shoved the man once more.

The man was tall and had blonde hair. He looked like he hadn't shaved in a few days, stubble across his cheeks and chin. He put his hands up defensively looking at Morgan and Gavin with his bright green eyes.

"I have a note from Claire that will explain everything. What this block head is refusing to listen to is Claire sent me." Dean said his voice calm and steady as he spoke to Morgan and Gavin.

"Claire was taken prisoner by these pirates." Jacob slammed Dean in the back once more.

"Aye but please read this note." Dean said as he went to reach in his pocket to pull out his note. Suddenly metal was pressed against his neck as Jacob threatened him with his blade.

Dean groaned frustrated. As he stopped and looked at Morgan and Gavin. Morgan stepped forward and placed a hand on Gavin's shoulder. Gavin glanced at her and reluctantly lowered his knife. Morgan then went to Jacob and touched his blade with her finger and ever so slightly lifted the blade away from Dean's throat.

"What's your name? She asked him.

"Dean Ma'am." Dean said softly to her.

"Dean, if this note is not true and you have my Claire I swear I will gut you myself." Morgan said as she held out her hand for the note. Morgan's voice was more deadly than any of the men present.

Dean nodded and quickly handed her the note. Morgan read the note quickly and her eyes shot to Gavin. She handed him the note and she walked over to the window. Looking out over to the harbor. She looked back at Gavin who finished reading the note.

"Jacob get back on The Crown and get her ready. Tell the other boys to ready The Star. Morgan." He said, turning around and looking at her.

She smiled weakly and looked down at her pregnant belly. She let out a deep sigh and shook her head. She cleared her throat as she held back her fears.

"Just bring her back and Jackie too." Morgan said quietly, she would have been on a ship in a heartbeat but baby number three could come any day now.

He walked to her and took her in his arms. He kissed her forehead as the bedroom door off the kitchen burst open. The children came running over and grabbed onto his legs. Morgan placed a hand on his cheek.

"Be Careful and come back quickly." She said and kissed him.

"Daddy you're leaving?" Ariadne asked quietly.

Gavin pulled back from Morgan's kisses and squatted down to his daughter and son. Orion was still not old enough and didn't want to talk much. He pulled them into a hug.

"Aye I'm going to go bring back Auntie." He told her.

"Ok but next time I am coming. I'll stay and look after mom next time." Ariadne said firmly.

"Aye darling next time." He said as he placed a kiss on her forehead.

"And you rascal don't cause your mother too much trouble." He said as he tickled the raven hair boy.

Orion looked like his mother with her bright green eyes but had his fathers hair color. He laughed widely and tossed his head back. His eyes gleamed with mischief.

"Dada." Orion giggled.

"Aye, I know trouble is so tempting." Gavin laughed and kissed his son on the top of his head.

He kneeled bring his head to Morgan's beach ball size belly. He rested his forehead against it.

"You stay in there till I come back, you hear me." Gavin said as he spoke to her stomach.

Morgan laughed as she watched her husband and shook her head. This was everything he had wanted in life.

"She will come when she wants." Morgan laughed.

"She?" Gavin asked as a smile smirk on his lips as he looked at her.

"Aye Danica." Morgan smiled.

"Orion, didn't you place an order for a brother." Gavin smirked.

"Yeah but I said sister." Ariadne spoke up.

"Hmm well then we will see. She or he needs to cook till my return anyways." Gavin said and poked her belly lightly before he stood.

"Love." Gavin said and couldn't help but kiss Morgan again.

"Go." Morgan said as she broke the kiss.

"I love you." He whispered to her.

"Always." She smiled back and squeezed his hand.

"Go get our girl." She said as she let go of his hand.

Gavin nodded and walked towards the door.

"You lad, you're with me." Gavin said and walked past Dean and out the door.

Chapter Eighteen

Brainless

Jonah struggled as he hung. The pain in his shoulder was unbearable. He attempted to break the rope to see if he could escape. He rubbed his hands back and forth in hopes that the hook that held him would fray the rope but the pain in his shoulder became too much. He thought any second his skin would rip and his shoulder blade would be exposed. He tried to stand on his tippy toes to ease the pressure but he could only attempt it for song. Sweat beaded across his forehead and dripped down into his eyes. It burned and stung. A light appeared at the far end of the hull and the sound of footsteps echoed to him. Johan took a deep breath in and mentally prepared himself for what may come. He knew Kenton wouldn't be able to stay away long. He had someone with him and the person was quiet as they approached. Kenton smiled sickly as he walked by Jonah.

"Over here." Kenton said was almost happy.

The man with him didn't say a word and Jonah could tell he was terrified. He walked over to the corner where the dead man was left impaled to the wall. The man began to gag as he saw him. He had to step away and try to contain himself.

"Come on get your captain, he's garbage. I would hurry up before you end up as my wall ornament too" Kenton laughed as he pulled the knife from the dead man's eye socket.

The body slumped forward and the man lost it.
He began to vomit where he stood. Kenton let out a
growl and grabbed the man by his hair and pulled him
up. Vomiting where he stood. He ran the blade ever so
carefully over the man's face.

"Get your trash or you will take his place." He
grinned

The man quickly nodded and scampered over to
his captain. He picked him up the best he could and
began to bring him with him. He had to stop once more
on the way out of the hull to vomit again.

"You stop one more time you stay!" Kenton
yelled to him.

The man slung the decaying body over his
shoulder and began to climb out of the hull. Kenton
chuckled watching the man struggle.

Jonah remained slightly as he could. The sicking
scene made his stomach turn. Kenton wandered over to
him and studied him.

"Shoulders hurt?" Kenton asked with a smile on
his lips.

Jonah didn't respond but locked eyes with a
small piece of light that danced in from above the ship.
Kenton pulled on his waist and applied more pressure
on his shoulders. Jonah cleaned his jaw as pain
screamed through his body. He would not yell, he would
not whimpered Kenton would not see any of that. He
would not give him the satisfacation. Jonah's eyes
remained locked on the one spot on the wall.

"Maybe I should add weights to your feet."
Kenton announced and walked over to the side of the
hull.

Jonah didn't say anything as he listened to Kenton shuffle around. Jonah glanced up at the ropes he hung from, He began to fantasize that he escaped. Wrapped a rope around Kenton's neck and strangled him. He then ran his blade through his belly. Left him hanging in his torture chamber to decay. Right now none of these thoughts looked like they were going to happen. Kenton stumbled back as he carried two large ball weights with chains attached to them. Kenton kneeled down and began to attach them to one of Jonah's ankles.

"Must be awful." Jonah said to him in his voice tried to hide the pain he was in.

"Come again?" Kenton said, the words intrigued him as she stopped and looked up at Jonah.

"It must be awful that you have to listen to Rowling all the time. Not able to do what you want." Jonah said quietly.

Kenton stood up and looked at him intensely. He hated that he had to listen to Rowling and was not free to go about and do what he pleased. Jonah had to hide the smirk that fought to come to his lips. He knew if he played to Kenton's ego he may be able to get out of this.

"What's it to you?" Kenton asked, slowly as he drew out his blade.

Kenton ran the blade down the center of Jonah's shirt, it cut through it like butter. Jonah did his best to ignore how close the blade was to his skin as he went to talk again.

"To me it means nothing, I was just pointing out what I've seen." Jonah said with an uninterested tone.

He could see the wheels as they spun in Kenton's head. He was not the brains in the operation but he craved to be the leader.

Kenton pressed the blade tip against Jonah's collar bone. He let the knife dig in and then drugged it down Jonah's chest. He stopped as the skin peeled away and left behind a long line of red. Kenton then ran his fingers over Jonah's ribs as if he counted them.

"He just doesn't seem as committed and forward thinking as you. He wants Jack so badly to join him. Jack hasn't done anything right in a long time. The obsession is strange. I think he'll put Jack in charge as second if Jack caves. Then we will both be out of a spot." Jonah said softly, his voice sounded sad and angry all at once as he blocked out the pain.

Kenton stops focusing on Jonah's ribs and looked up at him. Different emotions passed through him.

"You know there's a spot on this side of the rib that if you angle your blade just right and stay shallow you hit nothing important but it causes intense pain." Kenton said as he took the blade and pressed the tip of it into the spot he spoke of.

The tip began to enter Jonah's abdomen. He struggled to hide the pain from his face. It seems to fuel Kenton more. He made sure he pushed the blade into Jonah in the slowest way possible. He wanted to make sure it inflicted more pain and he could enjoy every moment of it. Jonah felt sick as the blade shredded away at his skin. He began to feel nauseous as the pain increased, he closed his eyes and told himself he needed to keep going.

"I bet Rowling doesn't know that." Jonah got out in a short painful voice

Kenton stopped the blade forward and looked at Jonah as if a light bulb had been turned on.

"No he doesn't." Kenton said shortly.

"I bet you always do the dirty work and clean up."
Jonah coughed out.

"Aye he has no stomach for what needs to be
done. He hands everything off to me and then I have to
clean up his messes. Kenton said, his tone annoyed.

"Then he tells you what to do." Jonah said out
loud a heavy breath.

"Aye. He doesn't lets me be my full potential."
Kenton said and pulled the knife out of Jonah's
abdomen.

Jonah had a rush of lightheadedness as the
blade left a small hole. Blood trickled down the rest of
his abdomen as he tried to keep his head in the game.
The pain stunned him as he tried to keep up with his act,
He had to focus. He shut his eyes as he tried to get a
hold of himself. He heard Kenton lit a candle.

"Jack does the same with me. I steer the ship,
tend to the ship, and give out orders while he does
whatever he wants." Jonah sounded upset as he spoke.

He could hear Kenton pause behind him as if
what Jonah had said meant something. Kenton picked
up something and continued to Jonah's back.

" I wish sometimes I could-

A painful yell escaped Jonah as he was not
prepared for the pain that hit his back. He could hear his
skin sizzle and smell his flesh burn. As Kenton chuckled.
The spot then became ice cold, the air stung the wound.
Jonah's head hung forward as sweat ran off his brow.
He tried to gather his thoughts. Kenton rounded the front
of him with a brand in his hand. It was the letter R.
Jonah became angry as he realized what was burned
into his back.

"Even with that right there. That is his, you do the work for it but look no K for Kenton. Not even an R with a K. No, it's just an R for Rowling." Jonah said as he locked eyes with him.

Kenton became angry and he knew it wasn't Jonah that caused the anger. Jonah's words hit him hard because it was true. All of it and he hated it.

"Sometimes I wish I was strong enough to do it." Jonah whispered loud enough for Kenton to hear him.

"Wish you could do what?" Kenton asked his eyes studied him.

"Get rid of them, sea law says that if you kill a captain. You get their ship and crew." Jonah said in a whisper.

Kenton turned sharply and now stood in front of Jonah. His eyes so intense Jonah was unsure what would happen next.

"So what you're saying is, we should take them both down." Kenton said with a smirk on his face.

"Aye Captain Kenton." Jonah said with a wink.

"Captain Jonah, I think we need to discuss plans then." Kenton said excitedly.

 Kenton in one quick movement cut the rope that held him up. Jonah collapsed to the ground like a sack of potatoes. Kenton laughed and reached down to help Jonah up.

"Here, here." Kenton said as he helped Jonah up.

Jonah reluctantly leaned against Kenton. With the weight and chains still on his ankle he couldn't go far. Kenton slid a chair over and helped Jonah sit. The skin of his back brushed against the chair and the sharp searing pain of the burn went through him.

"I think we should celebrate and you look like you could use a drink. You're very strong. I admire that." Kenton said as he slammed two glasses on the table in front of Jonah.

Kenton then began to walk away as he looked for something to drink. Jonah realized this was his opportunity. He fumbled his weak hand in his pocket and pulled the vial of poison out. He quickly sprinkled some into the bottom of Kenton's cup. He then slipped the poison up his sleeve,

Kenton returned with a bottle of whiskey in his hand. He smiled brightly to Jonah as he poured into his glass and then Jonah's. Kenton raised his glass and Jonah mimicked him.

"To new alliances and out with the old." Kenton said enthusiastically as he tapped his glass to Jonah;s before he took a long swig.

Jonah drank from his cup and prayed that it would work. He took another drink from his cup, the whiskey dulled the pain that he felt everywhere. He leaned back in the chair carefully.

"So when did you want to do this?" Kenton asked as he drank more.

"I figured let's have Rowling and Jack fight it out. They will weaken each other and then when they least expect it. I will go for Jack and you Rowling. Simply, we let the brainless do the job for us." Jonah smiled at him.

"Jonah I am glad I didn't- " Kenton began to say but his face fell forward.

Kenton's face smashed into the table as he began to convulse. Jonah pushed himself away from the table as he watched Kenton shake. Jonah took another swig of his drink as he waited for Kenton to stop. He looked around him and found a rag. He stood slowly as Kenton stopped twitching, his breathing began to slow. Jonah pressed the rag over his mouth and nose. Kenton tried to fight but couldn't. Jonah sat there and held tight. He suffocated him with the rag, his body twitch slightly. If he didn't have to poison in him Kenton would have put up a much bigger fight. Kenton stopped struggling and he slumped even more forward into the desk. His eyes glossed over as he let out a long breath. Jonah waited a few more minutes just to be sure. He slowly took the rag off of his face. He brought a finger to Kenton's eye touching his eyeball briefly, no response. If he was still alive his eyes would have blinked. He watched his chest to make sure it no longer rose or fell. Lastly to triple check he took his wrist in his hand and found where his pulse would be. He pressed lightly and began counting slowly. When he reached twenty and still didn't feel anything he knew with certainty he was dead.

Chapter Nineteen

Escape

Gavin boarded the Morning Star. His man came to attention as his feet hit the deck, he nodded briefly to them as he made his way up to the helm. Dean followed behind him. With each step Dean took he was more and more impressed with this man and his ship. Dean followed Gavin up the stairs to the helm. A tall man Gavin by the wheel, his face full of concern. Thomas met him by the wheel, his body tense.

"I just got a message from Jacob. He said Claire is in danger." Thomas glared at Dean.

"Aye." Gavin muttered as he ran his hand through his hair.

He looked across the harbor and The Crown was ready to go, they waited on the Morning Star and The Morning Star waited on Gavin. He looked at Dean. He frowned as he glared at him.

"You come with me. Thomas, you as well. I need to come up with a plan." He muttered and walked towards his cabin.

Thomas shot Dean with another threatening look before they followed after him. Gavin entered his cabin and walked straight for his desk. He began to fumbled

through maps. He studied each of them quickly before he pushed them off the desk and searched for another one. Dean went to step forward to help but Thomas caught him and shook his head at him. Dean hesitated but backed up behind Thomas. Gavin became more frustrated each time he scanned a new map. Time was of the essence. He searched each map and looked for Raven's Peak or Hang Man's Cove. He groaned and slammed his fist on the table. He needs his Morgan, he thought. She would find it in seconds. Maps spoke to her. He couldn't drag Morgan out here, not with the baby. He sighed frustrated. Dean stepped forward and scooped up a map off the floor. His eyes began to scan it.

"Where did Claire say to go?" Dean asked while he turned the map.

"Raven's peak." Gavin said his voice sounded threatening as he spoke.

Dean nodded and dropped the map. He picked up another and looked to Gavin.

"Find Port Sin. Raven's Peak is just south of there. Port sin will stand out more." Dean said, as he handed a map to Thomas before he got himself another.

Thomas raised an eyebrow and snatched the map from Dean. He didn't trust him.

"Exactly what does this guy have to do with Claire?" Thomas asked through his teeth.

"Long Story." Dean said, as he scanned another map.

"Damn how many maps do you have." Dean muttered as he got another.

"Well I would like to know this story." Thomas growled.

"There's a maniac sailing around making people pay him to use the ocean. My Captain, Jack, was trying to pay his dues. Attempted to rob your ship and found Claire. Now they are a thing, I don't know what else to tell you. Just that we need to hurry, the psycho has my friend hostage. Jack and Claire are going to save them and if we don't get there, we will lose people we all care about." Dean snapped, annoyed.

Thomas blinked a few times as he processed what Dean had said. He glanced down at his map.

"Jack..as in our Jack." Thomas asked quietly.

"Yes. Can you be helpful now!" Gavin yelled.

"Found it!" Dean yelled and brought his map over to the desk and almost pushed Gavin aside.

Gavin moved, his hand clutched in a fist. If he hadn't found the spot Gavin probably would have hit him. His eyes followed where Dean was pointing.

"Ok so here's Port Sin and then you follow it down here. Then around this bend here and ta da Raven's peak. I think we shouldn't meet right there. Rowling will be waiting there and if we all just meet there it's not going to be a surprise." Dean said as he babbled.

Gavin whacked him on the back to stop him from talking. He looked over the map and jotted down some coordinates. He handed them to Thomas.

"Have Billy run these over to Jacob. Tell him to stay with Jacob. We leave as soon as he's off the ship." Gavin said, as he walked to the door ahead of Thomas.

"Dean, make yourself useful. You've been on a ship before, find something to do." Gavin said over his shoulder as he walked out.

"You're welcome." Dean muttered as he followed behind Thomas.

Dean walked out onto the upper deck, the sunlight blinded him as his eyes adjusted. He watched Thomas call over a young man and hand him the piece of paper. The young man dashed across the lower deck and off the ship. Dean watched him run down the docks toward the other ship. He was so focused on watching the boy that when the coordinates were shouted out to the crew Dean jumped. He heard a small chuckle and he shrugged. He glanced over at a very serious Gavin before he headed down to the lower deck to find something he could help with.Gavin's eyes focused on the open sea as he pulled The Morning Star out of the harbor and set sail.

    Jonah struggled to stand, the pain made him light headed. He carefully ran his hand down his side finding the wound. It was an inch split in his abdomen. It was bleeding slowly but nothing that would make him critical, yet. It ached and throbbed every time he moved his torso. He took a deep breath and told himself he needed to get his head together. He pushed the lightheadedness from his mind. He looked around, he needed to get off this ship as soon as possible. He couldn't just walk up to the upper deck shirt ripped and bleeding. He glanced down at his shirt and pulled it slowly off his shoulder. He then ripped it long ways into a strip and tied it around his stomach. He applied a small amount of pressure to the wound. He then looked around. He needed another shirt or something. He glanced down at Kenton who was sprawled out face down on the table. Kenton wore a dark blue jacket. Perfect Jonah thought as he slipped Kenton's arms out of the jacket. As he tugged Kenton fell off the chair and

landed on the floor. Jonah stepped over his dead body as he slipped his arms through the jacket and then buttoned it up.

"Alright let's see how this goes." Jonah muttered to himself.

Jonah walked down the dark hall, walking into the wooden wall as he got closer to the ladder. The ship creaked and rocked which was making it hard for him to focus. Reaching the ladder that led up to the upper deck; He inhaled sharply as he grasped the rung of the ladder. He pulled himself up each movement causing pain to ripple through him. He could feel the blood seep through the ripped shirt. Finally he saw the light from the upper deck, he felt like this was the longest climb of his life. Sweat beaded across his forehead as he pulled himself up to the upper deck. He gritted his teeth and pushed the pain to the back of his mind as he looked around. He had expected the ship to be docked, he was hoping it would be docked. Or close enough to land where he could just swim. He didn't expect to see what he saw. Rowling was in the middle of boarding another ship. He then remembered the man who came down into the hull to retrieve his dead captain. He looked over at the ship. Its tall mass and simple striped flag called to him. He needed it. He began a slow but steady walk to the ship's railing. His stomach in knots and he prayed that there was so much going on no one would notice. He reached the railing and felt a rush of relief as he was almost there. A strong hand gripped his shoulder and Jonah felt his hope disappear.

"You better get across there before anyone else notices." The voice said.

Jonah looked at the man standing next to him. Questions flooded his face but the very tall and very large bald man just shook his head. He then helped Jonah onto the walkway. Jonah didn't look back as he quickly walked across the walkway. He didn't know if it would be safe on the other side but at least it was better than being Rowling's victim. He touched down on the other man's ship. He looked across at the very tall, very large man and nodded his thanks. The man nodded back and turned back to his duties. Jonah made his way to the back of the ship. Keeping out of sight. He didn't want to draw attention to himself.

He stayed in the background and watched the crew. They all seemed fearful and not sure what to do with themself. The captain's cabin door was kicked open as the poor man who had carried the body back to the ship was thrown out of it. He scrambled to get up off the ground but Rowling pinned him under his boot. He snapped his fingers as another crew member brought the dead body of the previous captain forward. He picked it up and threw it over the top deck railing. The body hit the lower deck as the men scampered to get out of the way. As the body hit the lower deck, it almost scattered, blood and pieces of body spread around the lower deck. Men ran to the sides of the deck and vomited up over the railings.

"Attention failures!" Rowling bellowed down to the men.

The men did their best to keep still, even the men who vomited struggled to keep still as possible. The amount of fear these men had for Rowling was overwhelming.

"Unfortunately your Captain is...unable to complete this task anymore as captain." Rowling announced with a chuckle.

"Your first mate is a sad excuse as well." Rowling said as he pressed his boot further down on the poor man's face.

Jonah watched as the men of the crew froze, and panic spread across their faces. Rowling enjoys every moment of it. The fear was a power trip for him. He glanced down at the first mate.

"Do you think you can do better or should I just kill the leadership here and start over again?" Rowling said and applied more pressure.

"No sir, I swear we can and will do better." the man under Rowling's boot begged.

"Do you hear what he says, you can do better." Rowling yelled down to the crew.

The crew was terrified to move but nodded in agreement saying that they would do better. Rowling growled and let the first mate up. He went to stand but Rowling pushed him down making him stay on his knees. You could see the wheels as they turned in Rowling's head. Jonah stayed back as he watched the scene.

"One week and I want double." Rowling growled as he brought his foot up and slammed his heel into the man's face.

As the back of his boot made contact with the man's face a tooth shot out of his mouth along with a glob of blood. The man was tossed back onto the deck. Rowling stepped over him. He kicked him in the stomach as he did. The man groaned and curled up as he held his gut, blood leaked out of his mouth. Rowling snapped his fingers and his crew made their way to his ship. Each man carried something that they had taken from the ship. Jonah sunk further back into the crowd as Rowling walked across the lower deck. The last bit of his crew left the ship. He turned and waved to the ship very

dramatically and walked across the walkway. The man
on the ship stayed still until the walkway was pulled
back. Each waited to see if Rowling would come back. A
small crowd began to gather around what was left of the
captain's body. Horror across their faces.

"We need to set sail!" Jonah yelled but shifted so
that the voice didn't seem like it came from him.

"Aye." Another man mumbled.

The first mate stood looking down at them
defeatedly. He went to the hull and took the wheel.

"Gather the remains of the Captain and toss
them overboard. He said he wanted to be buried at sea
if anything were to happen." The first mate said softly as
he pulled the ship away from Rowlings.

The man quickly and carefully began to scoop
pieces of their captain off the deck and toss him in the
ocean. Rowling's ship slowly faded from view. Jonah
looked about the ship, the crew was broken. They were
not sure what they were supposed to be doing and there
was no order. They all seem like they knew they couldn't
make the deadline and would most likely be facing
death. Jonah came up with an idea. Jonah walked up
the stairs to the upper deck and went to the railing. He
glanced back at the first mate who steered a confused
look on his face as he looked at Jonah.

"Lads! I have an offer for you all that will get you
out from under Rowling's thumb!" Jonah yelled down to
the lower deck.

The man stopped walking around like zombies
and all eyes locked on Jonah.

"Just who the hell are you and where the hell did
you come from?" A man from the lower deck shouted at
him.

"It doesn't matter, what matters is I have a way out for you all. You know that you cannot come up with double by next week to give to Rowling. Which means the first mate dies, several of you die and a handful tortured. I don't know if you want to waste your options and hope that you're not the lucky one this time around. He'll offer the same deal and the cycle will keep going until there's none of you left. Or just enough where he places a few of his men here and this becomes his ship." Jonah yelled down at them.

They all seem to nod in agreement, they all knew what Jonah said was true. There were some grumbles throughout the crowd.

"He's right, we're all gonna end up dead." The first mate yelled from behind him.

"We should just leave the sea." One man said.

"Say for yourself most of us are wanted on land." Another man grumbled.

"I have an offer for you. My Captain is going to take on Rowling. Our ship is much more capable than this one. However the back up would be nice. If you're all going to die anyways, why not die taking down the one man who has made your life hell. Murder your friends and brothers. Why not make sure that no one has to go through this again." Jonah yelled his voice full of excitement.

A cheer rose through the man as they agreed. A fire was put back in them and they awaited instructions.

"I need maps and someone to take over steering so the first mate and I can game plan. The mass needs to be drawn down. We need to put as much distance between us and Rowling before he gets too greedy. Prep your cannons were going to need them. Check all properties of the ship; everything needs to be top notch. For the love of god someone scrub the deck. Take pride

in this ship, men." Jonah yelled down at the before heading to the first mate.

A cheer was heard behind him as the man began to divide duties and go about the ship. The first mate looked at Jonah shocked and awe in his eyes.

"Who are you?" He whispered as Jonah approached him.

"Names Jonah." Jonah said and extended his hand to him.

"Marty." Marty replied as he shook his hand.

"Ok Marty, I need some medical supplies and to see your maps." Jonah said, mentioning his wound, his instinctively hand went to his side.

Marty raised his eyebrow at him as he glanced at his side. Questions went across his face as another approached Marty. He was a tall man with dark hair, he had a long scruffy beard and his hair was just as long. He kept both his hair and bread in a ponytail. He nodded to Jonah and extended his hand.

"David, I watched you come across from Rowling's ship. Were you part of his crew?" David asked with his hand out to Jonah.

"Jonah and no. I'm part of the Evening Star crew. I am the first mate. Jack is the captain, Rowling had me captured and I managed to escape." Jonah said and shook David's hand.

"No one escapes Rowling's ship." David said his voice was lined with amazement and distrust.

Jonah pointed to his face the long cut running down it. David seemed to shrug. Jonah rolled his eyes and unbuttoned the jacket. Another long slice went down over his chest and disappeared under the ripped shirt. The shirt was stained red. Jonah's face stated that he was annoyed with the questions. David looked at the wounds and looked at Marty.

"There's medical supplies in the captain's cabin."
David said quietly.

"Can I ask how you escaped?" David said as he
went to take the wheel from Marty.

"I killed Kenton." Jonah said shortly.

David and Marty exchanged shocked looks.

"Well if we were dead before we are now." David
muttered as he took the wheel.

"Come this way." Marty said and walked towards
the captain's cabin.

"I've heard of the Evening Star. People talk about
its massive black sails and ghost-like appearance.
Something out of nightmares. The story of its merciless
captain seems to add to the ghost tails as well. "Marty
stated as he opened the cabin door.

"Jack's a good man but he has no mercy for
those who wrong or harm people he cares about. The
ship's appearance is true. It's from a beautiful
nightmare." Jonah said with pride as he stepped inside.

Marty nodded understanding as he went to his
desk. He pulled open a draw and took out bandage
material. He set it down on top of the desk. He then took
out a roll of maps and placed them next to the
bandages. Jonah slid the jacket off and placed it on the
chair looking down at his wound. The long sliced down
his defined chest and abdomen didn't worry him but he
needed to clean out the puncture. He turned and started
to walk to the door but he paused as he saw Jonah's
back.

"He branded you." Marty whispered as he laid
eyes on the R burned that oozed from his skin.

Jonah tensed up; he had almost forgotten about it. He gritted his teeth as he tried to relax the anger coursed through him. He didn't respond but opened the door and yelled out that he needed clean water and clean rags. He then shut the door and slammed it a little too hard. He walked back to desk.

"Whiskey...Rum?" Jonah asked him quietly.

Marty nodded and pulled open the top drawer of the desk and took a bottle out. He placed it on the desk as well. Jonah opened it and took a long sip out of the bottle.

"Ok, two things I need you to do while I take care of my wound. One opens up one of those maps and find Raven's Peak. I heard Rowling and Kenton talking about meeting The Evening Star there. Two once I've had enough of this rum you're going to cut that R out of my back." Jonah said as he took another shot out of the bottle.

"Ok… wait what, no I can't do that." Marty said as he rolled out the map and started to look through it.

"I am not walking around branded any longer. It will be easy enough the flesh hasn't even started healing it should just smudge off." Jonah said, taking another drink.

"No I can't," Marty whispered.

"No wonder why this ship was an easy target." Jonah said, becoming frustrated.

"Here look, Raven's Peak." Marty said excitedly.

Jonah all but rolled his eyes at him. He was weak and a sad excuse for a first mate. This was the man that was supposed to take over when the captain failed or died. Jonah took another sip and looked at the man.

"Great go set coordinates for there and take over steering. Send David in here." Jonah said and

unwrapped the shirt from around his stomach.

Marty looked at the wound and looked like he was going to be sick. Jonah groaned seeing his face. He pointed to the door as blood seeped out of the hole, telling Marty to get out.

"Pathetic." Jonah groaned and took a sip of rum and then splashed some inside the hole on his stomach.

He let out a small yell and grabbed a hold of the desk as the alcohol burned and stung his flesh. A knock on the door came shortly after Jonah's yell.

"Come on in." Jonah said frustrated, he grew impatient with everyone on this ship.

If their leadership was weak and pathetic the rest of the crew might be. These men would be no use to him if they were like the first mate. The door opened and David walked in carrying a bowl of water. He didn't seem phased by Jonah's wound. He set the bowl down on the desk and looked at him. Seeing the brand on his back he grunted in disgust.

"That bastard branded you." David said, his voice almost angry.

"Aye please tell me you have some balls and will be able to cut it off of me." Jonah said and made sure to take a longer sip of rum.

"Or are all the men weak and pathetic on this ship?" Jonah groaned.

David did not respond. Jonah heard him pull something from his waistband. He held up a knife.

"Just sharpened." David said with a small smile.

"Thank god." Jonah said happy that someone on this ship wasn't a weakling.

"Give me the rum." David said, holding his hand out.

Jonah took another swig and handed it over to him. He expected him to take a drink but instead he ran it over his knife.

"Kill infection." David explained as he handed the rum back to Jonah.

"Alright boss, ready when you are." David said, and held his hands out.

"Aye, hold on." Jonah braced himself on the desk, he took a big sip of rum; the whiskey had started to work and he hoped it would numb some of the pain.

"Ok ready." Jonah said his stomach felt sick as he waited for David.

"Alright here we go boss. Hold tight." David said, as he walked up behind him.

Jonah nodded as Davd placed the knife above the brand. The skin was fragile and damaged. He hoped if he pressed above it and then swiped down that the brand would just slump off. David placed the blade on an angle and in a quick but steady motion moved the blade over the brand. The skin peeled off and disfigured the R but you could still see it. It was a burn and had damaged layers of skin. David pulled back this wasn't going to work. He could see Jonah shoulder shaking as he held in the pain he felt the best he could.

"Bad news boss. This isn't going to work, we can't cut this out. I have an idea though hang tight.' David said as he stepped away from.

Blood leaked from the brand now, Jonah could feel it as it dripped down his back. Jonah took small steady breaths as he tried to focus on anything other than the pain he felt. Jonah grabbed a hold of the bottle once more, one more sip he thought as he pushed the bottle to his lips. David lit a candle and began to heat up his knife. Jonah looked over at him and clenched his teeth.

"We're gonna have to burn it off boss." David said with a small weak smile.

"Great." Jonah grumbled.

"I have to go quick because the blade won't be hot for long." David said as he still held the candle to the blade as he walked.

"Just do it." Jonah said through a clenched jaw.

"Here we go." David said and took a step forward to Jonah.

He waited until the last second to remove the blade from the heat of the candle. He set the candle quickly down and then pressed the hot metal of the blade across the R brand. Jonah let out a loud groan as his head dropped forward. The smell of burning flesh circled around the cabin. David quickly took the blade off and studied the wound. It would be a burn but you would not be able to see the R any longer. David grabbed Jonah's shoulder to steady him.

"It's gone." David said to him.

Jonah nodded and tried to find the chair. David pulled it over to him and helped him sit. Jonah leaned forward as he tried to get through the pain. David watched him closely to make sure he wasn't going to fall out.

"Ok...now that's done." Jonah said as he tried to stand.

David stepped forward and helped him up. Jonah nodded his thanks and went over to the water dipping a rag in it and pressed it to the wound on his stomach. He cleaned it and winced a little bit from the pain. He patted the wound as he studied it before he grabbed bandage material and started to wrap his abdomen. David grumbled seeing him having trouble.

"Give it here. You are strong and stubborn." David grumbled again as he helped Joanh wrap his stomach.

David stepped back once everything looked good. He nodded to Jonah to let him know he was all set. Jonah walked over to the map and looked at it. He saw where Marty had found Raven's Peak. He traced it with his fingers. They need to meet up with Jack before this stop. They couldn't show up at the same time as everyone. It wouldn't be an ambush, it would be a free for all. Jonah felt a little woozy from the pain and alcohol catching up to him.

"Boss, why don't you rest. It will be a few hours before we get to where we're going." David said with a nod to the bed behind him.

Jonah wanted to disagree, he didn't know if he could fully trust these men but the way he felt he couldn't help but give in. He nodded.

"David we need to not go into Raven's Peak. If we do it will be a free for all. We need to stop just before it and try to catch the Evening star." Jonah told David as he sat on the bed.

"Aye boss, I'll make sure it happens." David said with a nod

"David, you should be the next captain not Marty." Jonah said as he laid back.

David chuckled as he walked out of the captain cabin. Jonah got as comfortable as he could and immediately passed out.

Chapter Twenty

Coordinates

ℛowling paced his cabin; it was taking so long to get to Raven's Peak. He knew Jack wouldn't be able to come up with payment and that's when he would make his offer. Join him or he would slaughter his whole crew. "Why do you care so much about him anyways." Kenton's voice echoed in his head. Rowling frowned for a second, he knew from the moment he saw Jack. He knew that Jack was his son. He looked exactly like his lost wife. The same bronze hair and bright hazel eyes. He had regretted leaving her. He could still see her standing on the dock, the baby wrapped up in a wool blanket as she cradled him close to her chest. Tears in her eyes as she begged him to stay. He remembered that he told her it was for the best. That he would return when he made something of himself. When he could be worthy of her. He never went back.

Years later he had found out she died of a fever and that the baby was given away. He had thought about looking for the baby now and then but never had a real urge to be a father. He had asked around about Jack's history and from what he could gather Jack was an orphan. It all fits. He remembers being proud when he found out he was a captain of his own ship but then rage filled him when he found he was caring and kind. He hated the relationship he had with the previous captain and knew the weakness had come from him. So he butchered him. He paused for a second as he realized something...Kenton...Kenton.. Where was that fool he thought walked to the door of his cabin.

"That mutt better not be torturing that boy just yet." Rowling grumbled to himself as he headed out of his cabin and down the stairs to the lower deck.

The men scampered out of his way and stood at attention. No one wanted to be in his way for fear of catching his wrath. A man stumbled and fell into him. He shrinks away as he apologized, he cowered deeply. Rowling snapped his fingers and a man next to him stabbed him. As he fell forward he was caught and hauled over to the side railing. Blood stained the rail of where they tossed him over. His screams echoed behind him as he was tossed in the water still alive.

Rowling went on his way as if nothing had happened. His footsteps heavy on the deck floor. As if he walked louder on purpose. He reached the small hole-like enclosure in the ground which led to the hull. He began to climb down the ladder. The hull had no natural light and the only way to see was to light a candle. He grasped a lantern that hung on the wall next to the ladder. Lighting the candle inside he began to walk towards Kenton's play area. He excepted to hear the sounds of pain and torture but everything was silent He felt something was wrong, something was off.

"Kenton!" He yelled out to him.

No answer.

"Kenton, I swear if you have started one of your projects on that man I am going to rip your lips off." Rowling roared.

No answer.

"Kenton!" Rowling yelled again as he reached the torture chamber.

He stopped as he saw Kenton on the floor. He placed the lantern down and leaned over him.

"Kenton you bastard." He grumbled as he shook him.

He shook him once more as he realized that he was cold and blue. He shook him again to confirm he was dead. He stood back completely baffled. He went to say something to Jonah who was supposed to be hanging from the hook.

"You lad what the hell-" Rowling said, as he turned to where Jonah was supposed to be and stopped.

He quickly began to search the small corner to find Jonah. As he searched rapidly for him, he slammed into the wall as he stumbled around. Jonah was nowhere to be found and Kenton was dead. Rowling growled and walked over to the table and flipped it. He then turned and struck the wall to the left of him.

"How!" Rowling yelled as he grabbed the chair and picked it up. He swung it hard and broke it across the wall.

---

*J*ack woke up with Claire nestled in his arm. She was still asleep, happiness spread across her face. He kissed her forehead lightly and slipped his arm out from around her. He covered her with a blanket and headed over to his clothing which was laid about the cabin. He slipped his pants on when there was a knock at his cabin door. He walked to it quickly not wanting the person to knock again. He opened the door and stepped out onto the upper deck. Sam waited for him.

"Aye." He whispered as he put a finger up to his lip as if to tell him to talk quietly.

"Sir, I was just letting you know that we will be at Raven's Peak within the hour. I didn't know what the plan was. Logan sent me to get more information." Sam said apologetically.

"Aye stay here." He whispered as he ducked back into the cabin.

Sam smirked as he looked at his captain with no shirt and completely disheveled. It was funny to see him like that. He was usually so uptight so on point that this was good for him. Jack emerged with the map tucked under his arm, still shirtless and shoeless. Sam wanted to laugh but held it in because he was the captain. Jack motioned for him to follow him as he made his way down the stairs to the lower deck. The fellow crew mates stopped to show respect that the captain was on deck but were also baffled about how their captain looked. Jack waved them off as he walked by and ignored their looks. He made his way up to the upper deck. He spotted Logan and brought the maps over to him. Logan couldn't help but cough out a laugh. Jack stopped and then unrolled the map and looked at him.

"Um Captain I mean no disrespect but you have no shirt or shoes on and um your…trapt door is open." Logan said as he kept his eyes on the horizon.

"Shut it." Jack said as Sam cracked up,

"Well we're in a hurry, we don't want to mess this up. " Jack said as he fixed his pants.

"It's a little bit refreshing to see you a mess Captain." Sam said being genuine.

"Yeah well if you keep it up you won't be seeing anything other than the depths of the oceans." Jack threatened as he rolled the map across the floor.

"Ok so Raven's Peak is here and we need to somehow find a hiding spot… Sam get down here!" Jack said, hitting the wooden deck next to him.

Sam laughed again as he kneeled down next to him looking at the map. Jack raised an eyebrow at him before he continued.

"As I was saying we need to find a hiding spot before we get to the peak so we can see what we're up against. I feel like Rowling will have one of his other ships with him." Jack explained.

"Captian." Sam said as he nudged him.

"Sam you're really not helpful, look at this and help me come up with a plan." Jack grumbled as he whacked him back.

"Captain." Sam said and nudged him again.

"Sam you're being useless right now." Jack said, and hit him back harder.

Claire cleared her throat as she tried not to laugh at the scene in front of her. A shirtless, shoeless Jack on the floor hovered over a map with his mate. They looked like two kids who were coming up with some crazy scheme. Jack recognized the noise as he turned around. His breath caught in his throat as he looked at Claire. She wore a light blue dress that hugged her curves perfectly along her bust line down over her hips and it flared out around her feet. She had a dark blue shawl covering her shoulders. Her golden locks flowed down around her, the sun danced off them and made her look radiant. He turned slightly, his mouth hung open slightly as he looked at her. She hugged a shirt and shoes to her chest as her lips had a playful smile on them.

"Lads, why don't we get up off the ground, find something to put the map on so we are not hunched over on the ground." Claire said with laughter in her voice.

"Aye..Aye you heard her Sam." Jack said as he shoved Sam as he stood up, his eyes still wandered over her.

"You look radiant." Jack said he went to her.

She laughed and shoved his shirt and shoes in his open arms. He grabbed a hold of them and continued to stare at her and then the thought of how every man on board must be looking at her.

"Claire, here you put my shirt on." Jack said,as he took her by the arm and led her towards the first mate's cabin.

"Jackie you're the one who's basically naked and you're worried about me" Claire said as she raised her eyebrows at him and smirked.

"Aye!" Jack said as he dragged her into the first mate's cabin.

"Do you not know what you're wearing?" He muttered as he shut the door.

"A dress...it was the quickest thing I could throw on." Claire said confused and became irritated.

"Aye and most of these men haven't seen a woman in a while." Jack said and held out his shirt.

"Well if your men can't control themselves because I am wearing what I am wearing then we have a bigger problem. Put your damn shirt on and let me see the map." Claire said with anger in her voice as she snatched the map from him.

Jack blinked a few times, not sure how to act. He glanced at Sam who shrugged and followed Claire over to the desk. Claire rolled out the map and began to study it. Jack quickly pulled his shirt on and headed over to the desk. Claire studied the map once more before she grabbed the feather pen from the desk and circled a spot.

"Here, this is the most likely spot everyone will stop at before reaching the peak. Gavin I know will pick here." Claire said and tapped the map.

"Now I am going to get some pants on. Not! Because I give a damn how me wearing a dress makes anyone of you feel but because it's much easier to fight in pants. And if the need arises to kick one of your rude asses then I can do so with less hazards. Tell Logan our coordinates." Claire said angrily and glared at Jack as she turned on her heels, walked out of the cabin, and slammed the door.

Jack blinked again, his mouth hung open slightly as he looked back to Sam.

"What just happened?" He asked Sam confused.

"Pretty sure she just gave us orders and you've royally pissed her off. That was all pretty much your fault." Sam shrugged.

Jack grunted and went to say something but Sam cut him off.

"I would do what she said before she gets even angrier." Sam chuckled.

"Sam!" Jack growled as Sam began to walk to the door.

"Aye I know captain bottom of the sea an all." Sam laughed on his way out.

Jack grumbled, he grabbed a hold of his shoes and slipped them on. He needed to go talk to Claire; he didn't mean to upset her. He needed to come up with a plan as well. Right now they were going in blind with the hopes of having back up. He wanted to discuss it with Claire because he wasn't exactly sure what she wrote to Gavin. Jack grabbed the map and rolled it up in his hand as he walked out the door. Sam and Logan were posted by the wheel. Jack went over to them with a frown on his face.

"Did you give coordinates?" Jack asked Sam.
"Aye Captain." Sam nodded.

Jack didn't say another word as he hurried down the stairs. He clenched the map in his han. A rush of emotions rushed through him. He was slightly angered that she embarrassed him and luckily it was just Sam. He was trying to protect her and she took everything the wrong way. He shook out his body slightly as he tried to release the anger before he got to her.

He stomped up the stairs to the upper deck after power walking across the lower deck. He headed to his cabin. He reached the door and took a deep breath in one last attempt to calm himself. He turned the handle and walked in. Claire glanced at the door as he came in. She looked forward and pulled on her pants, her back bare to him, his eyes traced every inch of her. The anger immediately left him. He shut the door quietly. He watched her wiggle just slightly as she pulled the pants up over her hips. He felt his pants immediately grow uncomfortable. Claire shot him another angry look as she pulled her shirt on. Anger rolled off her in waves.

"Claire-

"No, don't you Claire me! That was rude and completely uncalled for. What men on this ship do not have manners.' Claire yelled at him.

"Claire-

"What are we all just...just caveman ugh me see pretty girl ugh I take pretty girl." Claire said as she dropped her voice low.

"Claire!" Jack said and closed the distance between them.

"What!" She said fire burned in her eyes as she locked hers with his.

"No, my men would not dare touch or force or do anything to any woman on my ship. Most of them are good men and the rest would be afraid of the consequences for their actions. I was worried about myself. If I caught one look of wanting or needing or lust towards you I might not have a crew left." Jack said his hand went to her hip as he pulled her close to him.

Claire inhaled sharply, as she tried to hold on to the fact that she was angry with him and pushed thoughts from her mind about him being this close to her; her mind and body began to fight itself.

"Maybe I am still very much...caveman. In my head you're mine and I don't want to think about another hand or even eyes wandering over you." He whispered his voice gave away to how much he desired her, his finger tip tugged on her lower lip as he spoke.

Chills shot through Claire like electricity. Part of her loved his statement she wanted to be his. She wanted him to not want her to be anyone else. Part of her liked the possessiveness. She shut her eyes and tried to regain her thoughts. She placed a hand on his chest and had to stop herself from running over his hard defined chest. She licked her lips and forced herself to push him back.

"Yeah well Jackie, I'm not property and if I wanted to run around in nothing but my boots, it's my say so." Claire said as she attempted to be firm with him.

"Aye gorgeous you're not property and I would never think of you as such but I promise you won't get out my door if you try walking out with just your boots on. I wouldn't be able to stop myself from kissing every inch of you." He said and pulled her back into him.

Claire shuttered in pleasure at the sound and promise of his voice. She smirked as she wanted to test him.

"You shouldn't make promises that you don't know if you can keep." She whispered back her voice sultrily.

"I always keep my promises." Jack dared her, the spark of mischief in her eyes made him want her so much more.

She glanced down and saw the map in his hand. The thoughts of Jack chasing her down in just her boots went to the back of her mind. She reached down, took the map from him and placed it on the desk behind her.

"Although I would love to see just how quick you think you are, Jackie, I think we better put that on hold so we can ensure it happens at a later time." She said as she motioned to the map.

He groaned but knew she was right he stepped away from her and went to the other side of the desk. He hoped that if there was something in between them he could stop himself. Claire began studying the map.

"I told Gavin that we shouldn't meet right at the peak. That we need some place just before but hidden. That way we can meet and all come up with a plan to ambush Rowling. That way we can also see if he has more than one ship with him. His ship versus just our two will be easy but if he has more, that's when it's going to become hard." Claire said her eyes still on the map.

Jack listened and looked over the map. She was right, if you knew what was about to go down this would be the most obvious place.

"You sure Gavin is as bright as he once was?" Jack smirked.

"Aye older but he's still sharp." Claire chuckled.

"Alright then we head here and wait for him. We should develop a signal, I feel the only real way to know how many ships Rowling has is if we go in as bait first. Then let Gavin know just how many he has." Jack said thinking about the plan to have Rowling chase them into Hangman's cove.

"Lanterns." Claire said as she thought out.

"It should be dark enough that if we hung Lanterns from the crow's nest that we would be able to see from afar. One lantern for just his single ship and two if there's more than one." Claire continued to explain.

"Aye that's perfect. You truly are amazing." Jack said as he admired her.

Claire blushed slightly as she brought her focus back down to the map.

"I bet you're glad I let you kidnap me uh." Claire said a playful smirk on her lips.

"Aye you let me, right lass." Jack chuckled.

"You really think you captured me?" Claire said her smirk grew and her eyes changeled him.

"Don't make me lunge over this desk and show you who captured who." Jack said and returned the stare.

"Hmm, I wonder where I put my boots." Claire said as she pulled her lower lip into her mouth and turned from the desk to walk away.

Jack did just that as he lunged over the desk as Claire took off laughing. She made a beeline for the door but Jack's arms wrapped around her waist and picked her up off the ground. She laughed and struggled lightly as he carried her to the bed. He laid her down on the bed as she laughed. He brushed the hair from her face. Her laughter made him smile.

"No Gorgeous you're right. The one who is captured here is me." He said as he brushed her cheek gently with his thumb before leaning down and kissing her.

Chapter Twenty One

Meeting

*R*owling stood at the bow of the ship as he watched the cliff. Two other ships pulled Raven's Peak. He ran his hand over the railing as he admired his ship. Rowling's ship was a deep dark cherrywood, he had liked the cherry color of it because it reminded him of blood stained wood. He wanted the fear aspect to be in everything he did. His sails were a deep dark blood red and his personal flag was white with a sword hanging above a headless man's body. He even named the ship Trepidation. It was written on the side of the ship in deep dark bold letters.

He studied the green mossy rocks that covered the side of Raven Peak. The excitement and anxiety that built inside of him as he waited was getting to him. He turned his attention to the two other ships. They were nothing great but they would outnumber Jack. That way if he even thought about fighting he would second guess himself. Rowling wanted to make his presence known when Jack arrived and show off his power. He walked anxiously to the upper deck railing and drummed his fingers on it. His men scattered about the lower deck making sure all the orders he had handed out were being done. He had yet to decide who was going to be his next first mate but part of him was leaving that open. Maybe he would offer it to Jack. He glanced back down at his crew and then to the two ships off in the distance. They were here for him but they weren't loyal by choice. They were loyal to him because they feared him. Everything he had achieved and accomplished was done by force and that is exactly how he planned to take Jack and his ship.

"Have those men hang out in the distance, I want it to be very dramatic when Jack realizes outnumbered and has no choice." Rowling yelled down to the lower deck.

A man jumped up at the sound of his voice and immediately went to do what was ordered. That is exactly how it should be. How the world should work. Those in power should be obeyed, loyalty was nothing and fear was everything. He thought as looked down at his crew.

"Ants. They're all ants." He said quietly to himself.

$\mathcal{J}$onah shifted in the bed and a pain shot through him. He groaned as he sat up, he held his side as he stood slowly. He needed to know where they were and what time it was. The pain in his abdomen seared and stung. It felt like each step he took it burned. His body ached from trying to hold himself in positions that wouldn't hurt. He made his way to the cabin door and leaned against the doorway as he tried to pull himself together and push the pain from his mind. He straightened up and opened the cabin door. The sun was setting as he adjusted his eyes and glanced about the ship as he stepped out. He saw the man following orders and had completed most of their task. The ship looked much better. The deck was scrubbed and cleaned. Someone had taken the time to do the railings as well. The ship seems to have come back to life. Jonah walked over to the rail and leaned on it. David walked on the lower deck while Marty steered. David caught his attention and made his way up to the upper deck. David stopped in front of Jonah and looked him over before he spoke.

"How are you feeling boss?" David asked and leaned on the rail next to him.

"Better, how far are we from the destination?" Jonah asked him, his eyes focused on the sea.

"We are about thirty minutes out." David said shortly.

"Are you sure you're up for this?" David asked him.

Jonah shrugged in response. He reached over and clapped him on the shoulder.

214

"We don't really have a choice now do we. Come with me to look at that map and we need to not just sail up to Rowling." Jonah said as he walked back to the cabin.

They walked into the dark cabin, it was hard to see inside. Jonah stumbled as he caught himself the pain causing him to become a little light headed. David turned to the desk and struck a match. He cupped his hand around the flame as he bent down and lit the lantern. Jonah unrolled the map he had marked with Raven's Peak as their destination. He studied as David looked over his shoulder.

"I'm afraid we're going to be too late. I feel like we're going to get there with the fighting already under way." Jonah said, his voice almost whispered.

"We will surely surprise them then." David said as he tried to add some hope into it.

"Or will get there and it will be over." Jonah grumbled as he looked for any other quicker way.

"You gotta have faith, boss. It will be ok." David said and tapped him on the shoulder.

"Or we could just not go." Marty's voice came from the doorway of the cabin.

"That's not an option." Jonah snapped and turned to meet his glare.

        "Well I don't know where you come from but on a ship the captain makes the rules. The captain defaults to me. I for one don't want to put myself in any more danger." Marty said loudly.

        Marty's voice drew the attention of the fellow crew members and some stopped to see what's going on.

        "So you rather sail around being Rowling's punching bag, then try to break free. You're a coward." Jonah spat as he stepped towards him.

        "Yeah well I'm captain so what I say goes." Marty snickered and folded his arms across his chest.

        "You know next time around it will be you down there in Kenton's hole. You will be the one to face the torment and torture. It won't be a quick death. Even with Kenton gone Rowling is just as sick. He likes to cut things and slice things. " Jonah said, walking towards Marty.

        "Not if we keep our heads down and do what we're told." Marty said, his voice cracked as he spoke.

        "Oh your right… wait…isn't that what your former captain did. Was it enough for him?" Jonah said stopping in front of Marty the urge to shove him and knock the coward on his ass was strong.

        "I…it will be different. We will….we will turn you in." Marty said with a bright grin on his face.

        "Yes..yes we will turn you in and join Rowling in his fight against your captain. We will help him and he will reward us." Marty said proudly.

        "I can't let you do that." Jonah said his voice deadly as he spoke.

        "Well you don't have a choice, my men and my ship." Marty said his voice was very childish.

        "Then I challenged you." Jonah said with a shrug.

"What?" Marty asked, surprised.

"I challenged you to a duel for your title and your ship. Winner gets to be or stay captain and we follow that person's plan." Jonah said as he held his hand out.

"You want to challenge me. You're all broken right now.' Marty said laughing.

"Well then it should be easy, what do you say?" Jonah asked

"Fine." Marty chuckled, grasping Jonah's hand and shaking it.

"Swords!" Marty yelled down the crew that had gathered.

Jonah pushed past Marty and approached the upper deck.

"We're going to have a duel. Winner is the captain. These are the terms we both agreed and shook on. " Jonah made the announcement to the crew as a man came up the deck stairs with two swords.

Several grunts echoed through the crew that gathered. The noise represented that they understood. Jonah and Marty took their swords and stood ready. Davd had come out to watch. Jonah nodded to him and he straightened up.

"On my mark, the duel will begin. Ready 1...2... 3...and beginning." David announced.

Marty charged at Jonah his sword. The sword slammed into Jonah's. The sound of the metal echoed through the ship. The crew was silent as they watched the duel begin. Their blows were hard and fast as Jonah's and Marty's swords struck each other with the first blow. Jonah was slightly surprised that Marty even knew how to weld a sword. As they began to move about the upper deck. Jonah was on the defense as Marty's attacks favored Jonah's left side. Jonah knew Marty did this on purpose, Jonah was still weak on that side thanks to Kenton. Marty continued to attack Jonah at his weakest point and Jonah felt his strength slip with each block he had to make. Jonah had to find a way around Marty and use his strength against himself. Marty charged at Jonah hard and fast. Jonah moved to the side and lifted his foot as Marty came across him. Marty tripped on Jonah's foot as he stumbled and hit the ground. Marty was back up on his feet in no time his eyes set on Jonah.

Jonah was saving his energy and waited for him to strike again. Marty came full speed at Jonah, angry and hate swirled in his eyes as he did. Jonah remained cool and calm and waited for the right moment. As Marty came towards him blade swinging; Jonah spun to the right. He caught Marty on his side. Jonah's sword sliced through his shirt and left a long cut against Marty's right side. He let out a yell, his hand went to his side and held it as his shirt slowly turned red. Mart'sy face turned pale as he saw the blood. Jonah raised an eyebrow at him and waited for him to attack. Sweat beaded across Marty's forehead as he stared down at his bloody hand. Jonah was confused but soon realized that the sight of his own blood made Marty sick. Jonah approached him waiting for some response. Marty continued to stare at his hand. Jonah brought his sword up and placed it under Mart's throat.

Marty froze as reality set in. He hung his head as Jonah waited for him to drop his sword.

"Marty, drop your sword." David said who leaned against the wall this whole time watched the sword fight.

Marty looked fragile and weak as he nodded and dropped his sword. Jonah sighed deeply as he bent down and picked it up. Jonah walked to the railing and held Marty's sword above his head to let the rest of the crew know that he was now captain. A cheer broke out on the lower deck as the man seemed to immediately accept the change in hierarchy.

Jonah walked back over to Marty who was now cowarded into the ground. It was typical to finish the job after a duel. After one captain took the place of another the previous captain was killed.

"Please." Marty whimpered as Jonah approached him.

Jonah sighed deeply and shook his head. He held his hand out to Marty who seemed to shrink even further into the ground. Jonah was getting sick of the way this man held himself.

"Enough, get up man. I am not going to kill you." Jonah said anger rippled through his voice.

"You're not?" Marty said as he slowly got up.

"No. The next docking point your days at sea are over. It's not for you. You need to go do something else. But in the meantime I need you to contribute to this crew. If at any point you do not contribute or if you try to betray or deceive or team up with Rowling. I will personally gut you." Jonah said his voice was deadly with his threat.

"No sir, I will make myself useful and I will follow orders." Marty graveled.

"Good, go on." Jonah dismissed him.

David cleared his throat from behind Jonah. Jonah glanced back at David who nodded his approval as he watched Jonah. Jonah went to stand by him, his pain tolerance had reached its point now.

"So Captain we've got thirty minutes till doomsday." Daivd smirked at him.

"Aye, get to the helm first mate." Jonah said, as he nudged him.

"First-'

"Oh don't argue, just go steer the damn ship while I pull myself together." Jonah groaned at him.

"Aye aye Captain." David chuckled and headed to the wheel.

Gavin sat nestled in the long span of cliff side just before Raven's Peak. The Crown was staggered behind The Morning star, this ensured they did not draw attention to themselves as they waited for Claire and Jack. This was the only route that would make sense for them to travel. Now they had to wait.. The Crown was directly behind The Morning Star. Gavin paced the floor of the upper deck anxiety twisted inside his gut. He every now and then stopped to look at the horizon. His gaze focused on the spot he thought Jack's ship would come from. He glanced back at The Crown. He could see Jacob as he paced almost the same path Gavin was on The Morning Star. Jacob was done with waiting as well. Gavin grumbled to himself about everything taking so long. His eyes snapped to Dean.

"Are you positive this is where Claire said?" Gavin yelled as he closed the distance between him and Dean.

Dean nodded quickly seeing the anger rolling off Gavin. He did not want to upset him anymore. It's been long enough. What if something happened to them? What if they went a different route and this Rowling character has them already? Surely they would hear the fighting, they were close enough? Gavin's mind raced as he left Dean's side and went back to pacing. He promised Morgan he would bring Claire back. Doom and dread pitted in his stomach as it took over the feeling of anxiety. He became lost in his thoughts of what if. A strong hand clapped him on the back nearly knocked him forward. He gritted his teeth and anger but something caught his attention on the horizon.

"Look, see there!" Dean said and pointed to the Black sails as they came around the corner.

Gavin grabbed a hold of Dean ready to throttle him but his words caught his ear. Gavin's eyes spotted the ghost-like ship as it glided across the ocean. It was still as haunting as the first time he laid eyes on it. It was a ship from nightmares. It was meant to install fear and cause panic but your eyes could not look away from its beauty. She stood at the helm, her golden hair down and blew behind her with the ocean breeze. The nerves in his stomach settled slightly.The Evening Star pulled up alongside the Morning Star day and night at a stand still.

Claire nearly jumped up and down as she spotted The Morning Star and The Crown. She spun to Jack who for the first time in a while seemed to feel at ease. The look of shock on his face he tried to hide. He hadn't seen The Morning Star since was young. The golden ship reminded him of the sun at dawn as it danced across the sky and across the ocean water. It was magnificent and majestic. Claire leaned into him happily.

"I told you this would work! I told you we could do this!" Claire said with a laugh.

Jack pulled her closer and wrapped his arm around her and kissed her on top of her head.

"Aye Gorgeous you were right but we haven't even begun so let's not get ahead of ourselves just yet. We need to talk with Gavin and see what he thinks of our plan." Jack said to the top of her head.

"Aye. We better get this going. We've already waited long enough. I hope for Jonah's sake it hasn't been too long." Claire whispered her heart heavy.

Jack stepped away from Claire and yelled orders to his men. They jumped to their feet and readied the walkway between The Evening Star and The Morning Star, He spotted Gavin just on the other side. Old habits died hard, Jack watched Gavin pace across the deck as he waited for the walk way to be secured. Gavin always ran his hand through his hair when he was frustrated and paced when he was upset. Jack smiled a little at the old memories that rushed forward but at the same time he prepared himself for whatever wrath Gavin had. Jack inhaled as he made his way to the lower deck. Jack stopped in the middle of his lower deck and waited for Gavin to come across. Jack's men stayed off to the side and awaited instructions. Claire stood next to Claire excited to see her family. Gavin began to walk across the walkway. Even after all these years Gavin's presence still demanded respect and attention. The way he held himself, the way he walked. Everything about him was all with authority. He stopped just short of Jack and Claire. Jack studied him and waited to see what his response would be. Jack noticed the little grays speckled throughout Gavin's hair and the few wrinkles around his eyes. He was very much the same captain he remembered but very much older. Before an exchange could even happen between the two men Claire darted out from behind Jack and ran to Gavin. She wrapped her arms around him like he was her long lost father.

"Gavin! I am so glad you got my message." Claire squeezed him.

"Claire bear are you hurt? Are you ok?" Gavin said as he took a step back to look at her, his voice worried.

"I am perfectly fine. Jack and I had a rocky start but he soon followed orders." Claire laughed with a wink.

Gavin smiled as he listened to her, he was still angry at Jack for the whole situation that he had gotten himself and Claire into but he felt relief that she was fine and happy.

"Come, we need to discuss our plan." Claire said as she took Gavin by the hand and walked him back towards Jack's cabin.

"Aye lass." Gavin said as he followed her.

Claire walked past Jack and tapped him to tell him to come. She paused and nodded for him to go on. Jack shook his head at her as she completely changed the dynamics of everything once more. He sighed as he walked past her and ignored Gavin's glare. He led the way up the stairs to his cabin. Jack opened the cabin door and walked over to his desk. He wasn't sure what he wanted to say to Gavin or what he could say after all this. He paused slightly in front of the unrolled map.

"Ok so we haven't much time but we were thinking the best course of action is this." Claire began as Gavin stopped in front of the desk with her.

He glanced down at the map as Claire spoke but his eyes found their way to Jack and burned a hole in him as he listened to Claire.

"So Rowling is meeting us here at Raven's Peak, my gut says he's already there and waiting. If you travel just a ways south from Raven's Peak there is a small passageway that will lead into Hangman's cove. This is where our ambush will be. Jack will act like he's running head down the passage into the cove, where the Morning Star and the Crown will be waiting. If there is more than one ship with Rowing, Jack will have lanterns lit on the crows nestle to let us know. We feel he

might bring it back up to show his strength." Claire explained.

Gavin nodded slightly. The plan seemed simple enough and Claire seemed to have thought everything through. He could see Morgan standing there with her, the way she went over the map and told her plan with authority. She wasn't a little girl anymore. He frowned slightly.

"So when do we go?" Gavin said as he took his eyes off Jack and looked at Claire.

"The sooner the better we have a man over there and need to get him back as soon as possible." Claire said with a frown.

Gavin nodded again. "Jack is Captain of The Evening Star, I will be manning The Morning Star, Claire are you-

"Yes, I am The Crown's Captain." Claire said as she cut Gavin off.

"Claire I-"

"Jackie, I am The Crown's Captain." Claire repeated and cut off his protest.

"Aye Gorgeous you are The Crown's Captain but I won't be able to ...to. I'd rather have you here." Jack said frustrated.

"Jackie, I am just as safe over there as I am here with you. The men on the Crown will make sure of it. I will be better helped over there being your backup versus being here and in the way." Claire said as she put a hand on his cheek.

"Jack, you made me hide in a closet the last time Rowling was around. He will use me against you this time and things will go south quickly and not according to plan. We need to be in control of this." Claire said softly.

Jack let out a soft sigh and nodded. He wanted to argue and protest but she was right. The safest spot for her was away from him.

Gavin watched the exchange between the two and the anger he felt towards Jack faded slightly. He could see how much he loved Claire and couldn't hold that against him.

"Claire, why don't you let the men know the orders? I need a moment with Jack." Gavin spoke up.

Claire raised an eyebrow at the two of them, Jack nodded to her to let her know it was fine. She frowned slightly before she squeezed Jack's hand.

"I need you both capable and functioning so do not do anything stupid." Claire warned both of them before she headed to the door.

Claire left and silence hung in the air. They weren't really sure where to begin. It had been years since Jack had seen Gavin. At one point in his life Gavin was a father figure or older brother. They stood there in silence, Jack shifted slightly.

"What the hell is this all about Jackie?" Gavin said, as he broke the silence.

"Rowling killed Jason." Jack the words busted out of his chest with such force, he thought his chest had broken open.

Gavin stiffened slightly and looked confused at Jack as he waited for him to continue. His stomach knotted up at being told his friend was dead.

"Jason was wanting to retire, he was training me as captain. For the longest time it had been good, adventures, treasure hunting everything we thought it could be. Then Rowling came, demanding payment for using "his ocean". I told him to get lost and he slaughtered Jason in front of me. Left him to bleed out on the deck. It's been a long two years, payments and more deaths and more pain. I was supposed to just rob your ship. I didn't even know it was one of yours. I was trying to find a way to come up with the ridiculous amount he thought I owed him. Then… Claire. And now we're going to end him." Jack said quietly.

"Why didn't you come home to us, we would have helped Jackie." Gavin said quietly.

"I didn't want to have anyone else harmed or killed because of me. Claire...she ..well she just happened. I knew she wouldn't let me drop her off anywhere once she found out and I knew once Rowling knew about her she wouldn't be safe anywhere." Jack expressed frustration and sadness in his voice.

"This ends. No one we care about is getting hurt anymore. Let's go kill this son of bitch." Gavin vowed and held his hand out to Jack.

"Aye." Jack said firmly and grasped Gavin's hand.

Chapter Twenty Two

Battle

Claire made her way across the lower deck. The Crown pulled up close to the Evening Star. Claire smiled as she looked at her ship. She missed being captain. She missed commanding a crew and a ship. It felt good to see it. As The Crown pulled up on the other side of The Evening Star Claire spotted Jacob at the helm, his eyes locked with hers and a rush of relief washed over Jacob. She was safe and looked good. Claire smiled and waved at him. Jacob nodded in her direction. Jack walked up to her from behind his eyes locked with Jacob as he slid his hand around Claire's waist and pulled her close to him. Jacob narrowed his eyes at Jack. He hadn't heard the full story yet but all Jacob knew was Jack was the reason Claire was in danger. Claire looked from Jack to Jacob confused.

"So your first mate, he feels….. protective over you." Jack said as he glared at Jacob.

Claire laughed as she realized what was going on. She tapped Jack lightly on the cheek before she answered him.

"Jacob is my first mate and friend. He is nothing like ….what you are to me and he has never been." Claire chuckled again.

"If anything he's an older brother that wants to kick your ass." Claire laughed out loud as she looked to Jacob who glared more.

Jack nodded at him from across the way. Jacob frowned at Jack and then his attention was caught by something, Gavin came up behind Jack and Claire as he shook his head at the scene.

"Well if you love birds are done with your staring contest. Can we get to work?" Gavin cleared his throat and then spoke.

Claire laughed again as Jack snorted. He shook his head, his eyes left Jacob and paid attention to Gavin. Gavin tapped Jack on the back as if he said he was ready to get going.

"See you in the cove. Godspeed." Gavin said as he squeezed Jack's shoulder once more before he made his way across the lower deck.

Thomas leaned against the lower deck rail and waited by the walkway for Gavin. His thoughts elsewhere. Dean stood on the other side of the walkway as well, his eyes focused on the ocean. They both were waiting for orders as their captains decided the best course of action.

Thomas straightens up as he spotted Gavin make his way towards them. Gavin didn't say anything to Thomas, just simply nodded.

"Dean, you're staying here with Jack." Gavin said as he stepped onto the walkway.

"Aye sir." Dean said and he straightened up as Gavin and Thomas made their way to the Morning Star.

"I really wish you would stay here and I could make sure you're safe." Jack whispered to Claire, as he tightened his hold on her waist a little more.

Claire turned his arms and placed her hand to his cheek. She pulled his head toward hers and brought his lips to her. She kissed him. He pulled her closer, deepening the kiss. Claire smiled as she broke the kiss.

"Me leaving is keeping you safe." Claire said, as she tugged a small lock of his hair.

"I know.." He grumbled.

"Even if you don't see it this way. It still ensures us victory. Now let me go." Claire said softly.

Jack grumbled and squeezed her tightly once more. He fought with himself to let her go. He had spent years from her. She had always felt like home. He needed her. He kissed her forehead. He glanced over at the other ships, they all waited on them. He sighed deeply and loosened his grip.

"Let's get this over with so I can have you back here." He said pulling her in for another kiss.

She kissed him back once more. She wished that she could stay but she had a job to do. She was the one to break the kiss again. She glanced over to her ship and a smirk formed on her lips as she locked eyes with Jacob briefly and then glanced back to Jack. Jack brought his eyebrows together in confusion as he looked at her. Claire stepped away from Jack and towards the rail; as she did, she snapped her fingers. A rope from The Crown came swinging towards her. She grabbed a hold of it and stepped up onto the rail. Before Jack could blink she hopped off the railing and swung across to The Crown. She landed neatly on the other side. She smiled brightly at him and blew him a kiss.

"She's going to be the death of me." Jack sighed, his hand rubbed the back of his neck. He clenched his jaw briefly as she watched Claire hug

The crew looked happy to see her, each one nodded or shook her hand as she made her way to the helm. Jack stayed still as he watched her. He felt a sense of pride. She was in her element. She was remarkable.

"So what's the plan Captain?" Logan asked as he came up to Jack with Dean.

"Aye were all ready to go just waiting orders Sir." Dean said his voice trailed behind Logan's comment.

"Aye orders ... .well lads we're going to be bait." Jack laughed at the word bait and walked to the helm.

"Bait….great." Dean said as he followed after Jack.

Logan shook his head, he thought the same thing. As they reached the helm Jack turned to them and looked at them. He sized them up for the two jobs he had.

"Dean, I need you to go up to the crow's nest. When we get to Raven's peak if there are more than one ship your job will be to light the two lanterns I have up there. Only light them when we start making it through the passage. Understand?" Jack said firmly to him.

"Seriously crows nest." Dean grumbled.

"Dean." Jack growled.

"Aye aye Captain." Dean grumbled like a punished child.

"Remember to only light them when we get into the passage and only light them if there's more than just Rowling's ship." Jack said firmly again.

"Got it." Dean grumbled to himself as he walked down the stairs and headed to the center mass.

"Passage?" Logan asked as he watched Dean pout as he walked.

"Aye, we are going to Raven's peak but we are not staying there. There is a hidden passage just south of it. It leads to a cove. This is where we will flip the tables on Rowling. Gavin and Claire will be waiting there. What I need you to do is make the get away for me. I need to be down on the lower deck acting like I'm waiting for Rowling to board. As they start sending the walk way across; I need you to make a break for the passage. You will be at the wheel while I am down on the lower deck. Got it?" Jack said carefully to Logan. He prayed that the small amount of time Joanh secretly taught Logan was enough.

"Got it." Logan said as he processed the plan.

        "I am going to set it up so all you have to do is pull the ship away from Rowling's and take off. You will be pointed in the direction of the passage. I will be down on the lower deck so I will make sure that the sails get up and going." Jack reassured Logan.

        "Got it." Logan repeated.

        Jack went to the helm and took the wheel in his hand. He tightened his grip on the wheel, his stomach flipped inside of him with nerves. He watched The Crown and The Morning Star sail off. He waited until he couldn't see them anymore before he made his way towards Raven Peak. He wanted to make sure they had enough time to get to the cove. He gritted his teeth, his heart raced in his chest as The Evening Star rounded the cliff's bend. The sails caught the wind just right and allowed them just enough speed to make it feel like everything was happening too fast for Jack. He hadn't let the whole crew know what was about to happen. He only told a handful, he didn't need the crew's action to give anything away. Claire returning to The Crown made it look like he was just giving her back. He needed them to still act fearful. The silence that hung in the air of the ship was so thick you could feel the weight of it. The tension was high and the somber attitude of the men was the perfect touch. They all acted like they were sailing to their doom. her. They could very well be but Jack told himself that this would work. They're plan would work.

Jack studied the green mossy rocks as they sailed alongside the bend. The rocks quickly turned to a black slate as the peak came into sight. The rocks that built the peak were as dark as Raven's wings. Thick dark vines ran up the side of the peak laced with deadly thorns. The thorns were just as dark and cold looking as the rocks. As they entered Raven's Peak The blood red sails of Rowling's ship stood out like a beacon. Jack's grip tightened even more. Everything inside of him tensed. The silence of the ship grew louder as all the men paused to look at the haunting sight. Jack became frustrated seeing his men. They were the ghost ship, they were the ship to fear. He couldn't believe what they had come to. It all ends today. This would not happen any longer.

Jack bit his lip as he sailed the ship along the side of Rowling. The men on Jack's ship began to raise their sails to stay put. Rowling proudly waited in the middle of the lower deck. A wide smile plastered on his face. Jack glanced back at Logan and nodded for him to come take the wheel. Logan came forward and switched out with Jack. Jack patted him hard on the back. Jack took a deep breath and then walked down the stairs to the lower deck. His attention was not on Rowling but he looked to the crow's nest. He could barely make out Dean who surveyed their surroundings. Jack reached the lower deck and his eyes locked with Rowling. Rowling waved at him as the ships became lined up. Jack glanced around quickly and spotted two ships off in the distance.

They began to move in closer. Jack glanced back to Rowling who very childishly put a hand over his mouth as if to say "uh oh" when he saw Jack notice the other ships. Jack frowned, he didn't give his men any instructions. They all paused and waited for orders.

They looked at him, their eyes begged for some type of order. They wanted to fight. They hated Rowling and hated submitting. It made Jack proud but he still didn't give any orders. He stood solid in the middle of his deck. Rowling became frustrated and yelled a few orders to his own men who began to pull out their walkway and started to make their ways towards The Evening Star. As the board crept toward The Evening Star Jack glanced at Logan and nodded. Logan gripped the wheel tightly in his hand and then turned the wheel away. The ship yanked away from Rowling's ship and began to move. Jack sprung into action.

"Lower the sails!" He yelled to men that stood by.

Jack raced towards the center mass and pulled the rope to let the sail go. Two other men did the same to the other two masses. The wind caught sail just right and The Evening Star took off.

"Running, are we Jack!" Rowling yelled to him as he raced up his deck stairs and tried to get to his helm.

"Fire cannons!" Jack yelled as he hoped to delay Rowling.

"Cannons!" A man yelled Jack's order into the hull.

Within seconds several loud bangs were heard periodically one after another. Each cannon on the right side of the ship was fired as they pulled away from Rowling. The Evening Star shook as the cannons were fired. A wall of smoke covered the way from Rowling's ship to Jack's. A loud splinter sound was heard as one of the cannon balls broke through Rowling's upper deck and first mate's cabin. Jack smirked as he glanced back, and saw the wreckage. Rowling furiously yelled to his men.

"Reload!" Jack yelled to his men.

"Reload" The order was shouted down into the hull.

"Jack!!" Rowling yelled across the distance to him as Jack's ship began to get away.

Jack smirked as he heard the anger in his voice, he turned to Rowling and waved. He then made his way up to the helm. Logan knuckles were white and locked on the wheel. As he nervously glanced to the side of the incoming two ships.

"Captain." Logan said quietly.

"I see them, let me have her." Jack said and took the wheel from Logan.

"Make sure Dean lights those lanterns." Jack said to Logan as he glanced up to Dean.

"Aye." Logan said as he took off down to the lower deck.

Jack held tight to the wheel as his eyes searched the cliff side, he knew the passage would be small and almost hidden he needed to make sure he didn't miss it. He looked ahead and spotted a small gap. That had to be it. He glanced back and Rowling was gaining on them and the two ships coming for them may cut them off before they reach the passage.

"Fire the left Cannons at those ships. We need to slow them down!!" He yelled to Logan who was walked across the lower deck.

"Fire left Cannons!" Logan yelled.

"Left cannons fire!" The man yelled down into the hull.

The rattle of the cannons being prep for fire and then the sequence of booms as each of the four cannons were fired shook The Evening Star with force. Jack glanced at the incoming ships. He watched them try to swerve their ships out of the line of fire.

The incoming ships faced The Evening Star and cannons were on the sides of the ship. They had no way to return fire. They would need to turn, same as Rowling's ship. One of the cannon balls struck the base of a ship. He knew it wasn't enough to sink and if their crew was quick they could work to fix the damage but it would slow them down.

"Ready cannons!" Jack yelled.

"Prep cannons!" Logan yelled.

"Reload!" The man who stood by the hull yelled down to them.

At the speed they were going, it was going to be a tight and hard swing as they pulled into the passage but he couldn't slow down. He needed to stay this far ahead of Rowling. He couldn't risk it.

"Hang tight, secure the cannons in place. We're turning!" Jack yelled to the men below.

"Dean, hold on!" Logan yelled up to the crows nest as he wrapped his arm around a hanging rope to stay near the mass.

"Secure cannons!" The man yelled down into the hull.

Dean grabbed a hold of the sides of the crows nest and prayed they would make it. Jack saw the passage coming up. It was now or never. He cut the wheel hard and prayed he didn't scrap the side of his ship. The man stumbled across the deck as they tried to stay in their spots. The ship tilted slightly as they entered the passage. Jack swung the wheel back hard trying to get the ship straightened out again. The ship hit the ocean and caused waves. The wave caused by the ship bounced off the cliff's walls and back at the ship causing the ship to almost ping pong off the cliff side. Jack spun the wheel a he got a hold of it and took

control of the ship. They pushed on. Jack once he gained the ship's control back and looked up to Dean. He was straightening himself out.

"Lanterns!" Jack yelled to him.

"I know!!" Dean bellowed down at him.

Dean grabbed a hold of the lantern lighting it and then hung it off the side of the crow nest. He quickly lit the other lantern and did the same. The amber glow from the lanterns gave the passage an haunting glow as they sped through the passage. The passage was small and by the time Rowling was entering Jack could see the exit.

Claire stood at the helm of The Crown and paced. She knew that it would take a little bit to get the plan underway. She tried to calm herself although her stomach made her feel like she wanted to vomit. The wait made her skin crawl. What if he didn't make it to the passage? What if Rowling took over the Evening Star? What if Jack was in trouble? Jacob felt the anxiousness roll off of Claire in waves. He was anxious himself. Once Claire explained everything to him he hated Jack less. He remembers Jack as a lad and was loyal to Jason. He trusted Claire and Gavin's judgment. He would follow either of them to the ends of the earth if they asked.

"Captain!" Jacob said to her as he saw The Evening Star pull through the passage.

Claire's heart fluttered as she saw the ship. He did it! She thought as she rushed to the upper deck rail. She had stationed the crown in front of the exit of the Hangman's cove. If anyone tried leaving they would have to go through her. The Morning Star was to the right of the entrance with her cannons pointed at the

237

passage, drawn and ready to fire. Claire spotted the lanterns.

"He brought more ships! Be ready to fight!" Claire yelled out to her crew.

She watched her man nod, each one ready to fight hand to hand if they needed to. The Crowns' cannons were prep and ready to fire. Everyone's eyes were on the passage. Jack sailed The Evening Star to the left due to Gavin being on the right side. He spun his ship's cannons to face the passage. He looked to Gavin as he set up. Gavin nodded and signaled he was ready. Blood red sails began to pass through the passage exit. Jack waited until the ship was completely through. He locked eyes with Rowling.

"Fire!!" Jack screamed.

Jack could see the panic take over Rowling's face as it went from confident to now scared. The whistling of the cannons taking flight echoed throughout the cove. They landed full force into Rowling's ship. As the cannon balls punctured through the wood loud snaps and cracks rang out as the wood broke. One cannonball broke through the side rail and bounced across the lower deck. Screams were heard as the cannonball ripped through some of his crew and sent them into the ship with the cannon ball. Blood splatter onto the lower deck.

"Reload!" Jack screamed as the crew shuffled to hurry up and follow orders.

"Load the cannons fools!!" Rowling yelled to his crew as they were in a daze.

Rowling's ship powered through and tried to get out of the way of fire. Gavin's ship waited for him. Another ship had caught up to Rowlings.

The second ship approached behind Rowling and as he saw the cannon fire the ship pulled to the other side of Rowlings and used Rowling's ship to block any potential fire. The second ship began to make its way to Gavin's ship. The sails of the ship were gray with no special flag posted. It was a standard size ship, nothing special compared to The Morning Star, but it had cannons and was fully loaded. Rowling's crew finally pulled it together as Jack's crew was about to open fire again. Rowling's cannons fired.

"Move away from the lower deck!" Jack yelled to his crew.

"Fire!" Logan yelled down to the hull as he tried to move out of the way.

Rowling's ship only had three cannons for all the fancy touches he had tried to add to it; he did not add enough cannons. The first cannon was stationed just past the front of Jack's ship so its cannon ball missed. However, cannons two and three made an impact. The cannon ball shattered a railing and smashed across the lower deck. Jack's warning was enough that most men were cleared. Logan hit the ground just in time to have the cannon ball bounce over him. The loud whistle noise passed him. He tossed himself to the ground and he had to double check his heart was still in his chest. The third cannon ball struck the hull of the ship. Jack's men were prepared for this. While the rest of the crew was preparing to send off cannons again, the other half found the hole and began to try to patch it so they wouldn't take in any water.

A third ship came through the passage slowly; its sails were also dark gray. It did the same thing and snuck around Rowling's ship. Jack looked to Gavin's ship as they began to do battle with the previous ship. They were both actively sending fire each other's way. They were evenly matched. Jack needed to find a way to end this or they all would sink. As the dark gray ship peeked around Rowling's ship it started to make its way towards Claire. Jack looked over the rails to check the damage on The Evening Star. The water coming in concerned Jack but he could see his men working on it. Rowling on the other had ignored the damage his shop was taking simply.

Jack's crew sent another round of cannon fire. Each ship shook as the cannons went off. Rowling was sent commands and his men got the walkway ready. They were taking it to hand to hand combat.

"Logan, Dean get the men ready! They're coming!" Jack yelled.

He then watched the dark gray ship change its mind and went to flank the Morning star. They were going to try to take Gavin out two on one. Jack cringed. He looked to The Crown and as if he knew Claire must have sent commands to head to help, The Crown began to race towards them. He watched the dark gray ship try to come around the side of the Morning Star. Jack headed down to the lower deck. He needed to take Rowling out. He cut a rope from his mass and headed to the rail. The walkway from Rowling's ship to Jack was up and men started to come across. Jack's men came up from the hull swords drawn and ready to fight.

"Captain!" Logan yelled at him as if knowing what he intended.

"See you over there!" Jack yelled as he jumped and swung.

"Damn it Jack!" Dean yelled as he watched him land on Rowling's ship.

"We need to get over there!" Dean yelled to Logan.

As soon Jack's feet touched Rowling's deck a man charged at him with a sword drawn. Jack began fighting the man off as another man came up from behind. Jack heard him as he approached and side stepped as the man swung his sword. As the sword came down he sliced his crew mate by accident. The man looked confused at his sword as he was stunned that he sliced his crewmate. Jack took the opportunity and shoved his sword through the man. A third man approached and locked swords with Jack. Dean grabbed a hold of the rope that Jack had used to swing over. He stepped up onto the upper rail and swung. He landed next to Jack. Jack spun around to face off with the person behind him. Dean's sword blocked him.

"Captain!" Dean yelled at him as he pushed his sword away and blocked a sword that came for Jack.

"Thanks for joining me." Jack smiled as he went back to fighting the man Dean blocked. Dean and Jack stood back to back fighting off men.

Logan sighed deeply as he decided to follow suit. He grabbed a hold of the rope as well and swung across. He landed next to Dean and then placed his back towards him. The three of them made a triangle in order to fight off Rowling's crew.

"Nice of you to join us." Dean said to Logan.

"Yeah well now we're outnumbered and in a great position. What the hell is the plan?" Logan said as he blocked an oncoming attack.

Jack ran his sword through a man's belly and kicked the man's body away from him before answering Logan.

"I need to get to and kill Rowling before the other two ships sink The Morning Star." Jack said as he glanced at the scene across the way.

The Morning Star was still holding up and The Crown made progress toward it to help. Logan glanced about the ship. Where was Rowling?

"You would think he would be thrilled that we were on his ship and come greet us." Dean mumbled as he rammed his sword through another man's chest.

The man dropped to the floor in front of Dean as he yanked his sword from his chest. Blood sprayed out of the gaped wound as the man crashed forward.

"We keep this up and we'll have a wall of bodies around us." Dean chuckled.

"Rowling!!" Jack yelled as he was locked sword and sword with a red headed man.

There was commotion on the upper deck. Then Rowling began to make his way down the stairs as he clapped. His crew on the ship seemed to pause and wait for instructions. Jack headed butted the man whose sword was still locked with his. The man stumbled back and held his face. Rowling's man that was locked in battle on Jack's ship continued to fight.

"Jack ... .this ...this is fun. I still don't see this ending well for you." Rowling smirked as he motioned to the chaos around them.

"Where's Jonah?" Jack growled, he was done with the dramatics and games.

"We don't have him. Not sure what happened." Rowling grinned.

"You took him! What do you mean?" Jack bellowed back.

"Looks like we are both down a first mate…Maybe there's a solution in this for both of us." Rowling smirked as he implied Jack should join him once more.

"Rowling shut up for once and come fight me. You versus me that's it. The winner takes all." Jack said through gritted teeth.

"Really, your ship across the way is about to fail. My men will shortly be over running your ship and it's you three versus the rest of my crew. That one ship coming to the rescue will meet the same fate. Why should I fight you when I can just wait it out." Rowling said laughing.

"Coward." Jack called him.

"Coward! Me Coward! How dare you!" Rowling said the word instantly made him angry.

"Cowards wait." Jack said and shrugged.

Rowling growled and slammed his fist into the stair's railing. He hated to be insulted. Hated to be belittled. That was the thing that got Jack into this whole mess in the first place... He felt insulted.

"I mean if you want to wait by all means. Just saying how everyone will see it. Hell, I would be afraid to fight me too. " Jack said very nonchalantly, he knew exactly what to do to get under Rowling's skin.

"Winner takes all." Rowling said steam poured out of his ears.

"Winner takes all." Jack repeated.

"Come and get some boy." Rowling said as he drew his sword.

"Tell your men to stand down til we're done." Jack said not moving away from Dean and Logan.

"Aye, Stand down fools." Rowling yelled to his men.

The men shifted away from Dean and Logan. The men on Jack's ship froze as well. Jack double checked before he left Logan and Dean. He made his way to the center of the lower deck and waited for Rowling. Rowling took his time as he came down the stairs as if debated with himself. He crossed the lower deck and stopped in front of Jack. He held his sword out to him. Jack had just about enough of the antics. Jack stepped forward and hit Rowling's sword with his own beginning the fight.

For everything that Rowling was he did know how to use a sword. The crew watched them battle it out as they moved about the lower deck. Every strike Jack threw Rowling blocked or countered. Jack became frustrated as he knew the longer he took to win against Rowling, the longer Gavin was a sitting duck. He blocked Rowling's attack as he swung towards his rib and counted it, the blow landed a strike across his forearm. Rowling winced seeing his own blood spill. Jack smiled at him.

"You have her smile as well." Rowling said almost too softly.

His comment caught Jack off guard and as Rowling lunged at him he barely moved in time. The blade caught the outer part of Jack's shirt and just missed. Jack swung his blade at Rowling stepping towards him as he did to add more force.

"Her hair and eye color." Rowling said and blocked it but he looped his blade through Jacks to keep him in that position

"What in the hell are you talking about!" Jack growled as he pulled on his blade trying to get it free.

"Your mother." Rowling said as he still held Jack's sword locked with his.

"Aye what about her." Jack growled and this time he pushed forward with force. It sent Rowling backwards as he stumbled.

Just as Rowling stumbled away from Jack a ship came through the passage. The ship had tall blue sails, its cannon doors were open and it was ready to battle. Jack glanced back at Rowling. They could take on another ship. How did he have this much support. As Jack looked to him he saw fear flash across Rowling's face. Jack now was confused, was this not another one of Rowling's ships. He walked to the lower deck rails to get a better look and ignored Rowling.The ship sailed up the side of Rowling's ship and Jack tried to think of something to tell his men to be ready for. As the ship passed by he spotted Jonah at the helm. Jack's face lit up with excitement, his friend was alive, not on Rowling's ship, and coming to help!

"Jonah!!" Jack yelled to him excitedly, he couldn't even think of a way this would even happen.

"You started without me!" Jonah yelled to Jack.

"You're late!" Jack yelled back with a laugh.

Jack pointed to the Morning Star who was taking heavy fire. Jonah nodded back and began to head to assist. Jack was too excited to see Jonah that he forgot about Rowling. Rowling took this opportunity and rushed towards Jack, sword drawn and ready to attack.

"Jack!" Logan yelled as he tried to save him.

The yell almost came too late, Rowling's blade pierced the side of Jack's torso. It caught just the outer part of skin but enough that Jack grabbed his side in pain before he blocked the next strike Rowling was happily swinging at him. The cling of the blades echoing. Jack growled as he pushed forward. Rowling took a step back not prepared for the strength Jack was delivered after taking a hit. The wound just made Jack angry.

He began to fiercely swing his sword at Rowling. Each block Rowling made Jack swung harder and faster. He needed to end this. Rowling backed himself into a corner as he tried to get a handle on the incoming strikes. Rowling's back pressed against the railing and he found himself with nowhere to retreat to. Jack delivered another force blow and their swords locked once more.

"I...It wasn't supposed to go down like this boy." Rowling said as his sword held tight to Jack's sword.

"No...we're not there quite yet. Once you're bleeding out on your deck floor then it will be over." Jack said through gritted teeth.

Claire's heart was in her stomach as she pushed The Crown full speed as she tried to get to Gavin. The Morning Star was a great ship but there was no way it could take fire from both sides. She needed to get there and get there fast.

"Have the cannon ready!" Claire yelled down to her men.

Her grip tightened on the wheel as she watched the scene in front of her in horror. She had to do something quickly. She had to take out one of the ships as soon as she got there or The Morning Star did not stand a chance.

"Jacob, have the two middle cannons loaded with a ball and chain. If we can take out their center mass, the damage of it falling over and the chaos it will cause on ship, might give Gavin some time to recover!" Claire said as she judged the distance of how far they were from the gray ship.

Jacob didn't need anymore orders, he basically jumped to the lower deck. He raced to the hull and ducked into it. Panic raced through both of them as they waited. They couldn't do anything else. Claire counted the seconds. She needed her ship just a bit more closer before she could turn it and allow the cannons fire access. She watched as Gavin and The Star took another hit. She could hear the men as they yelled as the cannon fire wreaked havoc. Seconds turned into minutes and minutes felt like years but finally The Crown was close enough. Claire spun the wheel hard and fast and the ship turned, cannons aimed and ready towards the gray ship.

"Fire!" Claire screamed.

The cannon fire from the Crown began. Claire prayed it would work. The whistling noise was piercing as the cannon ball and chains flung toward the gray ship. Claire held her breath as she waited to see if she was right. Contact happened and the chains wrapped around the center mask and ripped through it. The first set caused their center mass to wobble and crack. The second cannon ball and chain came behind it and struck again. The center mass cracked more and like a tall tree in the woods. It came down in slow motion. The center mass crashed into the upper deck. The loud snap followed by the crashing noise of the wood on the lower deck cracking from impact echoed in the cove. Men jumped out of the way to avoid being crushed. Some drove into the sea, Claire literally jumped up and down seeing her plan work! Their destruction made the men pause, they would be fighting soon but at least the damage was done and gave Claire more time to get closer to help. She pulled The Crown straight and started towards them again.

Jack pushed Rowling into the rail of the deck and forced his sword to let go. Rowling collapsed against the railing tired and out of breath. Jack stepped back and drew his sword above his head and went to bring it down on Rowling. A loud bang echoed through the ship. Smoke masked Jack and Rowling. A sharp groan of pain was heard as the smoke began to clear. Rowling was still leaning back against the rail of the ship. Jack was on his knees holding an already injured shoulder. His sword was placed on the ground on the side of him. A hole was pierced in his shoulder and blood trickled out. Rowling smirked as he began to tuck his pistol away. Logan and Dean went to move towards Jack but Rowling's men stepped in the way.

"Jack, you were supposed to join me." Rowling groaned.

"You were supposed to be my first mate and we would take over. Father and son." Rowling said dramatically, moving his hand about.

"I have no father and he's certainly not you." Jack coughed as he applied pressure to the gun shot wound.

"Oh but I am. Your mother, you are the spitting image of her. The bronze hair, the hazel eyes, her long eyelashes, even her nose is on your face. That chin though that chin's mine. Your fighting spirit is mine." Rowling said as he took a step toward him and pointed at his features as he called them out.

"My parents are dead." Jack said again, this time more angry.

"Your mother is aye, I am not. Don't believe where's her necklace. Do you wear it?" Rowling said as he started to laugh.

Jack's eyes narrowed when he mentioned the necklace. It was the only thing he had from his mother. He glanced briefly at The Crown. The same necklace that hung around Claire's neck. The image of him clasping it around her neck on the docks that day flashed in his mind. He had said he fought a mermaid for it but in truth it was the only thing he had from his mother.

"I was there the day she got it. Some merchant on the side of the dock telling stories about it being made from mermaid's tears. So ridiculous. I left her shortly after that to pursue my dreams. I knew she was pregnant but it was better that way. Maybe if I had known she would have had a boy who would become captain of his own ship I may have stuck around." Rowling said and took a few more steps towards him.

Jack could feel his blood boiling. He shifted his gaze when a loud series of bangs raptured the cove. The Star and Jonah's ship had sunk one of the gray sail's ships. You could hear men yell as they tried to abandon the ship. The Crown had bordered the dark gray sails and worked on taking it down as well.

"So you've always been a coward. Thank god you left. I would rather have the life I lead and the people who helped raise me then grow up being your son." Jack said as he shifted slightly.

"I am more of a man than that poor excuse of one you mourned over as he bled out on your deck." Rowling spat through his teeth.

Jack saw red as he mentioned Jason. Rowling had not realized he was losing the battle in the sea, he was just focused on Jack. The word coward made him shiver with anger. He began to walk angrily towards Jack, his free hand clenched in a fist. He bent over to pick Jack up by the collar. His fist coming down and connecting with Jack's face. His head slumped to the side as Rowling's fist connected with his cheek. Rowling raised his fist back again to hit him once more. Jack grabbed a hold of his sword and as Rowling's fist was coming to connect with his face again; Jack pushed his sword upwards as he stood. Jack's sword pierced through Rowling's abdomen. Rowling stopped where he stood, his face in shock as he inhaled sharply. Rowling's face instantly turned white. Drool began to leak from his mouth as he placed a hand on Jack's shoulder. The drool turned to blood. Rowling blinked as he looked down at the sword in his belly and then to Jack. He did not understand what happened. How?

"Well that's not how this was supposed to go." Rowling coughed weakly and more blood began to pool out of his mouth.

Rowling tried to push himself off of Jack's sword but didn't have the strength. Jack pulled the sword slightly out but not all the way. Anger flooded through Jack. Images of Jason dying in his arms flooded his mind and all the rage he had in him came to surface. Jack twisted the blade inside of Rowling. Rowling let out a scream as it happened. With all his force Jack pushed the sword sideways and walked away from Rowling. The blade cut through Rowling's side. He dropped to his knees, blood and organs spilled out from the large gaping hole and what was left of his body.

Jack didn't look back as Rowling dropped to his knees. His entrails leaked on to the dock as blood washed down over him. His eyes went vacant as he slumped forward and then collapsed. His face in the deck floor as his body empty of blood.

Rowling's crew went lifeless. They didn't know what to do or say or even how to respond. Logan pushed past the men who were once blocked their way and rushed to Jack, Dean followed behind him.

"Jack your shoulder." Logan said he hurried to look at it.

Jack waved him off the adrenaline still rushing through him, he felt nothing. The pain was no longer there. His eyes looked past Dean and Logan to the scene in front of him. Dean went to see as well and Jack swatted him away. Jack's eyes shifted upwards.

"Take those bloody sails down, take that flag down!" Jack's voice echoed throughout the ship as he commanded respect.

Rowling's crew, as if snapping out of a spell, began to follow Jack's orders. The blood red sails were pulled from the masses. A man in the crow's nest reached out and yanked Rowling's white flag down and dropped it. The flag floated down to the floor of the ship and landed in the pool of Rowling's blood. As the flag nestled in his blood a cheer rose up from Rowling's crew. Followed by shouting and cheering from Jack's. The cheering echoed in the cove and all went still for a moment. The captain of the remaining gray ship saw Rowling's ship dismantled and his colors no longer flying.

"Host the white flag, surrender!" He yelled to his men.

Gavin watched he white flag go up on the ship. His eyes scanned the cove, a smile on his face as he looked over and saw that they had won. A cheer rose up from The Morning Star, The Crown following suit.
It was over.

Chapter Twenty Three

Flames

*J*ack stood in the center of Rowling's ship and looked around. All eyes were on Jack. All men stood still, his crew Rowling's old crew. They looked to him and waited for orders.looking around.

"Captain?" Dean asked the question that was on everyone's mind.

Jack cleared his throat as he glanced around the ship. He hated this ship, hated everything it stood for. He glanced at the men who he hoped were just victims as well.

"You all have ten minutes to gather your belongings and get on the Evening Star. From there you can get on whichever ship you please and head to wherever. This ship doesn't leave this cove." Jack shouted.

"Dean, Logan I need you to round up whatever treasure he's got laying around here, have other men help you haul it over to the Evening Star. I am looking for a ruby. Find that if anything." Jack said to them as he tiredly began to walk across the lower deck.

He stepped up onto the walkway and made his way across to his ship. His shoulder throbbed intensely, now that everything was over the pain came to forefront. He could feel his warm blood as it dripped from the open hole in it. The wound on his side stung fiercely but the shoulder pain canceled most of that out. He couldn't wait for everything to be finally finished. He was tired. Tired deep down in his bones. He walked across his lower deck, the men around him cheered and saluted him.

They were free. Jack kept his promise and returned them back to what they once were. The ocean was for anyone. He nodded his head in acknowledgement as he walked by. He slowly and painfully walked up the steps to the upper deck and helm. He slouched back against the rail and looked out over the cove, his eyes settled on The Crown. He just wanted Claire.

Claire stood at the helm of The Crown, the noise from Rowling's ship echoed out over the cove. Her eyes watched as his flag was torn down from the mask and floated to the deck. She watched the white flag rise and she felt her chest settle. The weight was gone and she could breathe. The lone gray ship quickly surrendered as it followed suit, no hesitation no fight. They wanted no part of this fight now Rowling was gone. She was eyeing the blue sail ship carefully. She wasn't sure who they were but was happy they came to assist. Several questions she wanted answered came to her mind. Who were they? How did they know what was happening? Maybe they were part of Rowling's fleet that turned. She wouldn't know till she got there, her guard slightly up at the potential of a new enemy. She looked to The Evening Star and without a word turned her ship toward it. She wanted nothing more than to see Jack and make sure he was ok. The gray ship began to help the crew of the ship that sank out of the sea. She glanced at the Morning Star as she began sailing towards Jack. Gavin was assisting the other ship as well. Without Rowling no one was enemies any longer.

Claire pulled The Crown adjacent to The Evening Star, she nodded to Jacob summoning him to take the wheel and hold her steady. As soon as Jacob had the wheel in his hand Claire made her way as fast as she could down the stairs to the lower deck. As she walked towards the rail, her hand went to a rope that hung from the mask like it had been waiting for her this whole time. She was not waiting for a walkway. She needed Jack and she needed to see him now. She grabbed a hold of it and ran towards the rail. Gracefully she hopped and swung across the distance between the two ships. She landed neatly on The Evening star. Jack couldn't help but smile as he watched her. He shifted his weight as he began to slowly try to make his way to her. The pain from the gunshot wound started to make him feel nauseous. He pushed it aside because everything he wanted and needed in the world was racing up the stairs towards him.

Claire rushed toward him with every intention of wrapping her arms around him. She came to a halt as she came to him she stopped short. Her eyes wandered over his wounded body, her hand covered her as she saw his shoulder. She inhaled to keep herself in control of the panic and fear that rushed into her. She walked to him.

"I'm fine Claire." Jack smiled weakly.

She ignored his comment and carefully looked at his wound. There was a good size hole from the gunshot. She immediately started to look for an exit wound. She needed to see the back of his shoulder. She grabbed his hand and started towards Jonah's cabin. Jack didn't fight her and followed slowly behind her.

Claire led him to a chair at the desk and started to search for her bag that held her medical supplies.began looking around.

"Jack, I need to take your shirt off, I need to see if there was an exit wound. The bullet could still be in there." Claire ordered as she continued to search.

Jack began trying to lift the shirt over his head but now that he was no longer fighting Rowling and the adrenaline left him he was in too much pain to lift his shoulder. He went to raise it and let out a groan. He couldn't. Beads of sweat dotted across his forehead, his shoulder burned and felt like something inside of it was ripping through it every time he moved it. Claire frowned and motioned for him to stay still. She needed a knife. She glanced about the cabin, seeing a knife on the nightstand next to the bed. She went and fetched it.

"Hold still." Claire said as she brought the knife to the small rip in the shirt and began to cut the fabric away from Jack's shoulder.

Once the fabric was cut away Claire was able to pull the shirt up over Jack's head without hurting his shoulder. She studied the wound. The blood was clotted for the most part. There was a small trickle coming out of the hole. Just as she thought there was no exit wound which meant the bullet was lodged in the shoulder. She frowned thinking to herself; the bullet needed to come out, but most likely was part of the reason it had stopped bleeding. She glanced at Jack who was looking worse as the minutes went by. The pain was getting to him. She knew removing the bullet right now would cause him more pain. Her stomach knotted knowing it had to be done. She looked him over once more and noticed a blood spot on the side of his stomach.

She slowly pulled up his shirt and saw another wound. She relaxed a little seeing that it was not as deep.

"Well, doctor, what's your plan?" Jack said with a small smile on his face.

"The bullet is still in your shoulder. I'm not sure where or how deep but it needs to come out. It's going to be painful trying to dig it out." Claire said her voice was full of hurt as she spoke about what she had to do.

"Well I trust you. Do what you need to do." Jack said and grabbed her hand with a soft squeeze.

"I need to go get my bag, it's not in here, it's still in your cabin across the way. Stay here and don't move too much." Claire said as she stood up.

"I'll be right here. Claire when you go out there yell at them to hurry up with my previous orders. They're taking too long." Jack grumbled.

Claire shook her head with a small smile on her face as she walked out the door. The fact he still thought about his commands made her feel a little better.

Jack closed his eyes and slumped against the desk. He did not know why everything hurt but now he was weak enough where he could just fall asleep. He closed his eyes and focused on breathing. A few seconds later the door of the cabin opened up and Jack listened as the footsteps walked towards him. He smiled slightly, not opening his eyes.

"I missed you. You took far too long." Jack said his voice was sleepy but a smile danced on his lips.

"Well I am sorry I kept you waiting. I had a lot on my to do list." Jonah said with a half laugh.

Hearing his voice Jack sat up, regretting the fast movement and the instant pain. He looked over to Jonah and tried to hide the pain with a grin.

"Jonah! I thought you were still stuck on that piece of shit. We tried our best to get there as quickly as we could I was…. I thought Kenton-

"I killed him." Jonah smiled satisfied.

"Aye!" Jack said with the same satisfied tone Jonah had.

"It felt good." Jonah said with a smirk and nod.

"So you have a ship now?" Jack asked as he shifted slightly.

Jonah walked the rest of the way across to the desk and sat against it. Jack's eyes searched over him seeing how he really was doing. He spotted the wound and went to ask but Jonah started talking first.

"It's not mine, well technically I took over captain but I don't want it. You're welcome for saving your ass, by the way." Jonah chuckled slightly.

"About that, can you explain? Don't get me wrong I am thrilled that you're standing here in front of me but how did you pull all of that off." Jack asked.

Before Jonah could get started telling Jack, Claire walked in. Seeing Jonah, Claire let out a loud yell and rushed towards him happily. She wrapped her arms around his neck and squeezed him. Jonah laughed and hugged her, he winced from his wounds but ignored the pain.

"Hey, that's a long enough hug." Jack muttered.

"She can love us both, Jackie." Jonah said with a smirk his voice teased him.

"She can-" Jack began but was cut off by Claire.

"Jonah you're hurt too." Claire said her eyebrows came together as she studied him.

"It's ok really Claire." Jonah said as he nodded to Jack who was in worse shape than he was.

"I will fix you both but I might need your help with fixing Jack. If you are able to." Claire said as she walked beside Jonah.

Jonah nodded as Claire emptied her bag out to gather all the supplies she needed. Jonah glanced down at everything she had laid out, all the tools and then to Jack. There was a lot and none of them looked nice. He was going to need something. He walked over to his

night stand and pulled open the drawer and grabbed a bottle of rum out of it. He walked back over to Jack and handed the bottle to him. Jack laughed as he took a sip and nodded his thanks to Jonah/

Claire took a deep breath in as she grabbed a long slender tool, she turned towards Jack. Jack looked at the tool and her, he took another sip of rum.

"Ready?" Claire almost whispered.

Jack nodded. Claire grabbed a cleaned rag, dunked into the water she had bright and rinsed off the wound. She hoped and prayed she could maybe see the bullet. That it was just under the surface but frowned as she saw that she could not and would have to probe for it.

"Jonah I am going to ask you to hand me things so be ready." Claire said her voice was quiet and calm as she spoke.

She placed the small slender tool inside the hole and began to feel around. Jack grabbed onto the sides of the chair as he fought through the pain. Claire felt the bullet she pressed to the side of it trying to get the tool around it. It began to slip forward and with the slow pressure began to come into view.

Jack fought hard to stay still as sweat began to roll down his back from the pain. He dug his fingernails into the chair, he felt pieces of wood splinter into them as he tried to block out the pain.

He felt his face grow hot and warmth rushed through him. The rum in his stomach begged to be released. The pain burned and tore through him. He shut his eyes trying to focus on anything but his shoulder.

"Jonah, I need the tweezer looking tool and the clean rag." Claire said to him as she could see the bullet, blood slowly started to seep around the wound.

Jonah handed her the tweezers and the rag. Claire lightly dabbed the wound with the rag. While she still held pressure on the bullet with the slender tool her free hand took the tweezers and grabbed a hold of the bullet.

"Hang on, Jack almost got it." Claire whispered to him as she glanced at his very pale face.

She slowly pulled the bullet forward and out. The bullet dropped into Jack's lap with a heavy thud. Then a flash of bright red blood began to pour out of the wound. The bullet had kept pressure and slowed the bleeding down. Now it was gone, the flood gate had opened. Claire handed the tools back to Jonah and applied pressure to Jack's shoulder. Jack gritted his teeth against the pain.

"Jonah I need the rum, the small vial of powder, suture with the tool next to it. One thing at a time in that order." Claire glanced to see how Jack was doing.

Jonah nodded and went to take the rum. Jack took a sip of it before he handed it over to Jonah. Jonah gave it to Claire who removed the rag that was held pressure and poured some into the wound. Jack inhaled sharply as the burning sensation took over.

"Sorry." Claire whispered as she placed the rag back over the wound to apply more pressure.

She handed the rum back to Jonah and held out her hand for the next item. Claire removed the rag once more as blood began to leak down Jack's shoulder. She hoped the powder would be enough to stop the bleeding because the only other way she could think of doing it would be to burn it. The hole was too small for her to try and find the bleeder. The powder burned just as much as the rum did. Jack's face flushed again from pain. The bleeding slowly began to stop and Claire felt relieved. She held her hands out for the other tools

and Jonah handed them to her. Claire began working to suture him up.

"Jonah, tell me….about...Kenton." Jack said through a clenched jaw as he tried to distract himself.

"Right so, they have a lovely torture room down in the hull. Lucky me that was my own personal suit, once the other guest left. It was quite lovely, dark, smelly, the maid service was top notch." Jonah said with a smirk.

Jack rolled his eyes at Jonah and motioned for him to get on with it.

"Well I convinced Kenton that he should be captain and that I could help him. He offered me a drink and then I used the poison that we had got from the bar and put it in his drink. He drank it and I suffocated him. There was another man down there when I got there. He had been keeping him and torturing him. He sent the body back with a crew member of the ship I came to recuse you all on. I managed to sneak out of Rowling's ship and get on that ship. Without a captain they were all over the place the first mate was pathetic so after winning a duel. I became captain." Jonah said like the story wasn't interesting at all.

"Oh is that it?" Jack said with a small laugh.

"Yeah and you're welcome again for saving your asses." Jonah smirked.

"Done." Claire said and leaned away from Jack's shoulder.

"Good." Jack whispered, as Claire stood and pressed her lips to his forehead.

"You need to rest." Claire said and pointed to the bed.

"I need to see what's the hold up with my men." Jack growled.

"Go lay down until I'm done fixing Jonah then." Claire said firmly as she glared at Jack.

Jack muttered something to himself as Jonah offered him help to get across the room and settled on the bed. Claire cleaned her tools off and gathered more items from her bag. Jonah sighed and he had thought about arguing with Claire. That he was fine however before he could utter a word she gave him a look that said don't you dare. Claire snapped her fingers at him and motioned for him to remove his shirt.

"Shirt off." Claire demanded sharply.

"Yes Ma'am." Jonah smirked as he looked over to Jack and wiggled his eyebrows.

"I'll kill you." Jack growled.

"No one is killing anyone. Shirt off, we don't have time for jealousy or games." Claire scolded them.

Jonah laughed as he took off his shirt and dropped it to the floor. Claire began inspecting his wound. Jonah's wound almost matched Jack's on the side of his stomach. His wound however was deeper and older. It was becoming infected. Claire leaned forward and touched his forehead with her hand. The action surprised Jonah and he stood still.

"No fever." Claire out loud to herself.

The wound had started to try to close on its own. Claire could see a green discharge almost trapped behind the new tissue starting to form. She sighed heavily once more.

"Ok so your wound is trying to heal, unfortunately it's trying to heal with a nasty infection. I need to clean out the wound by opening it up, flushing it, and then close it. It's not going to be....pleasant." Claire frowned as she told Jonah the plan.

"Whatever you say doc." Jonah said and leaned back in the chair, he placed his hands behind his head so Claire could get better access to the wound.

Claire grabbed a small blade and looked at Jonah who nodded. Claire made an incision across the tissue trying to heal. Green and yellow puss came seeped out. Jonah winced and shut his eyes as Claire began to press on the sides of the wound trying to drain as much of the puss out.

"So the ship that looks like yours but opposite." Jonah said through his clenched teeth.

"That was Claire's help, her cousin. We all met on that ship. Claire and Morgan snuck aboard it several years ago. I was a cabin boy." Jack said, resting his eyes.

"Going to burn some." Claire said to Jonah as she began to flush the wound out.

Jonah sucked in air through his teeth as he tried to think of something else to ask.

"Did you..... Rowling?" Jonah asked as he tried to get the sentence out through the pain.

Claire flushed the wound once more and then began quickly working on suturing the wound close. She glanced at Jonah to judge how he was doing. He nodded to her telling her he was ok.

"Aye. I rammed my sword through his belly, turned it sideways and walked away slicing him out the side. He laid there in a pool of his own blood as he deserved." Jack said the hatred in his voice would make anyone's hair stand on ends.

"He deserved much worse than that but I am glad....you did it Jack. you stop that mad man. Jason would be proud of you." Jonah said softly.

Jack smiled faintly and didn't say anything. He didn't feel better, he was glad Rowling was dead and glad he would never hurt anybody again. He could go back to the way things were before but he really couldn't. Things were not the same as they were before. He opened his eyes and watched Claire finish sewing Jonah up. He sat up and swung his feet off his bed. He had one last thing to do as far as it concerned Rowling.

"Jack?" Claire asked as she watched him stand.

"You fixed him right." Jack smiled as he walked to the door.

Claire growled as she watched a shirtless Jack walk out the cabin door. She enjoyed watching him walk away. His shoulders and back were absolutely perfect. She had an image of her holding on to his shoulders as he picked her up and placed her on the desk. Her cheeks flushed red as the image crept into her mind. Jonah cleared his throat and went to stand as well. Claire shook her head as if it would chase the thought away. She could hear Jack yelling to his crew about how they were taking forever. Jonah stood up and shook his head hearing Jack yell, as he walked away from Claire he heard her inhale.

"Jonah, your back." She said as she saw the burn mark.

"It's fine Claire." Jonah said, his shoulder tensed as he spoke.

He bent over and quickly picked up his shirt and pulled it over his head. He heard Claire rummaging around in her bag. She walked over to him and stopped him from walking out the door.

"I won't ask but here put this on it. It will help it heal quickly and help with the pain." Claire said her voice was sad.

"I'm sorry we didn't get to you. I'm sorry that you were taken." Claire said to him and handed him the jar.

Jonah smiled weakly. "That's enough of that, let's see what Jack's doing before he falls over."

Claire laughed as she followed Jonah out the door. The Morning Star had made its way over as well as the other dark gray sail ship. Jack seemed to be giving orders and sorting Rowling's crew. The men were then making their way over to a new ship or standing off to the side. Claire shook his head at his action but I guess it was better than killing them. Jonah saw the man who didn't tell Rowling he had escaped. Jack was in the middle of telling him where he wanted him. Jonah walked to the upper rail.

"Captain, if he would like to he should stay." Jonah yelled down to Jack.

Jack nodded and turned back to the man. The man nodded and stood off to the side. Dean and Logan pulled the last pieces of valuables from Rowling's ship onto The Evening Star and the last man was sorted. Dean showed Jack a small maroon bag. Jack nodded and took it.

The walkway was up and across The Evening Star to The Morning Star. Gavin walked across and everyone knew when he was on board as his feet touched the deck. Jack and Gavin exchanged looks and Jack nodded to him. No words exchanged and Gavin walked to Claire.

"See you at home?" Gavin asked her, as he said the word home he squeezed Jack's good shoulder as if telling him he should also come home.

"Aye send Morgan my love. Have Jacob take The Crown back. I'm going to stay with Jack" Claire said to him firmly.

Gavin smiled with a raised eyebrow and nodded. Jack heard the words and his chest fluttered, his eyes locked on Claire's and all the hatred and anger he was feeling from Rowling, the pain and exhaustion from battle all disappeared. Gavin smiled seeing Jack's expression and Gavin patted him on the back.

"See you at home then." Gavin said to Jack before making his way to his ship.

"Aye." Jack said and drew his attention from Claire and his eyes going back to Rowling's ship.

Jack began to gather some lanterns and oil. Claire watched him confused. He orders two men to take two barrels of rum and roll them across the walkway to Rowling's ship. Claire then watched the men leak the rum all over the ship. Claire then realized what Jack was doing. Claire nudged Jonah and started down to the lower deck. Jonah followed. They both stood on either side of Jack. Claire glanced off in the distance and as the other ships left the cove. All that was left was The Evening Star, Rowling ship and the blue sailed ship, which seemed to be waiting on Jonah.

"Are you staying?" Jack asked Jonah as he watched his men come back over from Rowling's ship.

"Aye." Jonah said, he moved closer to the railing as he waved to David telling him to go.

Jonah could see David frown but that wasn't his crew and it wasn't his ship. The blue sail ship began making it's way out of the cove. The Evening Star was his home and he wasn't going anywhere. Jack smiled seeing his friend staying. As the men pulled up the walkway from Rowling's ship. Jack picked up three lanterns, he handed one to Jonah, one to Claire, and kept one for himself. He looked up to the helm

Logan was awaiting orders. Jack struck a match and lit his lantern. He handed the match to Jonah and Claire. He glanced up to the helm and nodded to Logan. Logan began to pull the ship away from Rowling's. Just when The Evening Star was far enough away Jack flung his lantern across the way. It landed on Rowling's lower deck, the glass shattered. The flame hit the alcohol and fire raced about. Claire and Jonah followed suit. Bright red and orange flames covered the ship, black smoke raced to the sky. As The Evening star began to pull out of the cove. They watched Rowling's ship go down in flames.

Chapter Twenty Four

Home

As The Evening Star pulled out of the cove Claire glanced at Jack who tried his best to keep himself up right. Claire sighed and shook her head, she glanced over at Jonah who looked just as worn out as well.

"All right to bed boys." Claire said as she crossed her arms in front of her chest.

"What?" Jonah said confused with a scowl on his face.

"Are you coming with me?" Jack smirked, and stepped closer to her.

"No. You both need rest. I can handle the ship with Logan. You both need to actually relax." Claire said and swatted Jack lightly as he came to her.

Jack sighed and pulled her closer to him and pressed his lips to his forehead. Jonah gagged before he turned in the direction of his cabin. He was truly tired. Claire laughed at Jonah as he simply gave in.

"Jack-

"Alright Gorgeous you win. But only for a little bit." Jack said as he cut her off before she could begin to lecture him.

Claire smiled happily as Jack kissed her forehead once more before he made his way to his cabin. Claire went to stand by Logan as he steered the ship. She waited to take over as they made their way home.

$\mathcal{D}$ays had passed since Gavin had returned home. He looked out the kitchen window and saw Morgan. She was down at the dock again, she paced back and forth, her eyes flickered to the horizon as she did. He frowned seeing her distressed. He told her Claire was capable but as each day passed he became more worried himself. He would give Claire till the end of the week and then he would take the ships out to look for her. He hoped it wouldn't have to happen. He felt a small tug on his shirt as he looked down at the top of his daughter's bright red curls.

"Aye little one?" Gavin said as he reached down and patted her head.

"Auntie still not back yet?" Ariadne asked softly.

"She will be back soon. Let's go get your Mother." Gavin said softly as he took her hand.

Gavin and Ariadne walked down to the docks. The sun was setting and the harbor grew dark. Morgan stood at the very end of the dock and looked out over the sea, Orion tugged on her hand as she sighed heavily. Gavin walked up behind her and put his arms around her waist.

"She will be back soon, Love."Gavin said as he took a step back and reached for her hand.

" I know I just wish I knew she was ok and was coming back." Morgan sighed once more.

"She's coming back but you can't spend every minute out on this dock waiting for her. You have to think about the babe, Love." Gavin said and began to guide her away from the dock.

Morgan, Orion, and Gavin began to walk back towards the house. Ariadne hung back. As she watched the stars start to twinkle in the night sky, dark sails came in view on the harbor. She gasped at the ghostly sight as it sailed almost motionless towards the dock.

"Momma." Ariadne squeaked with happiness.

Morgan turned seeing the sails and her heart fluttered with happiness as she started back to the end of the dock. Gavin scooped up Orion and followed behind her. Morgan stopped at the end of the dock and grabbed Ariadne's hand with a soft squeeze as the ship came closer. The only color on the ship that could be seen was the gold from Claire's hair. She stood at the helm guiding the ship into the dock.

"She's home." Morgan whispered as a smile came to her lips.

The walkway was dropped from the ship and she could see Claire's hair racing behind her as she made her way down it. Claire reached the bottom and all but jumped into Morgan's arms. The two women laughed as they held each other.

"What on god's good green earth took you so long Claire!" Morgan said as she took a step back and looked at her.

"Well I never got to deliver the Queen's gift to our contract renewal. I figured I had to smooth things over first to ensure the contract and to make sure Jack wasn't an enemy of the Queen." Claire chuckled.

"I was so worried." Morgan said and squeezed her again.

Jack made his way down the walkway slowly, he wasn't really sure how to act. He felt happiness as he spotted Morgan. She had saved his life when he was a boy and he has always admired her. He just didn't know if that happiness would be reciprocated back to him. He stopped behind Claire silently and waited. Claire sensed him, she smiled, stepping back from Morgan and her arm looped around Jack's as she pulled him close to her.

"Morgan, you remember Jack." Claire said.

"Jackie, I swear I could kill you but I am so happy to see you again. I don't know whether to shake you or hug you." Morgan said as she stepped forward towards him.

Jack paused waiting for either and was surprised when Morgan wrapped her arms around him. The shock wore off quickly and he squeezed her back.

"It's good to see you again, Morgan." Jack said with a smile.

Morgan stepped back and put a hand to his face. He was not the little boy she once knew. She patted his cheek lightly.

"You're so grown up now. Come let's get you fed. If your men need a place to sleep if they don't want to sleep on the ship, the inn down the road is great and will gladly take and feed them. Let Joyce know I sent them and it will be all set." Morgan told him.

"Thank you." Jack smiled and nodded to Jonah to let him know to relay the message to the men.

Ariadne wrapped her arms around Claire's leg and eyed Jack suspiciously.

"Who are you?" Ariadne asked from behind Claire's leg.

Jack squatted down to talk to her. He smiled as he noticed the little girl was the perfect combination of Morgan and Gavin.

"I'm your …

"Auntie." Claire said to Jack,

"I'm your Auntie's...friend." Jack smiled at her.

"Friend uh." Ariadne said as she came out from behind Claire's leg more.

"Aye her friend." Jack smiled, his eyes flickered up to Claire.

"Is he really Auntie?" Ariadne said now out from behind Claire hands on her hips staring him down.

Jack couldn't help but laugh, she had both her mother and Claire's fiery personality. Ariadne narrowed her eyes at him for laughing at her and Jack quickly tried to cover it with a cough

"Aye Ari. He's a good friend." Claire smiled.

"If Auntie says you're ok then you're ok." Ariadne said with a shrug.

"Come on, let's go then." Aridane said and walked after her mother.

Jack chuckled whole heartily at the little girl. Claire slipped her fingers into his hand and began to lead him down the dock. Claire glanced over her shoulder at Morgan who had a smirk on his face and raised her eyebrow at her. Claire smiled back and continued to the house.

They walked into Morgan's and Gavin's home and Jack was taken back. It was everything a home should be. It was warm and it was loving. He glanced about and saw all the little trinkets and tokens from their adventures. He watched Claire laugh with Morgan as she began to tell her about her own recent adventure. They fetched food from the fire, placing it in bowls as they talked and laughed. The kids running about their feet. Standing there watching everything, a strange feeling came over Jack. In that moment as he watched Claire's smile and the kids clinging to her, he realized this was everything he was missing. Everything he wanted and needed. He thought it was adventure, the thrill of the sea but as he watched Claire he realized that she was going to be his greatest adventure, if she would have him.

"It's something isn't it?" Gavin said as he came up next to him.

"Aye your home and family is beautiful." Jack said as he watched.

"Thank you. You won't ever regret it." Gavin said, and squeezed his shoulder before he went to sit at the table next to Morgan.

Claire tapped the seat next to her as she called Jack over. He smiled and sat next to her and began to eat. He felt like he belonged.

He stood on the docks a few weeks later his eyes watched the waves that rolled in and out against the shore. His stomach in knots as the nerves settled in. He had already planned to make Jonah captain. Gavin had offered him a position in the company commanding one of his ships if he wanted it. He would miss The Evening Star but she was not a trade ship. She was a ship built for adventure. He twirled the simple silver band in his hand. If all goes well she would say yes.

"Jackie?" Her voice stirred him from his thoughts as he quickly hid his hand behind his back.

"Gorgeous." He smiled and held his hand out to her.

"When do you leave?" Claire said sadness in her voice.

She didn't want him to go, she didn't want to be without him but she couldn't ask him to stay. She wanted to but she couldn't take away the life he was used to. The life she knew he wanted. A small fear pitted in her stomach, images of the last time they stood on this dock saying goodbye. He never came back. What if it happened again.

"About that...what if I stay?" Jack said softly and put his hand to her cheek.

"Stay? How? Why?" Claire said confused questions fumbled out of her mouth.

"Aye stay and I would make Jonah captain." He shrugged.

"No." Claire blurted out firmly.

Jack's hand dropped away from her cheek as his eyebrows came together, confusion masked the hurt he felt. Did she not want him? Was he wrong about everything?

"No..no as in don't stay?" Jack asked.

"Jack The Evening Star is...is yours. She's your ship. You are meant to be her captain. Why would you let that go? The adventure of her?" Claire said as she caught his hand as it dropped.

He smiled and shook his head. Relief rushed over him. She was worried about his happiness, not that she did not want him. He cleared his throat and slowly got down on his knee. The sun begins to set in the background. The ocean shimmered gold as the warmth of it skimmed across the dock. Claire tilted her head trying to figure out what was going on.

"Claire, the only adventure I need is you. Today, tomorrow, and forever. If you'll have me?" He said to her his eyes searched hers as he opened his closed fist to reveal the silver band.

Claire's hand went to her mouth as her heart and stomach began doing backflips. She looked down at him, tears formed in her eyes.

"Are you..are you asking-

"Claire, will you be my wife?" Jack asked as he nodded.

"Yes...yes!" Claire said starting out softly and then almost yelling yes.

Jack laughed happily and slipped the silver band on her finger. Once the ring was on he quickly stood and scooped her up off the ground and kissed her deeply. Claire's hands wrapped around his neck and hugged him tightly. He set her down and kissed her once more.

"Wait...wait why would Jonah be captain." Claire said that part just hit her.

"Because I am going to stay here, I asked Gavin if it would be ok to ask for your hand and he said yes. After he offered me a position with the company." Jack smiled and explained.

Claire began shaking her head.

"No, no I can't let you do that." Claire smiled.

"Claire what do you mean?" He asked, confused.

"Jack, you promised a girl on this dock several years ago a lifetime of adventure. I am going to hold you to that. We aren't anywhere near old or ready to settle. You are not giving up The Evening Star just yet." Claire said with a smile.

Jack grinned and then frowned as he looked back at the cliff side house.

"What about your family?" Jack said softly.

"I know my way home Jackie and as long as we visit often they and I will be fine. Jacob Can handle The Crown for a few years. There's so much I want to see and do." Claire smiled.

"I wanted The Crown because I saw it as my only way of seeing the world and having my own adventure but now the possibilities are endless." Claire continued.

Jack blinked as he listened to her not excepting any of this to come out of her mouth. He studied her face as he made sure he understood her.

"Besides you need me. Who's going to keep saving your life if I'm not around." Claire smirked.

Jack laughed as he pulled her against him and wrapped his arms around her.

"Well where to Gorgeous?" He asked as he leaned down and his lips brushed the skin of her neck.

"Wherever the wind takes us." Claire said breathlessly, his lips sending chills racing through her.

"Then we leave at dawn." He said as he placed small kisses along her neck and up to her mouth and captured her lips.

Claire smiled at the word dawn before kissing him back. Their adventures were just beginning. She couldn't wait to see what the world had in store for them.

S.E Dymek's other works:

The Alpha's War Series:
Between the Alpha's War
Breaking the Alpha Council
The Beta's Betrayal

The Trilogy of Light and Dark:
Falling in Love with Death
Keeping you
Saving Hell

The North Star Final book in The Star Saga:
Danice and Ariande are the daughters of Morgan and Gavin Abner. They come from a strong and proud family, with huge foot steps to fill. Morgan and Gavin leave their trade company in the hands of their children as they leave on a sea voyage. As quickly as Morgan and Gavin are out of reach, the world begins falling apart on the girls. A new trading company opened up on the other side of town. This new company seems to be out to destroy the Abner family and everything their parents have built. With contracts being stolen out from under the girls and funds dwelling away. They must do something before they are left with nothing.

Ariadne the oldest, is very mature and trying to handle everything in a business manner. The stress is eating her alive. She is her family's rock and will stop at

nothing to figure this out. Will she be able to hold her ground and defend her home from their rivals?

Danica is a rebel, wild heart, and has another way of thinking. With the deadline fast approaching Danica stumbled upon one of her Father's old treasure maps. She sneaks off one night stealing one of their trade ships in search of the treasure. Will Danica be able to fight time and the unpredictable sea to get the treasure and obtain the funds?

When people are not who they seem to be and hidden secrets from the past emerge, Will the girls have what it takes?

Falling in Love with Death Book one in The Trilogy of Light and Dark:

"Shh. Get down." The warm voice said with urgency as her hand was tugged downward.

"Don't let them find you," he said as he crouched down with her.

She looked at him in confusion. He was still holding her hand. His touch made her skin come alive beneath his fingertips. He was covered in black and a hood was hiding his face…but she knew him.

"Who-" she started to ask but nothing came out. Her mouth just formed the word silently.

He pressed her hand into his cheek as he leaned into her touch and let out a small breath; like the breath he released was the only thing keeping him together. She

watched him closely. He was savoring every detail of this moment.

"Silas?" She whispered his name finally coming to her.

"You weren't supposed to see me, little dove." He said his face concealed as he went to stand up.

"Stay away from the crying. Do not help them. Do not go to them. Stay away from them." Silas ordered. His tone became very harsh as he spoke.

Ryan survives a horrible car accident. A car accident that was supposed to end her life, but Death had other plans. Death saves her and now the world is spinning out of control. Ryan has a huge target on her back as Death desperately tries to keep her alive. Find out what happens when Death falls in love.

 "I was torn between doing my job and rebelling against everything I stood for." -Silas.